Jaycee's Bakery

A Larkin Bay Romance

Leanne Stanfield

Jaycee's Bakery, A Larkin Bay Romance

Published by Leanne Stanfield

Copyright © 2024 Leanne Stanfield

All rights reserved.

No part of this book may be reproduced in any form or by any electronic or mechanical means, including information storage and retrieval systems, or for use in training AI systems, without permission in writing from the publisher or author, except by reviewers, who may quote brief passages in a review.

ISBN 978-1-7380659-0-5 (Electronic Edition)

ISBN 978-1-7380659-1-2 (Book)

Please do not participate in or encourage piracy of copyrighted materials in violation of the author's rights.

The story, all names, characters, and incidents portrayed in this production are fictitious. Any similarity to real persons, living or dead, is coincidental and not intended by the author.

Book Cover by Jenna Fifield

Printed in Canada

First printing March 2024

Visit: www.LeanneStanfield.com

For David, Jenna, Robbie, and Rebecca
with thanks and love.

Jaycee's Bakery
Leanne Stanfield

The stakes are high when you're playing with fire.

So great to meet you!
I can't wait to read your
book one day. I hope you
enjoy mine!
      xo
         Leanne.

Chapter One

The dish tumbled out of Jaycee's hand and hit the gleaming tile floor with a sickening crash.

"Crap," she said, glaring down at the pieces scattered on the floor around her feet.

"Now, now. Watch your language. This is a place of business, you know," the tall, dark-eyed man whispered into her ear as he tightened his hold around her waist and pulled her up against him.

Jaycee glanced up, then bit her bottom lip and looked down at the dish again. "But..." The rest of her protest died on her lips as Tony dropped his head to claim them. Closing her eyes, her fingers reached for his shirt, pleating its soft fabric between her fingers before tugging him closer and returning his caresses with equal enthusiasm.

A moment later, Jaycee's hand fluttered back, resting near her pounding heart for a second. Then she wrenched herself away and tilted her head back to gaze up at him.

"We're at work," she reminded him, reaching up to place a single finger on his lips to stop him from kissing her again.

"I know that." He pushed her hand away and dipped his head again so he could nuzzle a tender spot at the base of her neck.

She gasped and tilted her head back. "Mmm, Tony, no. Stop. What are you doing? I thought you didn't want anyone here to know about us," she exclaimed, wiggling out of his grasp. "There are at least three people who could come in here at any moment and catch us doing this." Looking down, she waved a hand at the broken platter pieces lying on the floor. "Besides" —she stepped back and placed both hands on her hips—"do you see this mess? You can't just come in here and grab me from behind! Look at what you made me do!"

His eyes were dark with desire and unapologetic as he glanced at the crockery pieces at their feet. "You did make a mess," he agreed.

Jaycee rolled her eyes. "Yeah, well, you startled me. Now, go away so I can get this cleaned up before my boss comes back and finds out I've broken one of his favorite display platters."

"Ah, your boss won't even notice. He's as blind as a bat and stupid as a tree stump," Tony replied. After a quick glance at the door behind him, he reached over and pulled her close once again. "You're too good to be working here, anyway. You let *me* deal with that fat old guy. I'll set him straight."

Jaycee laughed and ducked her head as she cuddled up against him. "You're not fat," she said, walking her fingers down the buttons of the shirt that hugged his tight, flat stomach. "But the stupid part? That we can debate," she teased, then stretched up on her toes and pressed her lips against his one last time before stepping away.

Turning to leave the kitchen, Jaycee exaggerated the sway of her hips under her snug-fitting apron, knowing Tony—her boss, her lover for the past year, and part-owner of the bakery—would be watching. When she got to the doorway, she flipped her thick, dark braid over one shoulder and gave him a flirtatious grin before disappearing down the back hall to the closet where the cleaning supplies were kept.

When she returned with a broom and mop, she saw the room was empty and the door to the front of the bakery was gently swinging. Tony may have returned to the retail area of the bakery to serve customers, but the tangy smell of his cologne still lingered, and that, along with the anticipation of their planned rendezvous for the next day, had Jaycee humming as she cleaned.

Quickly, she swept the floor twice and then damp-mopped it to ensure no stray shards of glass from the platter were left behind. Nodding in satisfaction at the results of her efforts when finished, she held the broom out in front of her and did a quick waltz with it around the perimeter of the room. After several minutes of crooning along with her Barry Manilow iPhones playlist to her pretend broom partner, she ended her dance routine with a deep dip and gave a loud "Whoa-oh-oh-oh-oh" before returning the cleaning supplies to the back storage closet.

Stepping into the bathroom, Jaycee looked at her reflection in the mirror over the sink and wrinkled her nose. Grabbing a few stray curls that had escaped their clips, she coiled them back into her braid and pushed everything into a hairnet that she knotted tightly against the nape of her neck. After washing her hands twice, she returned to the kitchen, where she slipped on a pair of long oven mitts and slid a tray of dough out of the warming oven. Grabbing a section of the pale, rising dough, she plopped it on the table in front of her and began to rhythmically knead it into shape.

As her fingers flew, working the sweet-smelling dough into perfect loaves, she tapped her foot and sang along with her iPhones playlist. Her words were a little off-key, but she made up in volume for what she lacked in tune.

"Well, aren't you sounding all sunshiny today," Lisa, the bakery's assistant manager, announced as she banged open the swinging door that led to the front of the bakery and strode into the kitchen.

"I *am* happy," replied Jaycee, glancing up and shooting a grin at her friend before giving the loaf she was forming a quick slash of a design on top and placing it alongside the others she had prepared on the baking sheet. "I am doing what I love with wonderful people and I'm almost done for the day, so soon I can return to my little oasis called home—it doesn't get much better than that."

Lisa rolled her eyes and grimaced. Going over to the side table, she turned down the Barry Manilow playlist before thoroughly washing and drying her hands. Taking some of the unfinished dough from Jaycee's tray, she hip-checked her friend to nudge her over and began kneading a portion of the dough alongside her.

"Well, as your bestie, you know I only wish you well, and I'm glad you're having such a good day. But just be careful. The happiness sprites can be a mischievous bunch when they think you're too content. They love to mess with cheerful people."

"I'll take that chance. But honestly, what could go wrong? Surely, the sprites have someone more important to wreak havoc with than little old me," Jaycee said, grinning at her friend as she placed a finished loaf beside the one Lisa had completed.

"You never know, and you don't want to tempt them or fate," the pretty brunette replied, waving a hand at her. "What are you doing tonight, anyway?"

Jaycee looked up from counting the bread loaves they had prepared and shrugged. "Nothing too exciting. I'm actually kind of tired, so I think I might just pick up a box of Chinese food and go to bed early. I'm off tomorrow, and honestly, I'm looking forward to doing nothing." A contented smile settled on her lips as she contemplated the pleasures her downtime might hold, especially if Tony slipped away from work and spent some time with her, as he had promised.

Wrinkling her nose, Lisa frowned at the countertop in front of her as she wiped it. "That seems to be all you ever do," she complained. She shook her cleaning cloth at Jaycee. "You really should come out tomorrow night with the other girls and me instead. We're going to hit some bars in town, do a little flirting, and see who can get the most drinks bought for them by some poor, unsuspecting men. You'd have more fun with us than you would sitting home alone with some dull old movie."

"I'll think about it." Pulling up a list on her phone of the things that needed to be done to close the bakery, Jaycee held it close to her face to hide her expression while she imagined what Tony would say if she told him she couldn't see him tomorrow night because she was going out with Lisa to flirt with men.

As they continued chatting, the two women worked through their list of closing tasks and had just finished everything on it when they heard a high-pitched nasal Bronx twang coming from the front of the bakery.

"Crap. I'm out of here," Lisa exclaimed, her eyes growing wide and her mouth pinching into a scowl. Rinsing her hands, she hurried to trade her cleaning cloth and apron for the light jacket and handbag she had brought that morning. After pulling open the back door, she raised her eyebrows in mock horror and looked over at Jaycee. "The crazy monster lady has arrived, and I am in no mood to be nice to Rhonda this late in the day." She paused in the doorway to call over her shoulder, "Have a good day off and text me if you change your mind about going out with us tomorrow night." She then gave a brief salute of farewell before disappearing out the door.

"I will," Jaycee said. Sighing, she reached up to untangle her hairnet, then removed her apron and shot a longing look at the steel door that had slammed closed behind Lisa. Biting her bottom lip, she shook her heavy curls free from their braid and moved closer to the door that separated the kitchen from the bakery's retail area.

"We don't pay you to stand around dusting. We pay you to serve customers," she heard Rhonda scold from the other side of the door.

"Oh no," Jaycee moaned. She peeked through the slats that crisscrossed the top of the door. Squinting, she saw there was only one customer in the storefront, and she watched as the man took a bag filled with the bakery's distinctive dark green and gold cardboard boxes from Tony. The customer had also heard the criticism, and Jaycee smiled when she saw him shoot Rhonda a dirty look and Katelyn, their part-time employee, a sympathetic one before leaving.

The teen's lower lip was trembling, and Jaycee raised a hand to cover her frown, wondering what else Rhonda had said to the girl. She started to push open the swinging door, fully intending to intervene on the pretty teen's behalf, but halted when she saw Tony stride over and grab Rhonda by the arm. After giving Katelyn a reassuring smile and saying something Jaycee couldn't quite make out, he propelled the scowling woman by the elbow out of the shop and into the kitchen. Jaycee stepped back as they entered, and Tony's eyebrows rose in surprise when he saw her standing there.

"Hello," Jaycee said. Shuffling farther back into the prep area, she bit her bottom lip and watched as Rhonda yanked her arm out of Tony's grasp.

Rhonda Benoit was a tiny, raven-haired woman who always wore impractical high stiletto heels at the bakery. Jaycee's feet often ached just watching her hobble around in them. Today, the shoes were shiny black and embossed with some sort of lizard pattern.

Perfect.

Jaycee sighed and raised her chin when she realized Rhonda was scowling at her.

"You look ready to leave," the other woman admonished her, waving at Jaycee's tousled, unbound hair. Glancing around the spotless preparation area, she sniffed at the sugary smells of the kitchen. "Have you checked today's receipts yet? Did we make our sales quota?" she asked, placing her hands on her hips and narrowing her eyes.

"Yes, I did," Jaycee replied, taking a deep breath so she could respond in a calm and professional tone. "And we had a wonderful day. We're well above where we projected we'd be for the entire week already. The big police conference next door at the convention center has been great for sales."

Rhonda's frown deepened as she heard this good news. "So, what are we baking for tomorrow morning's rush? I thought we might want to make apple pastries. They're always popular in the fall."

"They are, and we are," Jaycee assured her. "Oh, and do you know how to make an apple turnover?"

Rhonda's brow furrowed as she shook her head.

"Push it down a hill."

Tony's deep chuckle rolled out from somewhere at the back of the kitchen, causing Jaycee to smile.

Rhonda continued scowling as she tapped one set of lizard-clad toes against the tiled floor.

"You didn't think that was funny? Okay. Well..." Jaycee swallowed her grin. "We're actually doing apple turnovers *and* apple fritters for the morning and lunch crowd." She gave a quick nod in the direction of the bakery's refrigerator, where the pastries were being stored, fully assembled and ready to be baked early the next morning by Michael, the night baker. "You're right, they do go over well when the weather cools. And good quality summer fruits are becoming harder to buy fresh now, so it's a great idea to switch over to apples."

Rhonda muttered something unintelligible under her breath.

Jaycee's forced smile turned to one of relief when she saw Tony was returning from his routine evening check of the bakery kitchen. He stopped beside Rhonda, and Jaycee blinked in confusion as the other woman glanced up at him and slipped her arm through his to tug him close to her side.

"Did you hear our news yet?" Rhonda asked, giving Jaycee a smug smile that caused her to flash back to all the mean girls she had known in high school.

Jaycee gave her a bewildered frown, shaking her head as she watched Rhonda wrap both arms around Tony's waist.

"You should have told her," Rhonda scolded him with a teasing laugh.

He lifted both hands in the air, shaking himself free from her hold as he stepped back. "No, I shouldn't have," he replied, his eyes wide as he looked from her to Jaycee. "And really, this isn't the right time.

Jaycee's ready to leave, and she won't be interested in any of that stuff, anyway."

Jaycee shot him a puzzled look.

"Oh, you! *Men.* They know nothing. Of course she will. All women love to hear happy news like this," Rhonda said, winking at Jaycee, then smiling up at Tony. She didn't seem to notice that his face had lost its color as he inched even farther from her side.

"No, Rhonda."

"I'm telling her," the other woman declared, swatting Tony's hand away as a brilliant smile brightened her face, turning her usual sour expression into something resembling pretty. "Tony and I are having a baby! We're getting married!"

Chapter Two

Jeremy Matthews clicked the remote to display the slide on the overhead projection screen that would conclude his presentation. "Thank you for your time. I hope this was helpful," he said, setting the small plastic controller down on the wooden podium at the far side of the stage. "And if you have any questions, I have a few minutes now to answer them. Or you can reach out to me at the email address shown here," he added, waving a hand at the overhead screen, "and I'll be happy to help in any way I can."

After picking up his reference notes from the lectern, he walked back out to center stage and clasped both hands in front of him. Every chair in the oversized room of the sprawling conference center was filled. Looking out just over the heads of those seated in front of him, he smiled steadily, and when the applause finally decreased in volume, he acknowledged the attention with a modest bow. As people turned to talk to their neighbors and an inaudible murmur filled the room, Jeremy turned and hurried down the side stage steps.

"I just have a few minutes," he said, a sincere smile lighting up his eyes as he addressed the small group that had gathered there. "I've got a flight to catch."

Glancing down at the chunky watch on his wrist, he did a quick calculation and confirmed that he had about fifteen minutes to answer questions. Then he would need to grab his bag from the back of the room and find a cab in order to meet the check-in time the airline had recommended.

He stepped forward. "How can I help?" he asked, ducking down to better hear the question from the policewoman at the front of the line. After answering her, he stretched back up to his full six-foot-two height and handed her his business card. "Call me or reach out through my email if you still have questions or want me to expand more on what I suggested," he said, smiling at her. The woman nodded her thanks and moved away to allow another officer to take her place.

"I'm sorry I can't spend more time with you today," Jeremy apologized a short time later to the rest of the group gathered around him as he handed out his remaining cards. "But please," he said, "feel free to use the contact information on these to reach me, and I'd be happy to answer questions or help in any way I can."

Turning away, he began zigzagging through the crowd toward the exit. He had almost reached the door when one of the event organizers stepped in front of him. "You did a great job here today," the pretty woman said, and Jeremy couldn't help but notice how her glance dropped to his left hand. He winced.

There might not be a band on my ring finger any longer, but that doesn't mean my heart is available.

"It's been my pleasure," he answered, peering over her head and grimacing when he glimpsed a taxi speeding by.

"How long have you been specializing in arson?" she asked, shaking her long, shiny blond hair back as she tilted her head and batted her long eyelashes at him.

"It feels like too long, but it's been just over six years now. And honestly, I just wish my expertise wasn't necessary at all." He nodded briskly and stepped around her. "But now, if you'll excuse me, I have a flight to catch."

"Oh," she said, her smile fading.

Jeremy flinched. "I'm sorry," he said. "But I really need to get going if I'm going to make my flight. If you ever need help with a case, please reach out."

The woman nodded and pursed her lips as Jeremy hoisted his duffel bag high onto his shoulder and hurried out the conference room's back doors.

The downtown roads were congested, and the air around the tall buildings was thick with smog. Jeremy wrinkled his nose against the rank, sooty smell that had him clearing his throat as he stopped at the curb. Squinting, he searched through the four lanes of traffic rushing by him, hoping to spot a free yellow taxicab.

He tapped his foot impatiently. Now that the conference was over, he was eager to get to his next assignment. He was heading back to a town, just one over from where he had grown up, to help the police catch an arsonist who had already struck twice. The mayor of Larkin Bay, a very pleasant woman, had sounded desperate in her call, and he wanted to get there as soon as possible to help. Arson was a horrific crime, and while no one had been hurt yet, both he and the mayor knew it was only a matter of time before someone was.

Scanning the busy street in front of him, Jeremy let out a sigh of relief when the heavy traffic parted to reveal a yellow cab with its light on. His piercing whistle caused the pedestrian standing beside him to startle in surprise, but it caught the taxi driver's attention. The cabbie was just pulling over to the curb when Jeremy caught sight of someone rushing toward them out of the corner of his eye.

A teen waiting to cross the road farther down cried out a warning, and Jeremy dropped his bag, instinctively reaching out to grab the woman's arm and jerk her back out of the path of the oncoming cab. The shriek of locked car brakes on asphalt rose above the usual afternoon traffic noise, causing the other pedestrians around them to turn and stare.

"Hey! Watch where you're going! You were almost hit by a car." Jeremy yelled, clutching the woman's arm and pulling her farther onto the sidewalk, out of harm's way.

She gave a small cry of distress, and Jeremy's eyes widened as he realized she was crying.

"Are you okay? What happened? Do you need help?" he asked, gentling his hold on her.

The woman shook her head but continued to tremble. A moment later, her legs seemed to give out beneath her, and he tightened his hold once more, pulling her closer so she wouldn't fall. "Look, it's okay. The cab stopped. Everything's fine. You're safe now," he said, carefully keeping his tone soothing while he frowned down at her.

When she finally looked up at him, Jeremy was struck by the heartbreak in her eyes. He then blinked as he realized he knew her, or at least recognized her. She was the pretty brunette who had served him the last few mornings when he'd stopped by the bakery next to the conference center. He had gone there for the delicious pastries and coffee and returned after lunch for their delectable peanut butter cookies. But also, if he was honest, after the first visit he had returned because he appreciated her open, bright smile and friendly chatter. Now, however, her welcoming demeanor was nowhere to be seen, and tears streaked her cheeks while her shoulders trembled in distress.

She's in shock.

Jeremy stared down at her wide eyes and unfocused gaze as she used both hands to push away from him. Instantly, he released his hold on her and stepped back, his police training kicking in as he looked around and assessed the situation.

Now that the woman was safe, the small group of people that had gathered around them dispersed. Jeremy stretched up to his full height but didn't move away. He didn't know this woman well, but the several times he had talked to her this week, he had been drawn to her pretty eyes and welcoming smile. Besides that, her thick, curly hair and long legs would attract the eye of any straight man, even if she hadn't been so charming.

He shook his head.

What the hell am I thinking?

He had always prided himself on being a calm and detached professional when dealing with the public. Clearing his throat, he pulled his shoulders back and forced himself to address her in a brisk and courteous tone. "Are you sure you're okay?" he asked. "Do you need any help?"

The woman looked up at him, her eyes narrowing. "Help? Huh. Probably." Her tone was bitter as she reached up and rubbed a faint scar on her cheek. "Maybe it would have been better if I had been hit," she replied, straightening her purse on her shoulder. Her expression was grim.

"No, don't say that," Jeremy commanded sharply. He glanced over his shoulder at the shop he suspected she had just come from. "Should I get someone from the bakery for you?"

The woman's eyes grew wide as her hands fluttered down to smooth her white apron. "Omigod! No! That would just make things so much worse."

Jeremy frowned at the intensity of her tone, watching as she looked down at her apron and startled, as if she was surprised to find she was wearing it. A moment later, she had untied it, bunched it up into a hard knot, and tossed it into the nearest public garbage can.

He stared at her. Obviously, something traumatic had happened to her at the bakery. He frowned and wondered what could have occurred that was bad enough for her to almost run blindly into traffic. He cleared his throat and turned to look at the buildings behind them as he reached for his phone to take notes. Something was definitely wrong, and his instincts were telling him to investigate.

The woman reached over and lightly tapped his arm. "No! Please. I'm fine, really," she said, straightening next to him and drawing her shoulders back. "There's nothing the staff at the bakery can do. I'm really all right."

Studying her through narrowed eyes, Jeremy could see from the telltale curl of her lip and inability to meet his eye that she wasn't telling him the truth, but she did seem calmer and more in control now. He was trained to recognize hidden trauma and while the woman appeared to be far steadier, she was also trying a little too hard to act like she was fine, which made it even more evident to him that she wasn't. His brow furrowed as he considered his options. She might not be steady by his personal assessment, but she didn't seem to want his help, and she wasn't in any danger.

His thoughts were interrupted by the taxi driver shouting through the open back window. "Hey, buddy? Do you want a cab or not? I got lots of people who'll pay me to give them a lift today if you don't need a ride."

Jeremy glared at the driver and then looked back at the woman. She smiled shakily at him and stepped back as she waved a hand at the taxi. "Thanks for your help and for, um, stopping me from being hit by a car, but I'm fine. Honestly, I don't need anything else. You should go now. You don't want to miss your ride."

"Are you sure you're okay?"

"Of course. I just received some news that upset me, so I wasn't thinking or acting clearly. But I've got everything under control now."

Jeremy nodded and reached for the cab's back door handle, then pulled his hand back. He didn't want to leave this woman alone. He turned around to speak with her again, only to discover that she'd already disappeared into the crowd.

The cab driver tapped his horn twice and glared over his shoulder. Jeremy shrugged and yanked on the door handle. After tossing his large carry-on bag onto the back seat, he climbed in.

"The airport, please," he said sharply. As the ancient taxi heaved and moved away from the curb, he turned to look out the window, searching again for the beautiful woman. When he couldn't find her in the crowd, he was surprised to discover he was disappointed. Funny how holding her had felt so comfortable, he thought. Her hair had smelled like apples and sugar, and even though she had obviously been upset, she was still very attractive.

Shaking his head, Jeremy sighed and settled back into his seat to watch the scenery go by as the driver sped toward the airport.

Chapter Three

As she crammed the last of her overstuffed bags into the trunk of her car, Jaycee felt the cell phone in her front pocket vibrate. She didn't need to look at the number to see who it was and, pulling her phone out, she stabbed the decline button. Scowling at the tiny screen, she decided it was past time to block Tony's number. Once finished, she shoved the phone back into her jeans and blinked back a few tears before loading up the rest of her belongings.

When she finally had the last of her things shoehorned into every available cranny of the car, Jaycee slammed the trunk of her ancient Honda shut and patted one of the many places on it where the paint was peeling. She hoped the vehicle would be up for the long drive home. Sadly, her cherished chariot was getting old. One of the many things she loved about living in the city was the excellent public transit system. And, since she had rented an apartment close enough to the bakery to walk to work, months had gone by since she had pulled her old, baby blue, bumper sticker–adorned car out of its parking spot.

The fall day was overcast, and the clouds were threatening rain. Jaycee shivered in the cool wind that had blown in overnight, but recognized her grimy Honda and the chill in the air suited her mood today. While her car might not be pretty, it was transportation, and she wanted nothing more desperately than to put as many miles as she could between herself and Tony right now.

Turning away, Jaycee hurried back up the steps of her low-rise building so she could finish gathering her things and say goodbye to Lisa.

"I can understand why you're going," her friend said a short time later. Carrying the two potted ferns she had agreed to plant-sit, she followed Jaycee out of her tiny, one-bedroom apartment. "But I'm going to miss you a lot. You know when I go into work later today I'm probably going to say something to Tony that's pretty awful." She gave her a sad smile. "You're leaving me in a terrible position."

"Well, trust me, I feel bad that it ended up this way too," Jaycee replied, biting her lip as she jiggled her apartment's door handle to ensure it was locked behind them. "But I'm long overdue for a visit home, and I can't go back to the bakery anytime soon. Honestly, I've got to leave before I do something crazy. I refuse to become roadkill because of a man."

Lisa shuddered in sympathy at the reminder of her friend's brush with disaster the day before. Once they reached the car, she steadied the two plants on the curb, then turned to embrace Jaycee.

"I'm sorry," Lisa whispered as she held her friend close. "Tony didn't deserve you. But at least karma's going to get him in a big way because he's stuck marrying Rhonda, and that's the worst possible thing I can think of that could ever happen to a person."

Jaycee's laugh was flat. "Don't worry, they'll both get what they deserve," she said, pulling back and giving her friend a forced smile. "And, you know what they say—karma never loses an address. She just sometimes needs to finish her tequila and sharpen her nails before she gets to work."

"I hope so."

Jaycee watched her friend pick up and juggle the two plant pots in her arms for a moment. She tried to smile, but instead found herself wiping away tears that had sprung up behind her lashes. "You take care of yourself while I'm gone, okay?" she said, her voice hoarse. "I want a gazillion texts and pictures so I don't feel like I'm missing out on anything you're doing while I'm away."

"Promise," Lisa replied solemnly, pressing her lips together as she watched Jaycee climb into her car and honk twice in farewell before pulling out into traffic to start on her long trip home.

The sun was setting, and Jaycee was determinedly humming along with the heartbreak playlist that Lisa had made for her when she pulled onto Larkin Bay's Main Street. The furrow in her forehead deepened as she contemplated how she hadn't been back to her hometown in over a year. Since the car accident that had killed her parents eight years ago, she'd simply found it too painful to visit for any extended period. But she was now relieved to find the passing of time had dulled the hurt enough that coming home felt strangely comforting. She eased off the accelerator and peered out her window, reacquainting herself with Larkin Bay by taking long looks at the narrow streets, cobblestone sidewalks, and tiny storefronts.

The shoe store, where Jaycee had bought her first pair of high-heeled shoes—memorable because they had been made of bright glossy-red patent—caused a nostalgic smile to cross her lips.

The shop was tucked right beside her favorite store in town, the bookstore. It looked exactly the same as it had ten years ago when she'd visited it weekly.

As she reached the end of the street, her eyes widened, and she gave a sharp gasp. Tugging hard on the steering wheel, she maneuvered the car into a parking spot and stared at the place where a beautiful eighteenth-century brick, gargoyle-adorned building that housed the local hardware store had once stood. Now only two blackened walls remained standing, the glass front windows were boarded over, and its bright blue awning lay in an ugly heap by the curb. She shook her head in disbelief as she studied the devastation. Her sister had mentioned the fire when they'd last spoken, but Jaycee hadn't fully appreciated the extent of the damage.

The building had been so beautiful and was now destroyed. Jaycee sighed and collapsed back in the driver's seat. She swallowed hard past the lump that had formed in her throat.

So many precious things have been ruined this week.

After taking another long look at the devastation, she took a deep, steadying breath, reminded herself she was strong, and pushed the gearshift into Drive. Pulling back onto Main Street, she forced herself to look straight ahead as she drove away.

A short time later, Jaycee pulled into the driveway of the house where she'd grown up. She had only stopped a few times on the trip for bathroom and gas breaks and her body was now stiff and begging to move. She groaned as she snapped open her seat belt and unwound her tired limbs from the driver's seat. As she climbed out of the car, she looked curiously at her childhood home. A roomy lemonade porch ran across the front of the small brick two-story house, and an oversized wooden door surrounded by fancy hand-carved wooden scalloping sat at its center. The red porch swing that Jaycee's father had hung at her mother's request was rocking slowly in the gentle fall breeze. The tidy front lawn had been recently mowed, but she saw that the house's once bright cranberry-red door had faded. Jaycee made a mental note to remind Betty that it was okay to use some of the money from the trust her parents had left them for painting and house upkeep.

Suddenly, the front door flew open, and a wide-eyed teen peered out at her. Jaycee gave her a tired wave. A moment later, she was almost knocked off her feet as her little sister launched into her arms, squealing in delight as she engulfed her in a bone-crushing hug.

"Whoa," Jaycee exclaimed, struggling to keep her balance. "Hey there. Yes, it's me. Surprise! Don't knock me over!"

Holding Chandra in her arms, she felt her sister's head press up close under her chin and realized that the girl had grown taller since she'd last seen her. After a minute, the teen pulled back and swung her dark, waist-length hair behind her shoulders to look up at her older sister. Jaycee's breath hitched, and she blinked hard when she saw how much this curvy, petite, green-eyed beauty standing in front of her had grown seemingly overnight to resemble their late mother.

"When did you decide to come home? Why didn't you tell us you were coming?" demanded a beaming Chandra. Grabbing Jaycee by the hand, she started to drag her toward the front steps. "Betty will be so happy to see you!" she added.

Jaycee smiled in anticipation of a reunion with Chandra's guardian. Since childhood, Betty had been their mother's best friend and had always been an important presence in both girls' lives.

"It was a quick decision. I just decided yesterday that I wanted to see you both, so I got up early this morning and hopped in my car. It was, uh, spontaneous."

Chandra nodded as if this was the most natural thing in the world while Jaycee marveled how only to a seventeen-year-old would it seem perfectly reasonable for someone to travel over seven hundred miles on a whim. She'd have to come up with a better story for Betty, though, especially if she didn't want to tell her anything about Tony.

She pulled Chandra back to the car, and they each grabbed a battered duffel bag from the back seat. Jaycee then took a deep breath, straightened her shoulders, and followed her chattering sister up the wide front steps and into the house.

Jeremy stepped carefully over the piles of broken and blackened timber, picking his way through what had once been the town's hardware store. When he had arrived in town yesterday, Larkin Bay's mayor had shown him a picture of the original structure and Jeremy had whistled appreciatively under his breath. The senseless loss of the building was heartbreaking for both historical and aesthetic reasons.

"What makes you think it was arson?" he asked the fire chief, who was standing a few yards away. This was the first question Jeremy always asked local emergency responders when he visited a suspected arson site. The firefighters could usually provide him with the best insights into where to start an investigation.

Sterling Robertson, a portly white-haired gentleman, cleared his throat and drew himself up a little taller. "Well, we've ruled out all the usual things. There were no electrical or mechanical problems that we could identify. All the inspections were up to date and done in the last year. What really caught my attention, though, was my men told me that this fire didn't burn right. It flamed brighter and faster than it should have just from the structure alone, even when one considers the number of flammable liquids and such that are sold in a hardware store." Pausing, the chief chewed his lower lip for a second. "Before we knocked it down, my guys found a door upstairs propped open too, and the owner says he's sure it had been dead-bolted shut."

"Someone wanted a big fire and opened it for better ventilation. They wanted the building to go up quickly," murmured Jeremy, his eyes narrowing as he scanned the rubble again.

"That's what I think too. The smoke was also very thick, and it was unusually dark."

"Huh."

The other man nodded. "Yup, I saw that myself when I first got on the scene, and that, of course, raised a red flag. I waited a little longer than usual to get my men in there because of it. I had to sort out what exactly we were dealing with."

"Gasoline? Gas is simple to get, so it's often the fire starter of choice for arsonists."

"Probably. But there's no way to know for sure—there were just too many flammable products being sold here."

Jeremy shook his head as he kicked at some of the debris on the site with his steel-toed boot. Did the owners tell you anything else?"

Sterling shifted his hands into the pockets of his navy uniform overalls and studied Jeremy for a long moment before shrugging. "He told us exactly what we expected to hear—that he was home that night. And his wife confirmed it." Leaning over, he picked up a small piece of stone and rubbed it between his fingers. "You know how it is. This is a small town. Everyone here knows each other's business, and this was a family company—third generation, in fact. Tom, the owner, has twin teenage daughters who worked here and who he'd probably planned to pass the business along to, if the girls wanted it. At least before all this happened."

The older man looked away, scrubbed a hand across his beard, and lowered his voice. "But just to be sure, I checked all of Tom's accounts. He had insurance, but the place was doing well. Really well. He doesn't seem to have any motive for burning it down."

Nodding, Jeremy took another long look at the devastation around him and then took a step closer to the fire chief. "Well, you're the one in the know here. So, you tell me. Did arson cause this fire? And if so, who do you think started it?"

Sterling shook his head slowly. "We've never had any suspicious fires like these last two, at least not since I've been chief. Do I think this fire was started intentionally? Yep, unfortunately, I do." He sighed out a long, rattling, frustrated breath. "But I don't know who did it, and I've lived in Larkin Bay my whole life. I know just about everyone who lives here, but I still have no idea who would want to hurt Tom or his family by doing something like this. No clue at all." Turning to face Jeremy squarely, the chief looked him up and down. "So that's where we are, and that's the reason I suggested the mayor bring you here. We need you to tell us what happened, who did it, and how to stop it from ever happening again."

The fall sunshine sparkled on the lake and lit up Main Street's storefront windows. Strolling with her sister along the cobblestone sidewalk, Jaycee saw that most of the shop displays were decorated in bright, autumnal colors. A banner advertising Larkin Bay's Halloween parade and annual fall fair was strung between the lampposts and fluttered gently overhead. The busy city she had left yesterday morning was beautiful in its hectic, crowded way, but this cozy, clean, and simpler small-town style certainly had a great deal more charm, she mused.

Walking next to Chandra, Jaycee kept glancing over at her sister, nodding and smiling while listening to her cheerful chatter. When they reached the center of town, she put out a hand to halt the girl and waved at the blackened remains of the hardware store across the street. "Have you heard anything more about happened there?" she asked.

The teen wrinkled her nose and shrugged. "No. Not really," she replied. "There was a big fire, and the hardware store got absolutely destroyed. We all came out to see if we could help, but the whole thing went up really fast, so we couldn't do much." She turned away from the scene and looked over at Jaycee. "But you know what? Although it was horrible, it was beautiful too. The flames looked like they were dancing, and they were the most wonderful colors. I couldn't help but think that it was more lovely than awful, at least to watch."

Jaycee frowned. The fire may have been artistically beautiful in some ways, but the devastation was heartbreaking. Glancing down, she checked the time on her phone, then reached over and grabbed her sister's hand. "Well, I think it's just horrible, not beautiful. But, come on. I want to get to the butcher before it closes. You and Betty have nothing in the house that I can use to make dinner tonight, and I'm really looking forward to creating a healthy home-cooked meal, so I need ingredients."

Tugging her sister behind her, Jaycee started toward the stores she wanted to visit. As she did, she noticed one of the uniformed police officers investigating the fire scene across the street had stopped his deliberations and was watching them walk away. She glanced over at him curiously, then halted, shocked to stillness as she wondered if her eyes were playing tricks on her.

She blinked.

The darkly dressed man standing in the hardware store rubble looked just like the man who had stopped her from running into traffic and comforted her while she'd cried over Tony just a few days ago.

What is he doing in Larkin Bay?

Chapter Four

Jeremy nodded at Jaycee from behind the caution tape before he turned and disappeared behind what was left of the once-beautiful building.

Jaycee's eyes were wide as she stared. "I must be seeing things," she said.

Chandra pulled her hand away and looked over with a puzzled smile. "Who are you talking to?" she asked. When Jaycee didn't reply, the teen shrugged and returned to texting on her phone as she headed up the street toward the butcher's shop.

Jaycee watched her sister walk away for a moment, then took another long look across the street.

I saw him seven hundred miles away from here. It can't be the same man.

She shook her head and hurried to catch up with Chandra. Her sister had stopped to speak with Grayson Young, who was frowning as he swept leaves off his shop's front steps. The gray-haired independent bookseller housed his eclectic collection of books in what was once Larkin Bay's small, redbrick schoolhouse. The historic gargoyle-adorned property had been carefully preserved and turned into a bookstore after a new school was built just outside the downtown area.

"Well, hello there! Jaycee, you've come back? To what do we owe this great honor?" Grayson greeted her as she stopped beside them.

Jaycee blinked at his less-than-welcoming tone. "Well, hello to you too, Mr. Young. How are things at the bookstore? And it's an honor to have me home?" She chuckled. "I'm just happy to be here visiting with my sister and friends."

The older gentleman acknowledged her reply with a nod. "That's a good thing. This young lady has been on her own for far too long, with no finances or anyone to look after her. It's a crime, if you ask me."

Jaycee looked from Mr. Young to Chandra, her brows rising as she stepped back. "No finances? But Mom and Dad left Chandra a trust fund, and Betty's been looking after it. There isn't any problem with money, at least none that I know of. What are you talking about?" She glanced at Chandra, but her sister was studying her feet, scuffing her sneaker-clad foot back and forth on the pavement, and didn't look up.

Grabbing the girl's arm, Jaycee turned back to Mr. Young, whose eyes had widened at her obvious confusion. He held up his broom between them and stepped back. "I'm sorry," he said, raising a hand in apology. "But honestly, I thought you knew where things stood." After clearing his throat, he patted Jaycee's arm and mumbled something about giving her and Chandra some privacy. Turning away, he hurried back into his bookstore, stopping only for a moment to shoot one last concerned look at the girls before pulling the door closed behind him with a firm jerk.

Jaycee released her hold on her sister. "Chandy? What's going on? What was that all about?"

"Please, Jaycee, can we just wait until we get home to talk about it?"

She studied the teen for a long moment before nodding. "Fine. We'll go to the butcher's and grab a few groceries at the market. But as soon as we get home, you're going to tell me exactly what he meant and what's going on."

Chandra nodded her agreement and then gave a sigh that sounded suspiciously like relief to Jaycee's ears as she followed her sister to do their shopping.

Later that evening, sitting around their family's battered kitchen table, Jaycee was stunned into silence.

"Honestly, it's not as bad as it sounds," Betty reassured her, twisting her hands in her lap.

Jaycee closed her eyes, forced herself to count slowly to three, and tried to ignore the sprites in her stomach who were threatening an acidic mutiny after hearing Betty's story. "I believe you," she finally said, opening her eyes. She spoke slowly and enunciated all her words carefully. "But I'm not really sure I understand, either. Did you take all the funds from the family trust and give them to this investor, or just some? That money was supposed to pay for Chandra's college tuition next year and allow you both to live comfortably here for a few more years..." She snapped her mouth shut. Her words sounded harsh and accusatory, even to her own ears, so she bit her lip to stop from saying more.

"I know, dear," the older lady replied, her voice trembling. "And I wouldn't have touched the money at all, except this man assured me it was going into a very safe investment and that nothing could possibly go wrong. I only wanted to make sure Chandra had everything she needed for college and maybe even earn a little extra for both of you. I didn't suspect for a minute that all the money would simply disappear. I trusted him."

Jaycee studied Betty silently. The worry lines on the woman's face had deepened since she'd had last seen her, and her hair, once a youthful blond, had now faded to a snowy white. She took a deep breath and forced herself to gentle her tone. "Is all the money in the trust fund gone, then? Is there anything left for you and Chandra to live on or use for her college tuition next year?"

Betty gave a tear-filled laugh that died off into a sigh. "Well, I'm not sure, honestly. We've been keeping things going using my social security check, along with the little extra money you've been sending every month. We've managed fairly well, and I think there *might* still be some money left in the trust for Chandra's tuition..." Her words trailed off as she gave a shaky smile.

Jaycee put a hand up to ward off the pounding headache she could feel forming behind her eyes. She forced herself to smile at Betty. "Well, that sounds promising. Everything is probably fine. I'll just go over to the bank first thing tomorrow morning and see if I can find out exactly where we stand."

Reaching over, she gave Betty a long hug. Looking over the other woman's shoulder, she saw Chandra had been eavesdropping from the shadows of the back staircase. Jaycee sighed when she saw her own worries reflected back at her in the teen's expression.

After Betty had left to stay with her daughter for the night, Jaycee headed upstairs to her small pink-and-cream floral-wallpapered childhood bedroom and pulled on some pale green Lululemon running gear. When she was finished dressing, she clipped her iPhone onto her armband and quickly brushed her curls into a high ponytail. She peered into the large silver-framed mirror that hung above her dresser, swept on some waterproof mascara, and leaned forward to examine her reflection. Her nose was small and turned up at the end, her clear, dark eyes were serious under neatly tweezed brows, and the dimple in her left cheek flashed as she gave herself a crooked smile. Today, even the tiny scar at the corner of her cheek—usually a cause of distress and her last remaining physical reminder of the car accident that had killed her parents—was reassuringly familiar. Her entire world might have been turned upside down this week, but you wouldn't know it by looking at her, she decided.

"Blah," she said, sticking out her tongue and crossing her eyes at her reflection, hoping the silly gesture might make her feel better.

It didn't.

Heading downstairs, she laced up her running shoes, then left the house and was soon jogging through one of the pretty parks that led to the town's boardwalk. She'd run this route often as a teen, and within minutes, she was moving freely, her steady steps helping to pound away some of the stress from Tony's infidelity and Betty's financial misstep.

Jaycee saw very few people on the streets as she upped her pace. It was too late in the year for tourists to be out, and since it was a Sunday evening, most residents were still tidying up their dinner dishes or were busy inside preparing for the work and school week ahead. Her run took her quickly through the pretty residential section of town and into the small, historic downtown core of Larkin Bay. Running past the picturesque street of retail shops where she'd been earlier, she crossed over the bay's wooden boardwalk and onto the running path that was nestled up along the lake's shoreline.

After running for several miles, Jaycee made a sweeping turn at the end of the trail, gasping as she inhaled the pine-laden breezes. She had just slowed her pace slightly when a small ball of black-and-white fur darted in front of her, nimbly leaping over her feet and dashing into a thick line of shrubs.

"Whoa!" she cried, taking a quick step back to avoid stepping on the small animal. Holding her arms out, she pinwheeled them quickly to regain her balance. "Yowza! What was that?"

Regaining her footing, she looked toward the underbrush, curious as to what had startled her into almost losing her balance. "I hope it's not a skunk," she murmured.

"It's not. It's this little guy," said someone from the other side of the hedge.

Jaycee looked up in surprise. A man, also dressed in running gear, was leaning over the shrubs, holding a tiny mewing black-and-white kitten out toward her.

"Um, thanks," she replied, and quickly smoothed her disheveled clothes back into place before reaching over and taking the trembling bundle of fur that he was dangling by the scruff of its neck. The cat immediately gave a pitiful cry and burrowed himself headfirst into the crook of her arm.

"Ah," Jaycee exclaimed and smiled down at the kitten before turning her attention back to the man.

Wow.

She felt her eyes widen. The stranger had obviously been out running too, as his Nike T-shirt was soaked with perspiration. Stuck to his body, it showed off a well-defined chest and broad shoulders that tapered down to a rippling abdomen. As he turned away from her, Jaycee fought the urge to grab his arm to see if his biceps were really as muscular and hard as they appeared.

She checked his profile quickly and felt her cheeks warm as she realized that not only was this man very attractive, but he was also the same police officer she had seen earlier downtown. And he was definitely the man who had saved her from running into traffic in the city.

Crap.

Jaycee looked down at the kitten she was cuddling in her arms and fought to steady her breath. After a few moments, she peered back up to discover the cat's rescuer wasn't paying any attention to her, but was instead watching a dark-colored puppy playing at the lake's edge.

"Bo," he yelled, his tone sharp, but Jaycee also detected a hint of laughter in his call. "Bo! Come here. Now!" The empty leash dangling from his hand suggested the dog had somehow slipped his restraint.

Jaycee's lips twitched as she watched the puppy clumsily run free along the shoreline, chasing the squalling seagulls that had been peacefully catching their dinner in the waves only moments before.

"Silly mutt," the other runner muttered under his breath. After shooting an apologetic look at Jaycee, he hurried off toward the lake, whistling and calling for the dog as he strode across the rock-strewn shoreline.

Jaycee admired his toned backside for a moment, then tore her eyes away and turned her attention back to the kitten, who was busy trying to burrow himself even deeper into the warmth of her arms. She gently examined the cat and, after seeing his well-rounded tummy and soft, shiny fur, concluded that he was too healthy to be a stray. He was big enough to be away from his mother, she decided, and had probably found an open window or door, made his escape, and was now lost. The kitten had no collar, but he was obviously comfortable being around people because, after a moment of soothing coos, he lay back with his stomach exposed, yawning and blinking up at her with large, trusting eyes. Jaycee tugged her running jacket from around her waist and wrapped it around him. Snuggling in, he yawned again and settled in for a nap.

Jaycee quickly decided he couldn't have escaped from very far. He was too little. Smiling, she held her hand up to shade her eyes from the setting sun and studied the small apartments above the shops to see if any of them had a window or door ajar. She saw nothing that looked open. Scanning up and down the boardwalk, she spotted a few people, but no one who seemed to be searching for a lost pet. She hugged the cat tighter as the man, with a now securely leashed puppy bounding at his side, jogged back toward them.

"Is he okay?" he asked, nodding at the cat.

Jaycee pulled her arms up to hold the tiny kitten a little higher out of range of the dog's inquisitive nose. "He seems fine," she replied. "I'm just not sure where he came from. He seems too healthy to be a stray."

The man nodded. "I suppose you could knock on a few doors and ask if anyone knows where he's from," he said, frowning. "But I don't know who you'd find in the shops at this time of the evening."

Jaycee shook her head. "I think it might be best if I just take him home for the night and reach out to the animal shelter first thing in the morning. I'm sure that's where people would call first if they're looking for a lost kitten."

The man smiled, revealing two dimples. "I agree. I'd take him, but, well," he said, gesturing at the dog, "I'm afraid Bo here might eat him or bat him around thinking he's a toy."

"That's okay. I don't mind," Jaycee said, cuddling the cat closer as she leaned forward to scratch the dog behind his ears. "I guess I've just found myself a new pet, at least for the night."

"Yep, I guess you did. A cute one too."

Jaycee looked up, and her breath caught when she saw that his blue-gray eyes were studying her intently. Her heart rate accelerated as she met his gaze, but she couldn't read the emotions running across his strong, angular features.

A loud bark broke the moment as the dog leaped up, trying once again to get a closer sniff at the bundle Jaycee was cradling. Laughing, she held the kitten up high out of the dog's reach once more as the man pulled the puppy back down to his side. "But I'm being rude," he said once the dog was settled. "I'm Jeremy—Jeremy Matthews—and this is Bo," he added, nodding at the puppy.

"I'm Jaycee Laughton."

"So," Jeremy asked, motioning toward the kitten, "are you really okay taking this little guy home?"

"Of course. I love animals. It's no trouble at all."

"How about you give me your number and I'll text you later to see if you need any help with him?"

"That would be great," Jaycee replied, feeling a blush steal across her cheeks.

Jeremy pulled an older model iPhone out of the back pocket of his running shorts and handed it to her so she could input her number. When she was done, he saved her contact information and grinned as he tucked it away. "Well, it was nice meeting you. I'll call you tomorrow to check up on this little guy," he promised, reaching over and gently stroking the kitten between his tiny, pointed ears.

Jaycee nodded back, ignoring the happy dance the sprites in her stomach were doing as the kitten purred louder in her arms. Smiling, she gave Jeremy a small wave before following the boardwalk back in the direction she had come.

She hoped Jeremy didn't remember her from the city.

He had given no indication that he had, and, Jaycee reasoned, with her tear-stained face and slightly crazed look that day, maybe he really *hadn't* recognized her.

"I shouldn't even be thinking about him," she said to the little cat, now slumbering peacefully in her arms. "I have too many other things to worry about."

The kitten didn't stir. After she had walked a few more yards, Jaycee glanced over her shoulder and saw Jeremy was still standing in the middle of the boardwalk, holding Bo tight on his leash while he watched her walk away. He grinned when he saw her turn and lifted his hand in a quick salute just as the dog pulled him back to the beach to continue their run in the opposite direction.

Jaycee's breath caught as she smiled happily in return before turning and picking up her pace toward home.

Chapter Five

The kitchen had always been her mother's favorite room in the house, and because of that and Jaycee's love of baking, it was her favorite room too. The cabinets were still the same light oak they had been when she was young, and while the granite countertops were now dull with age, Jaycee knew she wouldn't renovate or update anything in here for a very long time. There were just too many cherished memories in this room. But right now, Jaycee was living in the present, and things were nowhere near as good as those memories.

"I really am sorry," Betty said, repeating her apology the next evening for what seemed like the hundredth time. "I honestly thought I was doing the right thing. I believed everything that man told me. I was just an old fool."

Sighing, Jaycee leaned over and placed her hand on the older lady's shoulder. "It's fine. We'll figure it out. I just wish you or Chandra had told me when the money was first lost so I could have tried to help sooner." She frowned as she settled back in her chair and looked down at the financial papers Betty had placed on the table in front of her.

Or at the very least, I might not have quit my job so quickly.

But that thought wasn't entirely fair, she realized. Jaycee knew she would have walked out of the bakery as soon as she had discovered Tony was cheating on her, whether she'd known about Betty's investment missteps or not.

I'll just have to figure this out.

When Betty cleared her throat a few minutes later, Jaycee looked up from the bank documents. "Oh no," she said, her eyes widening when she saw Betty's pensive expression. "There's more bad news?" she asked.

Betty winced. "Well, no. No more money problems that I know of, anyway. I think I've given you all the paperwork the bank and that investment man gave me."

"Well, that's good."

When Jaycee's parents had died, Betty had immediately swept in to take care of their orphaned daughters. She'd insisted that Jaycee continue with her plan to attend culinary school and had moved into the family home to be with Chandra so Jaycee would be free to leave Larkin Bay, finish college, and pursue her dream of becoming a professional baker. Because of this, Jaycee knew she owed Betty a good dose of forgiveness and patience now.

"It's Chandra," the older woman said in response to Jaycee's questioning look. "I'm worried about her. She's always been such a good girl—thoughtful and worked hard at school. But lately, she seems different—like something's bothering her, but I can't seem to get her to talk to me about it. She's been hanging around with a new group of kids too." Betty's hands fluttered up to her cheeks as she looked over at Jaycee, then fell into her lap again. "And since she's started dating this boy, Dean, she doesn't seem to see any of her old friends. I was hoping you might talk to her a bit about what she's up to."

Jaycee's brow furrowed. "Sure. Chandra seems more than willing to talk to me about most things. Is there anything specific that you're worried about?"

Betty looked down at the table and shrugged. "Not one thing in particular, no. I love her like she's my own child—you know that. It just seems like something's off, and I can't quite put my finger on what it is."

"Well, she's a teenager. Things being off with her is probably pretty normal," Jaycee replied with a small smile. "But if it makes you feel any better, I'll take her out and try to talk to her tonight or tomorrow. I had planned on it anyway, as we've got a lot of catching up to do. I thought connecting with her frequently on Snapchat and texting was doing that, but it doesn't seem like that's been enough."

Betty smiled. "I'm glad you've come home," she said, getting out of her chair and leaning over to give Jaycee a hug.

"Me too," she replied, feeling a small smile creep across her face. "Me too."

Jaycee glanced at the time on her car's dashboard as she drove to the hardware store one town over. She still had a few hours before she'd arranged to meet with the bank manager, so she strolled the aisles, carefully checking prices as she filled a shopping cart with the long list of things she needed to clean the house and do some odd jobs. Leaving the paint to get tinted, she loaded the rest of her purchases into her car and browsed through the two small clothing stores in town. She quickly realized she couldn't afford anything new right now, so after picking up a steaming cup of tea from the local coffee shop, she hurried back to the hardware store.

"I was shopping in town while I was waiting, and I didn't see a bakery here. Where does your family go to buy cakes or bread?" she asked the teen helping her carry her paint cans out to her car.

The lanky young man scratched his wispy beard. "Well, I guess either my mom makes them, or we get them at the grocery store. I never thought about having a bakery close by before, but now that you mention it, we don't."

"That's good to know. Thank you." Jaycee tipped him for his help, checked the time on her phone, and, seeing that she still had a few minutes to spare, set off down the street toward the town's large chain grocery store.

When she entered the brightly illuminated shop, she saw the bakery area was spacious, clean, and well-stocked with an extensive selection of breads, cookies, and other prepackaged baked goods. She picked up a loaf of bread and cringed at the list of preservatives and refined sugar at the top of the ingredient's list.

A pretty, dark-haired woman in a clean white apron approached her. "Do you have any questions?" she asked.

"No, but thank you. I was just admiring everything you carry." Jaycee bit her bottom lip for a moment. "But I *was* wondering if you're hiring? I'm a baker. I've just moved to Larkin Bay, and I'm looking for a job."

The cheerful expression on the other woman's face quickly disappeared. "I wish we were," she replied, shaking her head. "I'm the department manager, and I've just had to lay off some of our staff. The bakery is being downsized as we're selling so many prepacked goods now. It's a shame too. Freshly baked products are usually a much healthier and better-tasting option."

Jaycee's smile wilted. "I think so too. Thank you for the information," she added before turning away and hurrying to the other end of the store, where she picked up a bag of kitten food along with some eggs, flour, and yeast to make her own bread.

A short time later, settling in the driver's seat of her car, Jaycee gazed glumly out at the busy retail streets around her. She needed a job, but it didn't sound like there was much demand for bakers here.

I'll just have to find something else to do.

Sighing, she turned the key in the car's ignition. The engine clicked but didn't turn over. "Oh no," she moaned, tapping the gas pedal a little harder and turning the key again.

Nothing happened.

Putting her head down on the steering wheel, Jaycee groaned softly. She was supposed to be back in Larkin Bay to meet the bank manager in less than an hour. She didn't have the time, and she certainly didn't have the money, for car problems today.

When Jaycee got out of her car to greet the tow truck driver who had arrived to help her, she realized, with a smile, that she knew him. He had dated her best friend back when they were all in high school, and the couple had gotten married as soon as they'd graduated from college.

"Danny!" she cried, greeting him with a hug. "You own the towing company," she exclaimed when she saw his name scripted in neatly painted letters on the side of the truck. "That's so great! You always said you wanted to work with cars and trucks."

The handsome, dark-skinned, and spiky-haired man smiled back at her and returned the embrace. "Jaycee Laughton! Well, this is a pleasant surprise. I wondered if it was really you when I got the call." He released her and stepped back. "Yep, I own Larkin Bay's tow truck company, and the garage there too." He slapped a hand against his leg. "So you're back in town? What are you doing way over here? Doesn't Larkin Bay have everything your little heart could desire?"

"It has you, so that's a good start," Jaycee replied with a laugh. "But no, I needed some things from a hardware store for the house, and Larkin Bay, unfortunately, doesn't have one right now. But, how are you? And how is Amanda? I can't believe I haven't called my oldest BFF since I've been home."

Danny's smile wavered slightly at the mention of the hardware store, but broadened again as she asked about his wife. "Everyone's good. Amanda is just a little tired these days, with Ava not always sleeping through the night and crawling now too. She keeps us busy. But I know Amanda would love to hear from you."

"Maybe I'll drop by the house sometime this week. It's her birthday in a couple of days, isn't it? I'll have to come by and celebrate with her."

Danny's eyes widened for a second, and then, after glancing down at his phone, he looked back at her with a rueful grin. "The day after tomorrow, actually. Her birthday is in two days. Wow! I guess that means I need to get moving on a few things. It's a good thing I ran into you today, or I'd really have been in the doghouse."

Jaycee laughed as Danny turned to look at her car. "You still driving this old thing?" he asked, slapping the car's hood. "I think it's older than we are. What seems to be the problem with it?"

"It'll spark, but it won't turn over. So I don't think it's the battery. I need to get it to a repair shop and have them figure out what's wrong. I was hoping you'd drag it and me back to your shop."

"I can do that." Danny replied, then slid into the driver's seat to try and start the car himself. After a brief look under the hood, he hooked it up to his tow truck.

Jaycee climbed into the passenger seat beside him, snapped on her seat belt, and watched as he carefully pulled his rig out into traffic. "So, what have I missed since I left Larkin Bay?" she asked as they made their way through the backcountry roads toward home.

Danny rested one arm on the sill of the driver's side window and smiled as he glanced over at her. "That depends. What do you want to know? Small-town gossip, the state of the economy, or what's going on with me?"

She laughed. "Give me the highlights of all of it."

He nodded as he chuckled. Most of their high school friends had stayed in touch through social media, but Danny still patiently filled Jaycee in on all the marriages, babies, and graduations among her old friends. She looked out her window, and a lump formed in her throat as she listened. She had missed many special events in everyone's lives since she'd been gone, but after her parents had been killed, returning to Larkin Bay without them there had just been too painful.

"So do you think you'll be in town for a while?" Danny glanced over at her. His brow was creased, and he looked concerned by her silence.

"I'm thinking about staying for a few months at least. It seems like things have gotten a little off track for Betty and Chandra recently, so I thought I'd stick around for a bit and help get things sorted out. That is, if I can find a job here."

Danny nodded. "Well, it's good that you might stay in Larkin Bay. I know it hasn't been easy for you or Chandra since your parents passed. Many people here have been trying to keep an eye on her and Betty—but I'm glad you've come back to help. I mean..." Danny paused as he shifted slightly away from her in his seat. "If the things I've heard through the town gossip vine are true..."

Jaycee nodded and rolled her window down farther, so the wind could dry the tears that were suddenly stinging her eyes. "I've been learning all sorts of things since I got back. I made an appointment with the bank to see just how bad things are." She grimaced as she glanced at the time on her phone. "But I guess I'll need to call and reschedule that now. I just wish I'd known what was happening sooner, so things wouldn't have gotten so out of hand."

Danny reached over and patted her arm before returning both hands to the steering wheel. "Let us know if we can help. You still have plenty of friends here, Jaycee."

She nodded and took a deep breath. "Thank you. What I really need is a job, though. Unfortunately, there doesn't seem to be a great demand for bakers around here."

"Well, there's definitely a demand for baked goods all right, especially for guys like me who have to get birthday cakes for our wives," Danny replied as he glanced over at her and grinned.

"I'd love to make Amanda a birthday cake. Let me know if I can help."

"Really?" Danny asked, turning slightly in his seat to look directly at her. "You're serious? Because if you could bake her a cake, that would be great. It would mean a lot to Amanda if you made it too. All of us used to love coming to your place after school and devouring whatever you and your mom had made."

"Those were the good old days."

"They sure were."

The drive continued in comfortable silence for a few minutes, then Danny cleared his throat. "I have an idea. How about we barter?"

Jaycee wrinkled her nose as she looked over at him. "What did you have in mind?"

"I'll tow your car back to the shop, and you bake me a birthday cake for Amanda."

She laughed. "Well, I know my baking is great, but honestly, I think you're getting the raw end of the deal with that proposal. A tow probably costs double what a birthday cake does."

Danny furrowed his brow. "Well, how about two cakes, then? Ava's first birthday is a few months away. How about you make two cakes in exchange for today's tow job? One cake for Amanda and another one in a few months for Ava's first birthday party?"

Jaycee chuckled, her heart swelling in gratitude. "That sounds perfect. It's a deal."

"Yee-haw!" Danny cried out happily, causing Jaycee to jump in her seat and laugh in surprise. He chuckled at her response and stepped a little harder on the gas to speed them back to Larkin Bay as she relaxed into her seat and enjoyed the ride.

Chapter Six

"Crap. Crappety. Crappety. Crap. Crap. Crap, Jaycee muttered under her breath as she scowled at the bank statements on the desk in front of her.

"Oh. Excuse me." She felt a blush rise to her cheeks as she ducked her head to avoid the eye of the man sitting across from her.

The white-haired bank manager gave her a grim smile and shook his head. "Don't worry about it. I think I would have said something along the same lines if I was in your position. Possibly worse. I'm just sorry I can't do more to help."

Jaycee sighed. "All the money in the trust is gone, then?" she asked. "This is all that's left?" Her voice trembled as she asked the question.

He shot her a sympathetic look and cleared his throat before answering. "I'm afraid so. Betty invested everything and from the very start, this was a very risky venture. It's definitely not something one of our advisers would have recommended. Both the trust lawyers and the bank's assistant manager tried to talk her out of it, but she was very insistent that this was what she wanted to do."

Jaycee rubbed a hand across the scar on her cheek.

"Did you still want to see the deposit box?"

She shut her eyes briefly, then nodded and followed the portly manager out of his office and into the vault, where he showed her the location of her parents' safety-deposit box. "You have the key?" he asked.

"I do," she replied, pulling the long, old-fashioned key out of her bag and holding it up for him to see.

He nodded at a set of doors behind her. "The viewing rooms lock from the inside. Take all the time you need."

"Thank you."

After giving her another sympathetic smile, he walked away.

Jaycee pulled the safety-deposit box from its slot in the vault and, after closing the door to the viewing room, locked it behind her. Setting the box down on the room's small desk, she settled into a plastic chair and stared at the metal case for a long moment. Leaning back, she looked up at the stucco ceiling and sent a silent prayer to her parents before taking a deep breath and releasing the lid.

Papers.

Her hands shook as she gathered the few flimsy sheets together and carefully set them in a pile on the far side of the desk. Tucked underneath them was a small, dark purple velvet pouch that she instantly recognized. It had belonged to her mother. Picking it up, she laid it flat in her palm and held it there for a long moment. She then drew open the ribbons and turned it upside down. She gasped as her parents' wedding rings fell out. Slowly, she closed her fingers around them, pressing them hard into her palm as a single tear ran down her cheek.

I had no idea these were here.

She unfurled her fingers and looked at the rings. The heaviest had a single diamond at its center—her mother's engagement ring. Her hand trembled as she slid the narrow gold band onto her own ring finger and centered the stone. Spreading her fingers apart, she stared at it for a long moment, remembering all the times she had seen it on her mother's finger—usually when her mom's hand had been lovingly clasping hers. Picking up the wedding band, Jaycee slid it on and nestled it next to the other ring. She then pulled her father's wedding band onto her thumb. The three rings looked perfect this close to one another, she decided. She held out her hand to admire them for a long moment, then wiped away another tear. Gulping hard, she closed her eyes and breathed deeply, cherishing all the bittersweet feelings and beloved memories the rings summoned of her parents.

Leaving the rings on, she turned her attention to the slim stack of papers. The legal-sized form at the top of the pile was the deed to the house, and it showed that the mortgage was paid in full. Jaycee let out a long sigh of relief. No matter what else they had lost, at least they still had a home. Flipping through the rest of the papers, she saw they were all statements that confirmed what the bank manager had already told her. The family's trust fund held shares in a company that had recently filed for bankruptcy.

Her hands dropped to her lap. Jaycee hadn't expected a large wad of cash to be sitting in this box, but more tears welled up in her eyes as the last of her hopes were dashed. All the money her parents had left them for the upkeep of the family home and for Chandra's college education was gone.

The next morning, Jaycee sipped a cup of coffee and tapped her foot on the kitchen floor as she watched her sister finish her breakfast. She was waiting for one of Larkin Bay's top-selling real estate agents to arrive. While the bank manager hadn't been able to give her a lot of good news, he had pointed out that the house could be remortgaged. This would give them enough money to live on short-term and help pay for the first few years of Chandra's college tuition. He had recommended a real estate agent, and when Jaycee had reached out, the other woman had immediately agreed to come over and meet with her this morning.

"Just because Cindy is a real estate agent, it doesn't mean we're going to sell the house," Jaycee reassured Chandra. "She's just coming over to help us decide what needs to be done to spruce things up a bit before the bank sends an appraiser. I just want to get a loan to tide us over for—we can use this place as collateral."

Chandra looked up at her sister over her bowl of cereal. "Fine, I believe you. But you *are* going to stay in Larkin Bay for a while, right? I mean, I know you have a job in the city and an apartment..."

"I'm not planning on going anywhere anytime soon. And no, I don't have a job in the city anymore. I quit, remember? But I should go back to get my things and find someone to sublet my place." Jaycee bit her bottom lip briefly before summoning a smile to her face. "And when I do decide to go back, maybe you should come with me. It would be a wonderful opportunity for you to check out some of the city colleges."

Jaycee frowned as Chandra ducked her head and silently poked at her cereal with a spoon. "Chandy, you *are* planning on going to college next year, right? It was really important to Mom and Dad that we both got college degrees. Have you thought at all about what you want to study next year?" While waiting for her sister's reply, Jaycee tried to remember how she'd felt during her last year of high school. Both her parents had helped her through the college application process, and her mother had driven her to multiple campuses so she could decide which one she would feel most comfortable attending. Her heart constricted as she thought about all Chandra was missing.

"I'm not sure. There have been some announcements at school about it. I haven't really paid that much attention," Chandra said, intently studying her cereal instead of meeting Jaycee's gaze.

"Chandy, really? You should be paying attention and asking questions. Picking the right college is a huge decision!"

A light knock on the front door interrupted their conversation and announced the arrival of the real estate agent.

Jaycee frowned at Chandra's glum expression. "Hey, do you know why the sun skipped college?"

"No."

"It already has a million degrees."

Chandra rolled her eyes and looked pointedly toward the foyer. "I think there's someone at the door for you."

Jaycee laid a hand on her sister's shoulder for a moment. "At least promise me you'll think about it?"

"Maybe," Chandra replied with a half smile.

"Good enough," Jaycee said cheerfully and left to answer the door.

Cindy Pearson of Larkin Bay Realty was as lovely as she was terrifyingly efficient. After touring the house and talking to Jaycee for over an hour, she was gone, leaving behind a long list of home improvement suggestions.

"I can't help but think that if we had the money to do all this stuff—painting, roofing, landscaping, recarpeting, and decluttering—we probably wouldn't need to refinance the house at all," Jaycee grumbled to Betty later that afternoon when she joined her in the kitchen.

Betty chuckled, but Jaycee couldn't even summon a smile as she pulled out her mother's mixing bowls from the cupboard. After doing some quick synchronizing with Chandra's wireless speaker that was sitting on the kitchen counter, she smiled at Betty, who had sat down at the table and was pursuing the real estate agent's list while petting the kitten. "Close your ears," said Jaycee as the opening chords of Barry Manilow's "Mandy" rang out.

"Oh no. Please, Jaycee. Any song of his but this one," Betty wailed, covering her ears with her hands.

"Nope. This one is my best baking jam," Jaycee replied. "I need some hurting music right now and Barry always makes me feel better. Besides, it doesn't get much better than singing about a dead dog."

"That's an urban myth. 'Mandy' wasn't about a dog," Betty exclaimed, then, knowing what was coming next, scooped up the kitten and hurried out of the kitchen, escaping before Jaycee began belting out the song's opening words.

Later that afternoon, Jaycee had just finished piping the last of a series of pink roses onto Amanda's birthday cake when Chandra came in from school. "Hey, you," she greeted her. "How was your day?"

Chandra shrugged. "Okay, I guess. Same old." After dropping her bag on a chair, she came over to stand beside Jaycee. "This is really beautiful. I love all the tiny flowers."

"Thanks. It's fun making cakes for special occasions, and Amanda's favorite color has always been pink, so I think she'll like it. Are you leaving for work soon? Let me know when you're going, and I'll pack this up and keep you company. Amanda and Danny's house is along the way into town."

"Will do."

An hour later, with the cake carefully boxed, Jaycee joined her sister on her walk. After a few silent blocks, Jaycee spoke up. "You're not saying much today. Is anything wrong?" she asked, bumping her hip against her sister's.

Chandra looked up from her phone and continued shuffling her feet along the colorful leaf-covered sidewalk. She shrugged. "No. I'm fine. But would it be all right if I had a few friends over after school on Friday night? You haven't met Dean, my boyfriend, yet, and he doesn't have a football game or practice then, so he's free to come by."

Jaycee smiled with genuine delight. "Of course! I'd love to meet Dean and see all your friends. Maybe we could even have a cookout over the firepit in the backyard like we used to do when Mom and Dad were alive. Nothing fancy, just hot dogs, some veggies, chips, and pop. I can make cupcakes too."

Chandra blinked at the enthusiasm in her sister's voice. "Really? You'd do all that? That would be so cool," she said as a smile crept across her face. "My friends would love it too. But you don't have to go to all that trouble—frozen pizza or something like that would be fine."

"No, I think it would be fun. Besides, I'm planning on spending most of this week cleaning up the house and searching for a job, so I'll probably be more than ready for the distraction of a party by Friday. It'll be perfect."

"Okay. Thanks, Jaycee," Chandra replied and returned to texting on her phone.

"You don't have to thank me now, but you will when you eat my hot dogs," Jaycee continued. "I'm great at cooking over campfires, you know. The secret is to let the fire burn down to coals and use all-beef wieners. Our cookout will be a good time for me to teach you all the old family secrets."

"I can't wait." Chandra laughed and put her arm around her sister's waist, being careful not to jostle the cake box as they continued on their way.

After parting ways with Chandra and delivering the birthday cake to a delighted Danny, Jaycee retraced her steps home. A nostalgic smile crept across her lips as she remembered all the times she had rushed along these streets from one joyous adventure to another. She'd loved visiting Amanda's house when she was young and playing outside with her friend until one of their mothers called them in for dinner.

"Hey, Jaycee!"

She startled and turned to see Jeremy and Bo making their way toward her from the other side of the street.

"Hello, lovely," she crooned, crouching down to scratch the puppy behind the ears when they reached her. "How are you today? And what are you doing on my side of town?" she asked the dog.

"He's out for his morning walk, which turned into an evening walk because I was up too late last night and got busy with work again this morning," answered Jeremy, smiling down at her.

Jaycee looked up, and the sprites in her stomach did a dance of delight as she smiled back at him. Jeremy hadn't shaved, and the stubble from his beard gave him a sexy, unkempt look she found very attractive. His gray eyes were crinkling at the corners, and her breath caught as she tried not to focus too long on his dimpled grin. She groaned inwardly. It was both a blessing and a curse that Larkin Bay was so small. Repeatedly running into this gorgeous man was going to be inevitable.

"How is the kitten doing?" he asked her. "Have you found his owners yet?"

"Not yet, but I took *her* to the vet earlier. She's healthy and a little girl. They're pretty sure they know the litter she's from and who her family is too. I'll probably be hearing from them soon."

"That's nice. At least you can reunite her with her mom and siblings."

"Yup. But why were you up so late last night?" she asked, giving Bo a final cuddle before getting to her feet. "Are you working long hours?"

Jeremy grimaced. "As a matter of fact, I am. I can't stop working on a case easily most days, and I must admit, trying to catch the arsonist here in Larkin Bay has me putting in even more overtime than usual."

"You take your work seriously," Jaycee observed, watching him shorten Bo's leash so they could all walk comfortably together on the narrow sidewalk.

"I do. But it's not just that." He paused for a minute. His expression let her know he was searching for the right words. "Solving arson cases quickly is really important to me," he finally said as he pulled Bo off a front lawn and back to his side.

Jaycee raised an eyebrow at this solemn pronouncement and slowed her pace to match his.

"I know that might sound crazy, but there's a reason."

"Oh?"

He sighed heavily. "Yeah, and I guess I might as well tell you, as everyone else in town already knows the story."

"You don't have to. It's okay." Jaycee said, placing a hand on her stomach as his melancholy expression caused the sprites in her stomach to tumble uneasily.

"If you don't hear it from me, you'll just hear it somewhere else anyway." Looking away, Jeremy scrubbed his hand across the stubble on his cheeks and frowned.

"Honestly, it's fine," Jaycee said, holding up her hands.

"No." Jeremy glanced at her. "I want to tell you."

"Okay." She plunged her hands into her pockets and looked down at her boots.

"You see, I was married a few years ago. My wife's name was Marianne. She was my high school sweetheart."

"Wow, that's great. Sometimes you just know when you've found 'the one,' right? It doesn't matter how old you are."

"Yes, and that's how it was with us," Jeremy replied.

Jaycee glanced up and saw he was still scowling. She skipped a few steps to keep up with him as he increased his pace. Pulling her hands from her pockets, she balled them into fists and dragged down the sleeves of her sweater to cover them.

The sprites in her stomach were tap-dancing now, warning her that what he had to say probably wasn't going to be pleasant to hear. She hadn't missed the fact that he was speaking about his wife in the past tense, and she scrambled to find a way to change the subject, fearing what he might tell her next.

"But Marianne died," Jeremy said, pulling Bo up against him as he stopped in the middle of the sidewalk.

Jaycee halted too and looked up at him with wide, solemn eyes as a soft whisper of sympathy escaped her lips.

"And when she died, I wanted to die too," Jeremy added, looking away and rubbing his free hand across his eyes. "She was so sweet and beautiful, and it was just wrong that she died so young."

Jaycee reached out and touched him briefly on the arm. Her hand fluttered in the air between them for a moment before dropping back to her side.

"The worst part of it..." He swallowed hard.

Jaycee felt her heart tighten in her chest as she realized this big, strong man beside her was fighting to hold back tears.

"The worst part of it was she died because of me." He looked away from Jaycee's shocked expression to gaze up at the clear fall sky as he tried to compose himself again.

"No, Jeremy. That can't be true."

"It is. You see, there was a fire. And it was started by an arsonist. But it wasn't Marianne that the criminal wanted to kill. It was me—the investigating officer."

Jaycee raised a hand to her throat in sympathy when she saw he was struggling to speak.

He swallowed hard. "Marianne died from smoke inhalation. And, Jaycee? I can't go through that again. I won't. So now I always solve my cases quickly, so an arsonist will never have the chance to hurt anyone like that again."

He was silent for a long moment, and when he spoke again, it was in an anguished whisper. "You have to understand—in my heart I know Marianne died because I failed at my job. Marianne died because of *me*."

"No, Jeremy."

"Yes, it's true, Jaycee. I'm responsible. And I hate myself for it every day. I killed Marianne."

Chapter Seven

Perched on a wobbly stool at the kitchen counter the next day, Chandra shook her head emphatically as she watched Jaycee put the last layer of cream cheese icing on a carrot cake. "He thinks he killed his wife? Did he? I mean, that's just crazy!" she declared.

"No, he didn't, and, well, it's easy for me and you to say he's wrong, but he feels guilty about what happened, so he can't see it quite as clearly as we can."

Jaycee scooped more icing onto her knife and looked over at her younger sister. "Everyone else might see it as just a terrible accident, but he doesn't." She shrugged and spun the cake plate around to inspect her work. "Anyway, he seems really nice and was so devastated that the next thing I knew, I was inviting him to come over on Friday night to join us for the cookout."

As Jaycee went to the sink to wash her hands, Chandra pondered her sister's words.

"Is he cute?"

Jaycee's head was tilted down, but Chandra could still see a blush was staining her cheeks. "Yep, you could say that. He probably won't be ready for a relationship with anyone else for a while, though. He's still too consumed with guilt over his wife's death. But yep, he's good-looking, or at least, *I* think he is. But, more importantly, I think he could use a friend."

Chandra chuckled as she watched her sister dry her hands. "Uh-huh."

"You're such a typical teenager sometimes," Jaycee scolded, picking up her frosting knife and waving it between them. "Just because I think someone is attractive doesn't mean I'm going to ask them out or sit around pining over them. I was just stating a fact about his looks. Besides, I need to find a job here in town, not a boyfriend."

Rolling her eyes, Chandra leaned across the counter and stuck a finger out to steal some of the icing from the base of the cake.

"Hey! Stop that," Jaycee cried, smacking her sister lightly on the knuckles. "Don't you dare touch this. It's not for you. I'm bringing it to the coffee shop in town so they can sell slices of it. Cup of Joy is paying me thirty dollars for this cake, which is enough to pay off part of our water bill, so don't you dare muck it up."

Chandra drew back. "Thirty dollars for a cake? Really? You can get that much? That's great! You should sell more of them."

"Yep, I should. Actually, what I'd love to do is open a bakery here in Larkin Bay and sell a lot of them. But opening up your own business costs a ton of money, and we don't have that right now. So, I'll just have to settle for selling them to the local shops until I can find a proper job."

Chandra looked down and flipped over a few pages of the fashion magazine in her lap. When she looked up again, her expression was serious. "How much money would it take?" she asked.

"To do what?"

"To open a bakery here in Larkin Bay? Would it be a lot more than what we're going to borrow from the bank for my college tuition?" Jaycee gave a surprised laugh. "Probably not. But we are not using the money from refinancing this house to open a business," she said, her tone firm while she rubbed the back of her hand across the scar on her cheek. "It's much too chancy. Besides, you have to go to college, and you need a home you can return to during the summer break and other holidays while you're there. And we are *not* doing any more investing. We've already seen how risky that can be."

"But this would be different," Chandra protested, sliding off her stool to lean over the counter. "This would be a business you were running, and I could help you. I don't need to go to college. I could stay right here with you and Betty, and then you would have the money you needed to open your shop. And Larkin Bay needs a bakery! You said so yourself. It would all be so perfect!"

Jaycee put down her icing knife and pressed her lips into a firm line. "No way. I will find the funds to open my own bakery one day, but right now, we need to get this place cleaned up and reassessed so the bank will lend us money that we can use for you to go to college and to pay some overdue bills around here."

Chandra opened her mouth to protest, then closed it firmly and turned away to scoop up the kitten. It was probably best, the teen decided, to drop the subject for now. But she was determined to talk to her sister about it again soon. Staying in Larkin Bay to help Jaycee open her own bakery was really the perfect solution to all their problems.

The fire had been started deliberately. Jeremy was certain of that. Turning back to the singed bricks, he scrutinized the marks on the building one last time and sighed. It didn't seem right. Most people were trying to stop evil from spreading and make the world a safer and happier place, but others were just determined to wreak havoc. Thankfully, in this case, a police cruiser had gone by just as the flames had caught and called it in. The fire department had gotten everything under control before any serious damage was done.

Jeremy rubbed a hand through his hair. This fire was only two blocks away from the last one at the hardware store. He looked up at the art gallery's front window, which was showcasing a local artist's pictures.

I have to catch this guy.

He'd been narrowing down the possibilities of who was setting the fires for almost a week now, but he wasn't making much progress. The more he learned about the arsonist stalking Larkin Bay, the more challenging the case became. And now, with another store involved, the pressure to catch the arsonist had escalated.

He was also having trouble concentrating on the case—something unheard of for him. But ever since he'd run into Jaycee and told her about his past, he couldn't seem to stop thinking about her. Since then, he'd picked up his cell phone to call her several times, but had stopped himself. He didn't have time to date, and the memories of what he'd shared with Marianne still left him uncomfortable even thinking about being friends with another woman.

Moving to the far side of the building, he began to remove the police tape. As he stripped down the barrier, he pondered exactly what it was about Jaycee that had made him blurt out everything about his past so quickly. True, she would have probably found out from someone around town anyway, but he didn't talk about his guilt over Marianne's death with just anyone. *Ever.* He'd even refused the offer of more professional help after the first year of therapy. But with Jaycee, he had spoken freely about his feelings, and ever since, he'd spent an excessive amount of time trying to figure out why.

He was drawn to her in a way he couldn't explain.

Shaking his head, Jeremy forced himself to focus again on the destruction around him. In some ways, solving this case should be easy; he knew a lot about pyromaniacs and arsonists, having spent years studying people who lit fires for their own enjoyment or profit. He also had several clues.

The person setting the fires seemed to know a lot about the town. Jeremy had multiple eyewitnesses who confirmed they had seen a darkly dressed man lurking around the stores about the time the fires started. The arsonist had slipped in, lit the blazes, and left the area unseen. This meant the suspect was most likely a Larkin Bay resident.

Jeremy looked up and admired the building behind him. Located just off Main Street, the art gallery was a tall, narrow and solid brick building with wide windows and oversized black shutters. He had visited the gallery years before and remembered well its large open spaces that exhibited both international and local artists' work. It was a colorful and peaceful space. He was relieved that the fire had caused almost no damage.

Flipping open his notebook, Jeremy read through his notes on the fire once more. The early lab results had confirmed his suspicion that the fire here had been ignited using gasoline. From what they'd found left behind, he suspected it had been poured into plastic pop bottles stuffed with cloth and topped up with wooden matches. This unusual and juvenile method led him to conclude that the criminal was probably a teenager. Arsonists were often unsupervised youths who were fascinated by the destructive power of fire. The fact that no one had been hurt yet further substantiated this theory—the fire starter was only after the attention the fires received. He wasn't callously targeting innocent people.

Bowing his head, Jeremy closed his eyes for a minute. This arsonist had to be caught before anyone *was* hurt, though. It was only a matter of time before he or she harmed someone, accidentally or not. He had seen this before. And he had to ensure it never happened again. Jeremy owed his late wife that much, and perhaps he owed it to himself as well.

It was a beautiful fall night in Larkin Bay. The temperatures were comfortable and the breezes off the lake were still warm. The leaves on the trees were starting to show their autumnal hues, and the full moon reflected their dramatic colors onto the slowly darkening sky. While Jaycee filled a tray with paper plates, cutlery, and napkins, Chandra and a few of her friends grabbed platters of food and placed them on an old picnic table that Jaycee had given a fresh coat of dark red paint the morning before. Now covered with a cheerful, bright yellow gingham tablecloth, and canopied by twinkly lights that Chandra and Dean had strung in the trees earlier that day, the backyard had a decidedly festive feel.

Meeting her sister's boyfriend for the first time that afternoon had gone well. He seemed like a nice enough boy, had greeted Jaycee politely and even offered to help with the preparations for tonight. Still, Jaycee had been uneasy about Chandra being alone with him when they had disappeared up to her bedroom to play with the kitten.

"Leave the door open," she'd yelled, smiling as she heard her mother's words coming out of her mouth.

After tidying the kitchen, Jaycee went outside and saw most of her sister's guests were gathered around the firepit. She relaxed her shoulders when she observed someone had put buckets of water and sand beside the pit's rock border.

One of her most treasured childhood memories was having outdoor fires and cooking marshmallows and hot dogs over them with her parents. She'd been humming and smiling all day, delighted that she could share this family tradition with Chandra and her friends tonight.

Clasping her hands together, she sniffed the fresh fall air as she swayed in time to the music Chandra was playing through a small, outdoor speaker. Scanning the group of teens in front of her, she noticed Jeremy was standing outside of the group, and made her way over to him.

"Feeling old?" she asked him with a teasing smile.

He chuckled. "A little, but this is a nice thing you're doing. Teenagers need to have things like this to keep them busy and out of trouble."

"I think it's important too. My parents organized cookouts often for me and my friends when we were in high school. It never occurred to me that a big part of why they were doing it was so they could keep an eye on us, though."

Jeremy nodded. "My mom did the same, except my buddies and I were all in the kitchen making pizza at our house. It was, I guess, a throwback to her Italian upbringing." He gestured toward the teens, who were adding more firewood to the flames. "Do you have a garden hose? They're always handy to keep close by when you have an outdoor fire. There's very little wind tonight, but it's always good to be extra vigilant."

Jaycee frowned. "No. I assumed we did, but when I went to get it out tonight, I discovered it was cracked. I've packed it up with the pile of things I need to take to the town dump in the morning. It's now on my list of things to buy, but it's a little harder these days to get things like that with the hardware store closed."

Jeremy's smile disappeared.

Jaycee smacked one palm theatrically against her forehead. "Yikes! I didn't mean to bring up one of your cases when you're supposed to be having a night off," she exclaimed. "Here, have a hot dog cooking stick." She grabbed one from the pile lined up on the picnic table behind them and thrust it at him. "Chandra and I spent hours yesterday whittling the ends to the perfect point to use tonight."

"Really? Well, that's very impressive, thanks," Jeremy said, grinning once more as he took the stick from her.

Soon a few of the teens joined him in cooking their hot dogs over the fire, and Jaycee handed out paper plates so everyone could add salads and chips to their meals. When they had all eaten their fill, Chandra handed out the cupcakes Jaycee had made. Even the teens who usually said no to eating desserts couldn't resist the beautiful colors and designs she'd put on the little cakes.

When everyone had finished, Jaycee made her way over to Jeremy and handed him a small plate of peanut butter cookies. He smiled as he took them. "You remembered me buying these from the bakery every day of the police conference?"

"I did." She felt a blush creep up her neck as she met and held his gaze.

A blissful smile spread across his lips with each bite.

They stood in silence for a few minutes, and Jaycee tried to ignore how comfortable it felt to have him standing so close to her.

"So, what do you think?" Jaycee finally asked, gesturing at the small group of teens in the yard.

"They seem like nice kids," Jeremy replied. He grinned and motioned toward Bo, who was sprawled on his back in the center of the group. "Bo is certainly happy, and he's quite enamored by all the young ladies who have continually been giving him hot dog pieces and tummy rubs."

"He's so cute. But—no," Jaycee said and grimaced at her sister's pleading expression.

Jeremy chuckled.

"No, we *cannot* get a dog," Jaycee continued, raising her voice to cut off any discussion before the teen could start begging. "We have too much going on right now to look after a puppy. Besides, they are at least a ten- to fifteen-year commitment, and I have no idea where we'll be in a decade."

"Actually, I'm just fostering Bo until he finds his final home. He's a guide dog," Jeremy said, looking from one sister to the other. "I only get to keep him for a year, and then he'll leave me to start his training. He'll either be a seeing-eye dog, a seizure dog, a diabetic warning dog, or help a child with autism or hearing loss."

Jaycee turned to him, her eyes wide with surprise. "Really? I'm impressed. So you're not keeping him?"

"Nope, I just have him until he's ready to go to work for someone who really needs him. I'm just the puppy dad."

"But how will you ever be able to let him go? I could never let him leave me! I'd love him too much to give him away," Chandra cried, tugging the dog closer.

"I imagine it will be tough. And I'll miss him. But I'm giving him a good start, and he's going to live with someone whose life will be so much easier with him by their side. He'll help another adult or child live a more independent and satisfying life."

"I suppose." Chandra giggled as a wiggling Bo licked her face. "But I still think it would be hard to let him go."

Jaycee nodded in agreement before spinning quickly as a teen cried out in alarm. Someone had tossed a handful of paper plates and napkins into the firepit. The ash had toppled over the edge of the stone border and small flames were now licking the dry grass and a few articles of clothing that had been discarded close by.

"Watch out!" cried Jaycee. All the teens looked up from their texting and conversations to scramble to their feet.

Jeremy pushed through the group, reaching for the pails of sand and water. He threw them around the firepit and began stamping out the stray embers on the clothing.

Dean picked up Bo from Chandra's lap and put him in the house out of harm's way while the other teens followed Jeremy's lead and began trampling the glowing cinders around them. Quickly the live embers outside the pit were extinguished.

"Chandra? Are you okay?" one of her friends called out a minute later. The teen hadn't moved from where she'd been sitting cross-legged on the grass. Now, she still sat frozen and wide-eyed, gazing at the blackened grass around the firepit.

"Sure, I'm fine. But, didn't you think that was beautiful?" Chandra asked, blinking up at her friend.

Jeremy turned to look at her, his forehead creasing in confusion. "You thought the fire was beautiful?"

"Yes," Chandra replied, her eyes shining. "Fire is lovely when it dances and burns. I think it's one of my favorite things in the whole world to watch."

Jaycee grabbed one of her sister's hands and pulled her to her feet. "Well, it might be beautiful," she scolded, "but if there are ever flames around you again, you need to get up and help put the fire out—or at the very least, get out of the way! What were you thinking? You could have been hurt!"

Chandra rolled her eyes, then pulled away to join her friends at the picnic table, where they were taking short videos of each other and talking in low tones.

Jeremy watched the teens for a long moment, shifting his weight uneasily from one foot to the other before rechecking the firepit area to ensure no embers were still glowing.

Soon, with the fire out and all the food eaten, the teens started gathering up their belongings and getting ready to leave. After thanking Jaycee for having them over for the evening, some left while a few others lingered to chat and help clear up the remains of the get-together. Finally, Chandra and the last of her friends went into the house to play with Bo and finish putting away the condiments and unused paper products, leaving Jaycee alone with Jeremy.

"Well, that was fun," she said, shaking the crumbs from the tablecloth, wiping it clean, and folding it up into a neat square.

There was a long pause before Jeremy answered. "Yep, everyone seemed to have a good time."

"Well, since you're a cop *and* a guy, what do you think about Dean? He's the one Chandra is dating. Do you think I have anything to worry about?"

Jeremy stuck his hands into the front pockets of his snug-fitting 501s and considered her question. "Well, I didn't get that much time to spend with him alone, but he seems decent enough. They all seem like nice kids."

Jaycee beamed. "That's what I thought too. But I haven't spent any time with Chandra's friends since she was about ten years old, so I was afraid my teen boy radar might be off."

He chuckled, and they both turned as the door behind them was nudged open and Bo bounded over to Jeremy's side. The puppy gave him a look of adoration before yawning widely and lying down at his feet.

"Well, it looks like I should head out too," Jeremy said, reaching down to pet the dog on the head. "This little guy looks like he's ready for bed. Can I do anything else to help you here before I go?"

"No, I think we're good. The kids cleaned up most of it. But thank you for the offer."

Jeremy smiled and stepped closer to her. "If it'll make you feel any better, I can let you know if I find out anything troubling about any of the teens here tonight. In an arson investigation, we usually take a close look at all the young people in town. The profile of an arsonist includes teens, as they often experiment with fire." His forehead creased as he stepped closer to her. "You'd be surprised how many devastating fires are started by a youth just having *harmless* fun."

Jaycee's hand fluttered to her scar as her eyes widened in concern. "You mean the fires in town could have been started by one of the teens here tonight?"

"It's just a possibility. And it may not be the case here, but it's something we'll be looking at."

"Wow." She looked worriedly at the house.

Reaching over, Jeremy pulled her close to him. She looked up, and a moment later, she sighed and parted her lips as he leaned down and gently kissed her good-night.

Chapter Eight

As Jaycee's eyes fluttered shut, fireworks exploded in the pit of her stomach and vibrated through her entire nervous system. She gasped and wound her arms around Jeremy's neck tightly as she kissed him back.

Although the connection might have started as spontaneous and chaste, once their lips touched, lust, passion, and all sorts of other unidentifiable but delightful emotions swirled together, causing the sprites to do a full cha-cha dance of desire in Jaycee's lower regions.

And Jeremy felt it too. Jaycee could read it in his hooded eyes and hear it in the catch of his breath when he drew back for a split second before leaning in again. As he pressed toward her, every inch of him radiated urgency.

A few minutes later, she pulled away. "Wow," she whispered, dragging in a deep, unsteady breath.

Jeremy grinned, put one hand on her waist, and raised the other to her cheek as he bent to briefly touch her lips against his again. "Yeah, you could say that," he whispered hoarsely. "Wow, sums it up pretty nicely, actually."

Jaycee stepped away and smoothed her hair back into place as she tried to steady her breathing.

"I'll call you tomorrow."

Jaycee nodded and watched as he called Bo to return to his side. After the dog was leashed, Jeremy pressed his lips to her cheek, then gave her a long, searching look. As she stared into his eyes, he rubbed his thumb over her lips.

"Good night," he finally said and, tugging on Bo's leash, slipped silently away.

As he latched the gate behind him, Jaycee let out a sigh and rubbed the scar on her cheek.

That was nice.

Licking her lips, she sighed in regret.

I shouldn't do this.

As sensational as that kiss might have been, she couldn't swoon over Jeremy like some lovesick teenager right now. Her to-do list was just too long. She needed to focus on talking to Chandra about college, find a job, and start organizing a garage sale. The real estate agent had suggested that they clean out some of the clutter from the house, and having a yard sale would accomplish this.

She had no time for a man in her life.

But, again. Wow.

She cocked her head to one side and felt a smile creep across her lips. Brushing the tips of her fingers over them, she realized they were still buzzing. Her smile broadened. Perhaps all the things she had to do could wait until tomorrow. It couldn't hurt to allow herself the luxury of swooning over what had just happened between her and Jeremy for a little while. Her smile turned dreamy, and she was humming happily under her breath as she headed back into the house to check on what the teens were doing.

Jaycee got up early the next morning to start decluttering the house. Later that afternoon, surrounded by boxes, she was singing along to the local country-pop music station on the kitchen radio and packing some old plastic picnic cutlery away when she heard the front door open.

"It's me," Chandra called out.

"I'm in the kitchen," Jaycee answered. A moment later, the teen appeared carrying a stack of magazines. She plunked them in the center of the table before turning to the fridge to pull out a jug of milk.

"What are these?" Jaycee asked, examining the pile. "We're supposed to be getting rid of junk, not bringing more home," she said, raising a brow.

"I know," Chandra replied, grabbing a clean glass from the cupboard. "But these were all just going into the recycling bin at the pharmacy in town. Meghan saved them for me because she knows I love looking at all the fashion magazines but can't afford to buy them. She's always giving me old issues that would just be thrown out."

Jaycee checked the dates on the magazines. While many were from the previous month, a few were the most current issues. Meghan seemed to be supporting Chandra's love of fashion at the pharmacy's expense. Jaycee sighed and made a mental note to bake another cake or pie that evening to take over to thank the pharmacy owner for her generosity.

After setting down her glass, Chandra pulled out a chair from under the battered kitchen table and started flipping through a magazine. "Look at these shoes." She showed her sister an ad for a pair of silver, Swarovski-encrusted stilettos. "Aren't they gorgeous?"

Jaycee stopped sorting through the kitchen utensil drawer to look over her sister's shoulder. She shrugged. "I guess so. But honestly, I don't know that much about fashion. It's never really interested me all that much. I normally just wear black pants and a plain T-shirt and cover both up with an apron. That's always been stylish enough for me."

Chandra looked up at Jaycee with wide eyes. "Really? I love fashion. I could make clothes and put together outfits for people all day long. I help my friends look fantastic all the time. It's my thing," she said confidently, then turned back to flip through more magazine pages.

"I can tell," answered Jaycee, admiring what Chandra was wearing. The girl certainly seemed to have a flair for putting together unusual combinations and coming up with stylish and flattering outfits on a budget. This talent was plainly evident today by the colorful leggings, oversized sweater, multiple scarves, and high-heeled boots that the teen was wearing.

After a few minutes of flipping through one of the thick magazines, Chandra turned away from the pages. "You know, I could do something for you," she announced. "All you need is your eyebrows tweezed correctly, some natural makeup, and a different-colored top, and you would look, um...like yourself—only better."

Jaycee sighed and put down the bowl she was holding. She considered her sister's words. The last thing she wanted right now was to get a makeover. She had too much to do. But she also needed to talk to Chandy about her college applications, and one of the best ways to do that would be to spend some time with her sister doing something that she enjoyed.

"Sure."

"Sure?"

"Yep, right now. Make me look different. How did you put it... Me, only better?"

Chandra smiled uncertainly at Jaycee for a moment, then tilted her head to one side as she studied her sister more closely. Finally, she nodded and reached for her hand.

"Let's do it, then."

An hour later, the doorbell rang. Jaycee hurried down the front stairs to answer it, trying not to twist an ankle in Chandra's thrifted sky-high baby blue heels. They pinched her toes, but Chandra had insisted she try them on. Now Jaycee was regretting she had agreed.

Anticipating Betty's return from visiting her grandchildren, she swung open the front door with a welcoming smile.

Her mouth dropped open in surprise.

"Tony?"

Jaycee's ex-boyfriend stood on the front porch, looking very handsome and entirely at ease. A moment later, for the second time in twenty-four hours, she was caught completely off guard as an attractive man pulled her up against him and kissed her passionately.

Jaycee gagged and shoved Tony away with both hands. "Stop! What are you doing here? How did you find me?" she gasped, wiping her lips with the back of her hand.

He grinned. "You didn't make it easy. You blocked me on every social media platform, and Lisa wouldn't tell me anything, either." He waved a finger in her face playfully. "But when you're as smart as I am, anything is possible."

"Yeah, I think anyone with even a basic knowledge of how a computer and Google work can track down a person these days. You don't have to be smart."

"Jaycee, that's not nice," said Chandra, her eyes bright with curiosity as she came down the stairs and into the foyer to stand beside her sister.

"Some people don't deserve to be treated nicely," Jaycee responded. "But, Tony, this is my sister, Chandra. And, Chandy, this is my ex-boyfriend, who is also a two-timing snake, but you can call him Tony."

He smiled at Chandra. "You're just as beautiful as your sister," he told the teen. "And she doesn't mean that."

"Yes, I do," Jaycee grumbled. She caught a glimpse of herself in the front hall mirror. She was more than happy now that she'd agreed to let Chandra give her a makeover. It was comforting *and* empowering to know she looked her best for this impromptu and totally unwelcome reunion with her ex.

"What do you want, Tony? Why are you here?" she asked abruptly.

"Is there any place nearby where we can grab something to eat? I'm famished," he replied. His flashing dimple caused Chandra to smile sweetly back at him while the sprites in Jaycee's stomach retched.

She studied him quietly for a minute. She couldn't decide if she wanted to take the fireplace poker and brain him, or sit him down and talk to him for closure.

He is not worth going to jail for.

Jaycee tapped a finger against her lower lip. She could invite him into the kitchen and make him something to eat, but she didn't want him coming any farther into her home. "There's a pub downtown that makes good food," she finally suggested with a shrug. "Why don't we go there?"

"Sounds great."

Jaycee kicked off the stilettos she had been test-driving and slipped on her comfortably worn ballet flats. After shrugging on a warm sweater, she hugged Chandra goodbye.

As she and Tony walked along the quiet residential streets, he took her hand in his. She growled under her breath and pulled it away, glaring at him. He flashed her a condescending smirk in return. They walked the rest of the way to the pub in silence.

Most of the red leather booths at Sullivan's Place, Larkin Bay's eclectically decorated Irish-style pub, were filled with customers. Jaycee exhaled in relief when they were led to the last empty high-backed booth at the back.

"I'll just have a cola, please," she said to the pretty young server who came by a few minutes after they were seated.

"Whatever you have in a dark ale on draft for me," Tony added.

After the girl left, Jaycee stared at her fingertips, drumming them on the table. "So," she said after a few moments of silence.

Tony smiled at her and reached across the table to pull one of her hands into his.

Scowling, Jaycee pulled it away and folded both hands tightly in her lap.

Tony raised one eyebrow. "So I guess you're still mad at me?" Jaycee held his gaze for a long moment as she considered the question.

Am I still mad at Tony?

She nodded. Hell, yes, she was. But what was more hurtful was that she also felt betrayed, and that seemed as good a place as any to start the conversation.

"Of course," she answered. "And that's not unreasonable, don't you think? I thought we were in a monogamous relationship, yet you were sleeping with Rhonda too. There are words for men who do that, and none of them are nice."

Tony squirmed in his seat for a second before responding. "Well, okay. I guess I can see why you might say that. But we never really *said* that we were in an exclusive relationship. I wouldn't have been upset if I thought you were seeing other people."

Jaycee thought about how possessive and controlling Tony could be and shrugged. "Nope, I'm not buying that. You would have killed anyone else, and me too, if you had even suspected I was flirting with them. You acted like a first-class jerk by two-timing me, and I'm sure Rhonda will see it that way too once I tell her."

Jaycee couldn't read the specific emotions that flashed across Tony's face at her words—guilt, remorse, maybe even fear? It hadn't occurred to her before now that she had fled the city without telling Rhonda anything about her and Tony's relationship. And although he owned a small share in the bakery, Rhonda's family held controlling interest.

A smile spread across Jaycee's lips as she considered what Rhonda would do if she discovered her boyfriend, the father of her unborn child, had been cheating on her.

I have the power to destroy his world.

Misinterpreting her expression, Tony smiled confidently and, reaching across the table, gently ran a finger across the scar on her cheek. "I've missed you," he whispered.

Jaycee pushed his hand away and glared at him. "Well, I can't say I've missed you all that much." She smiled grimly at the waitress who had appeared beside their table to deliver their drinks.

"Are you interested in looking at some menus?" the girl asked.

"No, thank you," replied Jaycee tightly as Tony simultaneously answered, "Yes, that would be great."

He shrugged and looked across the table at her. "I've been driving since before dawn, and I'm starving. I know you're mad at me, but can I at least get something to eat?" he asked in a pleading tone that Jaycee remembered once finding endearing.

Wincing, she nodded at the server. "Yes, then, please bring him a menu."

The waitress hurried away. Silence fell between them as Jaycee studied Tony across the table. "So, how *are* things at the bakery?" she asked finally.

"Good." He beamed. "But of course, it's not the same without you there. We all miss you."

Jaycee just barely stopped herself from telling him he had only himself to blame for that. But with all modesty aside, she knew the bakery staff *were* probably missing her. She'd been the calm and steady hand that had handled the day-to-day management of the place. With her gone, things probably were a lot more chaotic.

A few minutes later, the server reappeared and dropped a menu on the table. She waited while Tony perused the options and then ordered a brisket sandwich and another beer. He sighed tiredly and ran his hands through his rumpled dark hair. "I guess you're probably wondering why I'm here," he said.

"The thought *had* crossed my mind."

"Well, like I said. I've missed you—a lot. And I hoped that if you hadn't found another job yet, you might come back to work at the bakery. I realize I let you down, and I'm willing to do whatever it takes to fix that."

"And what exactly would that be?" Jaycee asked, curious despite herself at how he thought he might atone for cheating on her.

He smirked. "Well, I figured we could start by going back to how things were—but better. I mean, I'd have to tell Rhonda something, and the baby would have to be looked after, but you could come back, and we could be together. You could manage the kitchen again and I, of course, would make sure you got a raise too."

Jaycee sputtered and then struggled to bite back a laugh of disbelief. "So let me make sure I've got this straight. You're telling me you're going to tell your pregnant fiancée that you were cheating on her? And then you plan on continuing to see me while she's carrying your child?"

"Well, sort of. I mean, I would still have to marry Rhonda. She is, after all, having my son and our families have known each other forever, so they'd kill me if I didn't. But none of them would have to know about us. Everything was working just fine the way it was until recently."

Jaycee gasped.

I was such a fool.

She sat up straighter in her seat and pushed her words out through her clenched jaw. "So, tell me, Tony. Exactly why would I want to come back and not only run the bakery but return to being your side piece too?"

Tony put his beer down, looking surprised by the question. "Well, because what we had was good, and you're never going to find a job managing a bakery as great as the one you had with me. I figured by now, since you've had some time to cool off, you'd see that what we had in the city was too good to give up."

"*Good?*" The word came out as a squeak.

"Yeah, way too good to just walk away from. It's certainly better than anything you'd ever find in a small, backwater town like this." He waved a hand to emphasize Larkin Bay's inadequateness.

Jaycee slid out of the booth. Both her hands were clasped into fists at her sides as she scowled over at him. "Well, Tony, let me tell you a few things. You are scum. And I *am* going to tell Rhonda you were cheating on her because she deserves to know and, even though I don't really like her, all women should stick together."

Tony's mouth dropped open in surprise. "What?"

She waved a finger in his face. "And as for this small town, you know nothing about it. Any bakery I work in, manage, or even own here will be an enormous success and worth ten of the one I left behind. So I suggest you take your cheating ass out of this backwater town, as you called it, as quickly as you can, because I never want to see you again."

She turned to the server who had come to drop off Tony's beer but was instead standing frozen in place after hearing Jaycee's speech. Taking the pint off the girl's tray, she slammed it on the table in front of Tony. The teen looked with wide eyes at the beer that had sloshed onto the table, stammered out her thanks, and fled.

Tony stared at Jaycee. She placed her hands on her hips, raised her chin, and glared back.

A slow flush rose up his neck and across his cheeks. "Scum?" he finally retorted. "You're calling *me* scum? Here I gave you the best job you're probably ever going to have and some of the most romantic moments of your life, and you're calling *me* names? And who do you think you are, saying any bakery of yours would be better than mine? You're nothing without me."

He continued, but Jaycee decided she had heard more than enough. She spun around on her heel to leave. Tony was a fool, and she had been an even bigger fool for allowing herself to be heartbroken over a man who could cheat on her and then talk to her this way.

She marched toward the pub's exit, her step only hitching for a second when she saw Jeremy was sitting on a stool at the bar. Jaycee averted her gaze. She was too angry to have a conversation with anyone right now. With her head held high and the sprites in her stomach cheering her on, she left the pub, letting the door slam closed with a satisfying clap behind her.

Chapter Nine

From his comfortable leather barstool, Jeremy sipped his pint of draft beer and watched a football game on the overhead television. He was also using the mirror above the bar to spy on Jaycee. When he'd seen the guy she had arrived with take her hand, Jeremy had risen from his seat to leave. But he'd settled right back down with a grim smile when he saw her face flush with displeasure as she tugged her hand away.

His gut was telling him that this slick-dressed stranger was the reason she had almost run out into oncoming traffic back in the city. Jeremy closed one of his hands into a fist and considered going over and confronting the guy, but he turned away, reminding himself that one kiss didn't mean he had that right.

He forced himself to focus on the game again until a sudden movement at their table caught his attention. He watched in the mirror as Jaycee stormed out the door behind him, her step stuttering for just a moment when she realized he was there. But she didn't stop.

Jeremy contemplated the meaning of this as he picked up his beer and looked up at the TV screen again. He frowned when seconds later he saw, in the mirror, Jaycee's companion smash a fist on the pub table, slide out of the booth, and charge out the door after her. Jeremy's jaw clenched. Pulling a few bills from his pocket, he threw them down on the bar and followed the couple outside.

Keeping up a brisk, rage-filled pace, Jaycee left the pub and turned toward home. A moment later, she heard footsteps pounding up behind her. Stopping in the middle of the sidewalk, she spun around and crossed her arms, waiting impatiently to see what else Tony might want.

"You can't just walk out when I'm talking to you," he growled as he got closer. "I've been driving since four a.m. to get to this stupid little hick town, so you should at least have the decency to listen to what I have to say."

"I listened, Tony. And I didn't hear a single thing I liked. You didn't apologize..."

"You insulted me!"

"You're darn right I did. And you deserve even worse than that."

"Everything okay, Jaycee?" asked a low voice from behind Tony.

Her frown softened slightly when she saw Jeremy striding up the sidewalk toward them.

Tony was a tall man, but Jeremy was taller and his police training gave him powerful forearms that he was now flexing as he passed Tony to stand next to Jaycee.

"I'm fine, thank you, Jeremy," she replied, her voice strained but steady.

Tony took a long, assessing scan of them, and a dark look passed over his face as he stepped back. "So is he the reason you've left everything behind and run off to this place?" he asked, waving at Jeremy. "It looks to me like I wasn't the *only* one who was seeing other people when we were supposedly *exclusively* dating, now, doesn't it?"

Jaycee opened her mouth to protest, but then closed it, deciding it wasn't worth the effort. Let Tony think whatever he wanted. She turned away from him and sighed. "Jeremy, would you mind walking me home?"

He nodded but didn't break eye contact with Tony.

"Goodbye, Tony. I'm sorry you drove all this way for nothing," Jaycee said and turned toward home.

"Nothing? Nothing is right. You are nothing!" he spat back. "And you're going to end up exactly that. You're nothing without me, especially if you're thinking of running your own bakery. You'll be begging me to give you your job back after you fail, and you know what? I won't."

Jaycee tugged on Jeremy's arm as he took a menacing step in Tony's direction.

Seeing Jeremy's intent, Tony held up his hands and backed away. He shot a hostile glare at both of them before turning away, striding down the street, and disappearing into the bar without a backward glance.

Jeremy stared at the closed door of the pub, his mouth tight. "Are you all right?" he finally asked, looking down at Jaycee.

"I think so." Her expression was grim but resolute. "We just had some unfinished business, I guess. But now it's done, and he's out of my life." She glanced away. "Forever, I hope." Straightening her shoulders, Jaycee started toward home again. Jeremy fell into step beside her.

"You don't need to walk me all the way home," she said after they'd gone a short distance. She gave him a smile that didn't quite reach her eyes. "I'm okay now, but thank you for being there when Tony was so angry. It was nice to have the backup."

Jeremy looked down at her and stuffed both hands in the front pockets of his jeans. "I didn't mind."

"Well, I truly appreciate the support."

They walked the final few blocks back to the house in silence. As they reached the driveway, Jaycee saw a pile of bikes on the front lawn, and her expression brightened. "Oh, good. It looks like Chandra's friends are here again."

Jeremy nodded. "It does," he said, raising one eyebrow. "Do you mind if I come in and check to see who's here?"

Jaycee's brow creased. "No? But, why?"

"The department is keeping a close eye on the whereabouts of all the teens in Larkin Bay for the next few weeks. We think whoever is starting all the fires is young, so we just need to rule out some of the kids as possible suspects."

"Are you kidding me?"

"I wish I was. I'd like to see if anyone we are monitoring is here, just in case there's any trouble tonight."

Jaycee placed her palm against his chest to stop him from saying more. "Wait, what?" she exclaimed. "You think Chandra is friends with the arsonist?"

Jeremy held up his hands. "No, not necessarily. But it would help if I could confirm all the teens' whereabouts this evening at least."

"Wow." Jaycee stepped back and her shoulders sagged. "Well, this has been a crazy last few hours. First there's Tony, who shows up out of nowhere and acts like a jerk, and now you're telling me I might have to worry about one of Chandra's friends possibly being an arsonist?"

Jeremy was silent as he looked away.

"So tell me, are you just being nice to me so you can get access to them? Did you just kiss me yesterday and now walk me home so I'd help you with your case?"

Jeremy's eyes widened. "What? No. Of course not, Jaycee. The case has nothing to do with what might be going on between us. I'm just trying to do my job. I need to clear as many people in town as I can, and a few of them might be here tonight, that's all."

Jaycee's face flushed as she stared at him silently for a long moment, then slowly she unclenched her fists and shook her head. "Okay, I guess I believe you." She looked away for a long moment and then gave him a half smile. "I'm sorry for not trusting you right away. It's just been a weird day. Come in and talk to them if it'll help. I really want this guy caught too, but questioning these teens while they're here seems like a bit much, don't you think?"

"Maybe." Jeremy sighed and ran a hand through his hair. "Let's not worry about it tonight, then. I can check up on the kids in other ways. I don't need to use your house to do it."

Jaycee's shoulders sagged. "Thank you. I guess seeing Tony tonight has me feeling all out of sorts and defensive."

Jeremy nodded.

"But I will go in and see what Chandra and her friends are up to. If I hear anything suspicious, I'll be sure to let you know."

Jeremy nodded. "Text me later, okay? Let me know how you're doing. Maybe we can go for a run together or something tomorrow?"

Jaycee flashed him a swift smile that didn't quite reach her eyes. "Sure," she mumbled before turning away and hurrying back into the house, leaving him standing alone, staring after her.

"No, we can't get a puppy. You're leaving for college next fall. Who will look after a dog when you're in a dorm?" exclaimed Jaycee. She scowled down at the book she held, not wanting to meet Chandra's pleading gaze. She knew her sister's sudden interest in adopting a dog had developed, in part, from spending time with Jeremy's sweet Bo, and after their last conversation, Jaycee wasn't sure how she felt about that.

Looking up a few minutes later, she saw her sister's sad expression and sighed. Hopping off the kitchen counter stool, she picked up the kitten from her basket and placed the sleepy animal in Chandra's lap. "Besides, we have this little gal now. A puppy would just eat her up."

Hope filled Chandra's eyes. "Does that mean we can keep her? I mean, keep her forever?"

Jaycee smiled. "I suppose so. The family she escaped from says she's from a litter of five, and they're trying to find homes for all of them. They'd be thrilled if we kept her, and cats are a lot less work than dogs."

"That's wonderful!"

"We can take her back to the vet tomorrow and see what she needs for shots and such. Then it's fine with me if she stays."

Chandra gave a whoop of joy and held the kitten up to her face, rubbing her nose against hers. "Did you hear that, Mew? You can stay! You can stay with us forever!"

"Mew? You've named her Mew?"

Chandra held the kitten close to her cheek. "Yep. When she first arrived, I asked her what her name was, and that's how she replied, so that's what I've been calling her."

Jaycee laughed and sat back down to continue flipping through the cookbook she had taken off her mother's shelf.

"What are you doing, anyway?" asked Chandra as she tried to cuddle the squirming kitten.

"I'm just looking for some recipes for different things that might appeal to a few restaurants and pubs here in town. When I was at Sullivan's Place, I noticed their dessert menu wasn't that extensive. So I thought I would talk to Mark, the owner, and see if he might be interested in buying something new to add to what he offers."

Chandra tilted her head to one side. "So you're going to set up a catering business?"

"Sort of. Just for baked goods, though. I'm not trained to do many main courses, although I could make those too in a pinch."

"Why don't you just open a bakery?"

Jaycee looked up at her sister in surprise. "Well, for lots of reasons, honestly, but mainly money. The equipment would cost a fortune, and then there's rent and utilities to pay too. I'd need to have someone back me financially to get started, and I don't know anyone who would do that. Besides, we need all the money I'm making right now to pay bills and for your college tuition next year. Baking and selling goods to the stores in town is just something I'm doing to tide us over until I find myself a real full-time job, preferably one that has benefits."

"I went down to Daisy's Dresses yesterday and applied for a job."

Jaycee smiled. "Well, that's wonderful—and very responsible of you too. What did they say?"

Chandra shrugged. "They just took my résumé and thanked me and told me they'd be in touch. I have lots of retail experience since I worked all last summer at the hardware store helping Mr. Thompson. But it doesn't look like he'll be back in business anytime soon, so I figured I'd better look for something else. Besides, I love clothes, so it might be fun to work there."

"That's a great idea. I do feel awful for the Thompson family, though."

"It is pretty horrible. But you should have seen the fire that night. It was so beautiful."

"I still can't believe you went down there and watched that poor man's business burn down," admonished Jaycee.

Chandra shifted in her seat. "Well, we all did. Everyone in town went to see if they could help, and then, when we couldn't, we all stayed on the hill at the park near Main Street and just watched. The fire department and police wouldn't let us anywhere near the actual fire."

Jaycee frowned at Chandra, whose face was tilted away, her long, dark hair hiding her expression as she cuddled Mew in her lap. "Well, that's good at least," Jaycee finally replied, closing the cookbook and picking up her mother's recipe file box. "But make sure that you're careful whenever you're around a fire. I don't want you getting hurt. Fires can be dangerous."

"You worry too much," announced Chandra, getting out of her seat and gathering together some of the magazines from the table. She turned to look at Jaycee with a half smile. "But that's okay. It's nice having someone here besides Betty worrying about me again."

Jaycee stared at her little sister and swallowed hard. "I love you too, Chandy," she replied.

Chandra's smile widened. "I'm going to do homework," she replied, and after picking up the rest of her magazines, she tucked Mew under her arm and left the kitchen.

Chapter Ten

Jaycee took a deep breath and pressed the doorbell beside the old-fashioned wooden screen door. She smiled when she heard the familiar chimes playing through the house announcing her arrival. At first glance, the place Amanda now lived in with Danny and their baby girl had changed very little since it had been bought by Amanda's parents nearly four decades earlier. It had a new roof, and the front door was painted a brighter shade of green, but everything else on the outside looked the same as it had in Jaycee's youth—well cared for and cherished.

"If you brought wine, come on in!" came a shout in answer to the bell's chimes. The command was greeted with a chorus of loud laughter, so Jaycee pasted on a smile and stepped inside to face her past.

As she entered the foyer, Amanda came around the corner to greet her and, in one smooth motion, took the container of cookies that Jaycee was holding and transferred her baby daughter into her arms.

"Hey, everyone, it's Jaycee, and she did better than alcohol—she brought cookies!" Amanda shouted over her shoulder. She turned to kiss her friend on the cheek. "And for this nursing mom, this is so much better. Thank you!" she whispered.

Jaycee nodded and gave the little girl she had been handed a tickle under one arm. The baby didn't seem the least bit concerned about being passed to a stranger. When she realized she had Jaycee's full attention, Ava rewarded her with a gummy smile and a coo.

"Well, hello to you too," Jaycee replied, patting the dark-eyed baby on the hand. "Do you remember me? We met last week when I dropped off your mom's birthday cake." The little girl tilted her head and gave her a serious scowl that Jaycee mimicked back as she followed Amanda down the hall and farther into the house.

When Jaycee rounded the corner, she felt an immediate, alarming sense of déjà vu. Her old group of high school friends were sitting on couches positioned just the way they had been when the house had belonged to Amanda's parents. The women all looked the same too. Except now, instead of holding cans of cola and bags of chips like they had in the past, they were all drinking from stemless glasses of red wine and passing around the container of cookies she had brought.

Jaycee stood on the fringes of the living room for a moment, studying the scene in front of her. She had once known everyone here very well; they had been her closest girlfriends throughout high school, but she hadn't seen most of them since her parents died. The women had all tried to stay in touch, but once Jaycee moved into her dorm, she'd been so immersed in her work and trying to contain her grief that she'd ignored all the emails, Facebook requests, texts, and well-intentioned calls from them. Now that she was back in Larkin Bay, however, she needed to face the guilt she felt, realizing she probably should have been in touch with everyone long before now.

"Hey, Jaycee, come sit beside me," Denise called over. "We have a ton to catch up on." Getting off the couch, Denise took the baby from Jaycee and handed her back to her mother. After giving Jaycee a quick hug, she pulled her over to the sofa and motioned for her to sit down. Jaycee sighed in relief. Denise had always had a knack for pulling people into groups and immediately putting them at ease. She was sure Denise's relaxed and friendly personality made her very popular in her current job as the town's high school guidance counselor. She made a mental note to ask Chandra if she knew her.

"Have a glass of wine," Amanda said, handing her a large glass of red.

"Thank you," Jaycee replied and, holding the wineglass close to her nose, took a long, appreciative sniff of the sweet, aromatic liquid.

"House Rules," Amanda called out, heading back to her seat.

Jaycee almost spit out her wine. "Really? You all still do this?"

Denise groaned. "She does. The rest of us just try to ignore her." But when Amanda yelled out, "Left Mittens!" Jaycee noticed that everyone in the group dutifully transferred their wine over to their left hand. Jaycee sighed and did the same.

House Rules was a game Amanda had invented back in high school. The rules were simple: the house owner would yell out a silly command every five or ten minutes, and the rest of the group would have to follow them. Over the years, the friends had developed a shorthand for many of the commands. Thus, Jaycee knew Left Mittens meant that everyone could only use their left hand until Amanda changed the instruction. The penalties when the girls were young for not following the directions ranged from being forced to tell secrets, to flashing the neighborhood boys, to drinking shots of alcohol. Jaycee gripped her glass firmly in her left hand, deciding she didn't want to know what the penalties were for not following the commands now that they were older.

As she and Denise caught up on each other's lives, her old friend confirmed she had, like Amanda, married her teenage sweetheart and moved back to Larkin Bay to work at the high school they'd all attended together.

"Mr. Frat finally retired last spring," Denise informed Jaycee, as the conversation turned to her work and she updated her on their former guidance adviser.

They both grimaced as Amanda yelled out, "Stand tall," but they still struggled out of the heavily stuffed couch to their feet. "He was seventy-eight years old."

"Really? Wow."

"Yep. Can you imagine working that long? Remember how he used to tell us that girls didn't need to go to college but should instead just find a nice boy, get married, and stay home to look after their husbands and children?"

"I do! That was hilarious. No one listened to him, though."

Denise nodded and giggled. "I should hope not. When I started cleaning out his old desk, I found pamphlets from the 1950s home economic classes saying the same thing! It was hysterical. I framed one and hung it up in my office."

Jaycee smiled. She had many fond memories of her high school years, and Mr. Frat was one of them. The older gentleman had approved of her choice of career, obviously considering baking an appropriate occupation for a young lady, and that had suited her just fine. A lump formed in her throat as she recalled the days when her mom and Mr. Frat had helped her make her college decisions. Blinking back the tears that suddenly formed in her eyes, she turned her attention to the conversations around her, determined not to allow her reminiscing to ruin the evening.

"Sit pretty," demanded Amanda, and everyone groaned in relief as they settled back into their seats and continued catching up.

Leaning forward to better hear what was being discussed around her, Jaycee overheard Tina mention decorating. Jaycee raised a hand to get her attention. "I need to do some painting and such, but what I really need is a handyperson. Do you know of anyone in town who might do some odd jobs for me at a reasonable price?"

"Why don't you call Hank? You remember him from school, right?" suggested Amanda. "He's been working as a carpenter in Larkin Bay for a few years now, and he does a good job. If he can't help you, he'll at least know someone who can. Here, hold the baby again for a minute, and I'll find you his card." Plunking Ava in Jaycee's lap, she strode off without a backward glance but yelled out, "Knees to the left," as she headed into the kitchen.

Like a well-choreographed synchronized swimming team, the entire group of women crossed their legs to the left. Sighing, Jaycee made a goofy face at the baby and bounced her up and down. The little girl rewarded her with a gleeful chortle.

"Is she always this content?" she asked Tina, the owner of Larkin Bay's Yoga and Pilates studio and a friend of Jaycee's since they'd sat next to each other in seventh grade science class.

"Nope. At least not with me. But after she was born, I explained to her I would help look after her, but I wasn't ever going to have children myself, so she shouldn't be looking for any playmates from my womb. I think she took offense because ever since then, whenever she's around me, she fusses."

Tina stretched her arms out as though she was going to pick up the baby, and sure enough, Ava pulled away and whimpered softly.

"Really?" Jaycee said to the baby, chuckling in mock horror. "You don't like her because she told you she doesn't want children? You are a sensitive one, aren't you?"

"Just like her mother," Tina kidded.

Upon returning to the living room, Amanda demanded to know what they were all laughing about and smiled good-naturedly when they told her. After putting the carpenter's business card on the coffee table in front of Jaycee, she sat down and took her daughter back to be nursed. "Game over. I'm tired," she said.

"Thank goodness," said Tina. "Aren't we getting too old for this, anyway?"

Amanda stuck her tongue out at her. Tina ignored her and turned back to Jaycee. "We've missed you here in Larkin Bay, honey. Are you home for a while now, or are you leaving us again soon?"

Jaycee smiled. Fully aware that everyone was listening, she used a light and dismissive tone to fill them in on the disaster of Betty's investment, her recent breakup with her two-timing boyfriend, and how she was now looking for a job.

The women sipped their wine and listened with wide eyes. "Wow. It sounds like you've had a tough time of it lately." Denise placed a hand on Jaycee's forearm. "Is there anything we can do to help?"

"Thank you, but no. There's nothing, really. We're all doing fine. I'm over the guy now that I've had time to realize what a jerk he is, and I'm sure I'll find some steady work soon. I'd just like to find something close by so I can stay here for at least the next year. I think a teenager is more than Betty wants to handle at her age, but Chandra still needs someone to keep an eye on her."

"I had some of Amanda's birthday cake, and it was delicious," said Tina. "Would you consider baking me a few dozen muffins every other day for the studio? I'd love to get them from somewhere close by for my morning sessions, and having something freshly made regularly would be amazing."

"Sure. That would be great, and I can deliver them too. I'd love to see your place and perhaps even join a class."

"Done," said Tina, slapping a hand on her thigh. "And we'd love to have you join us for a class anytime. Can you drop off the muffins in two days? I already have some for the early-morning group tomorrow. We'll devour any flavor, so whatever you want to bake is great—just drop by with a bill at the end of each week, and I'll write you a check."

Jaycee smiled at her old friend. "That would be marvelous, thank you."

"Not a problem. And thank *you*. You're making my life easier."

The rest of the evening flew by, fueled by laughter and wine. Before Jaycee knew it, the hour was late. When she saw Amanda stifling a yawn, she got to her feet and announced it was time for her to be heading home.

"I'll walk with you," offered Denise. "We live out the same way, and I shouldn't be driving after drinking so much wine. I'll just leave my car here until morning and pick it up on my way to work."

The two women thanked Amanda for hosting them and said goodbye to everyone. After pulling their sweaters on, they were soon walking home.

"Where do you live now?" Jaycee asked Denise. "Your family home used to be by the high school, right?"

"My parents still live there, part-time at least, when they're not in Florida. When James and I got engaged, we bought a house closer to where you are, on Oak Street." She waved down the road ahead of them. "Since I spend all day working at the school, I didn't want to live right beside it. I thought that might drive me a little bit crazy."

"That makes sense."

Denise gave a little skip over a crack in the sidewalk. "So how are you really holding up being back here, anyway?" she asked. "It must be a big change from the city. And how is Chandra? I see her around the school once in a while, but she never comes into the guidance department, so I don't get to talk to her very much."

"Everything is okay. It's sort of strange being back here without Mom and Dad, and the house needs some repairs, but other than that, we're doing fine. And as I told everyone earlier, I'm thinking of staying for a while. Until Chandra goes off to college at least, so I'm looking for work. The birthday cakes and muffins are fun to make, but I need to find something more substantial to do to cover the bills."

Denise's forehead creased. "Do you know what Chandra's plans are for college? I work with the seniors doing college prep, but I don't think I've ever seen her doing any of the testing or coming into the office to look at the materials. We would have sent all the information out to Betty as her guardian, but I'm not sure we've ever gotten anything back from either of them."

Jaycee looked over at her friend, her expression stricken as she touched the scar on her cheek. "Yikes. I actually don't know. I've been meaning to talk to her about it, but there never seems to be a good time."

"Well, if she's planning on applying to college for next fall, we had better get the paperwork together and look a little closer at what the deadlines are for where she wants to apply. Do you know what she's thinking about studying?"

"I have no idea." Jaycee sighed. "I really am an awful guardian."

"Well, you did come home to a bit of a mess. Why don't I look at her file tomorrow and see what classes Chandra is taking this year? I can also speak to a few of her teachers and see what her strengths are and what might be suitable. Perhaps you can talk to Chandra about what she wants to do too. Then we can all get together and make a plan."

Jaycee smiled gratefully at her friend. "That would be wonderful, thank you. I'm not even sure where to start with college applications, so it would be great to have some help."

Denise shrugged. "Don't thank me. It's my job, and I love doing it. Besides, I'm sure we can get everything sorted out in no time at all."

"You're the best," Jaycee replied, stopping just long enough so she could give her friend a grateful hug, which Denise warmly returned before they continued on their way home.

Jaycee's breath hitched as she rounded the last corner of the boardwalk. She loved to run beside the lake, but after being out late the previous night with her friends, she was tired today. Biting down on her lower lip, she pushed herself a little harder. A few minutes later, she was relieved to see Jeremy and Bo were waiting ahead for her on the boardwalk across from the children's brightly colored playground.

Jeremy smiled as she drew closer. "Hi. Want a quick break before we head out?" he asked.

"That would be great. I forgot how quickly one's endurance disappears when they're not running regularly."

He laughed. "I believe it. I've actually been pretty consistent with getting out lately since I have Bo to exercise too. But some mornings it's still not easy."

"I used to love running every other day in the city park, but now that I'm living here, I must admit I haven't gotten out nearly as often."

"That's understandable. You've been busy."

Jaycee looked up at him and felt a small part of her heart melt. She was always touched by how interested Jeremy was in what was going on in her life. The sprites in her stomach had bounced up and down with glee at his invitation for her to join him on a run today, and they were swooning happily now that she was looking up at him.

As she kneeled to pet Bo, Jaycee realized that although Jeremy was very attractive, what she liked most about him was that he seemed nice. Genuinely nice. Not only did he foster service puppies, but he'd been lovely to all the teens at the cookout and he seemed to love his job as a police officer, helping others.

Isn't this the type of man every woman is looking for?

Especially when she compared him to Tony, who, although he could be quite charming at times, now in retrospect, seemed mainly interested in gambling online, working, and cheating on her. Jeremy seemed much less self-centered in comparison.

I need to find out if he's really as great as he seems.

They strolled along the boardwalk in comfortable silence for a few minutes. "Are you ready to run again?" Jeremy asked.

Jaycee's heart rate had slowed back down, so she nodded. "Yep. I'm good."

"You set the pace, then, and I'll try and keep up."

She laughed and waited while he gathered up Bo's leash, then she stepped back onto the jogging path to continue their run. Her steps fell easily into a compatible stride with his. She had run with enough other people to know that this didn't always happen, and she looked up to see if he had noticed.

His answering smile let her know he was also enjoying the ease and for the next two miles they ran together in harmonious silence, only broken by Bo's panting and Jeremy's occasional correction as he taught the puppy how to run on a leash.

When they reached the end of the pathway, they stopped and Jaycee drank for a long moment from her water bottle while Jeremy gave Bo a drink. Only when the dog was finished did Jeremy open another bottle and quench his own thirst.

"How long have you been running?" she asked.

"Since high school. I used to run track and when I decided I wanted to join the police force, I knew I'd have to stay in shape, so running seemed like a good way to continue getting cardio in."

"That makes sense."

"How about you?" he asked, kneeling beside Bo and ruffling the dog's ears.

"Not until college. Once I started culinary school, I realized I was going to be doing a lot of tasting and eating, so I decided to burn off some calories to compensate by running. Once I figured out that it was also a great way to release stress and made me feel good, I was hooked."

Moving to the side of the running path, Jaycee took a seat on a bench. She stretched her legs out in front of her, smiling as Bo came and sat down between her feet.

"Do you like being a baker?" asked Jeremy, sitting next to her. His entire face was lit up with interest, brightening his gorgeous eyes and causing the dimple in his cheek to flash. That, combined with his toned abs, muscular biceps, and tight behind, made him very easy to look at and the sprites in Jaycee's stomach were once again very much enjoying the view.

She nodded. "I love the baking part and the testing and creating new things. I must admit, though, I don't like always working for someone else. My last manager was a jerk, and that made it difficult some days."

"So you quit?"

"I did. But for a lot of reasons. Not just because I didn't like Rhonda." She closed her eyes and lifted her chin to enjoy the soft breezes and smell of pine in the air. "But enough about me. How about you? Do you like being a cop?"

"Technically, I'm an investigator, not a police officer. But yes, most days I do. It's very satisfying to know you're helping people."

"That makes you sound very noble."

Jeremy cocked his head to the side. "I don't know about that. I just know helping others makes me happy."

"Me too," Jaycee replied. "But I do it by baking cookies."

Jeremy laughed and got to his feet.

Reaching down, he took Jaycee's hand in his and pulled her up, chuckling as she groaned in mock protest. A moment later, Bo was prancing close to his side as they all broke into a slow jog back the way they had come.

Chapter Eleven

Leaning back in the squeaky office chair in the corner of Larkin Bay's police station, Jeremy linked his fingers behind his head and studied the stucco ceiling. According to the fire marshal's report, the last three fires in Larkin Bay were all strongly suspected or confirmed to have been started intentionally. That was good to know, but what the information couldn't tell him was who had started them. Figuring this out was on him.

Fortunately, he had a few hints he could puzzle together. He knew, for instance, that several witnesses had seen a lanky, darkly dressed man hanging around the targeted buildings a short time before the fires were discovered. One report also stated that they thought the suspect was very young. Jeremy frowned as he considered this—he had never heard of an arsonist younger than fourteen, but he'd seen too much to not believe they existed.

Closing his eyes, he sighed heavily. It was taking him longer than he liked to narrow down the identity of this arsonist. Larkin Bay was a small town, and another fire could devastate not only its historical buildings, but the town's economy as well.

I need to find this kid.

Getting up from his chair, he walked to the coffee station. It was late, and the pot hadn't been refilled in a while. He sniffed the bitter aroma and poured the remains down the sink. The office had been deserted for hours. No one would be looking for more coffee tonight.

After wandering back to his uncomfortable chair, Jeremy sat down and pulled a pad of legal paper toward him. He didn't have enough evidence yet to make an arrest, so he needed whoever was starting the fires to make a mistake. He needed the arsonist to start a fire in a way that would give away who he was. Jeremy smiled grimly.

I need to set a trap.

Jaycee gritted her teeth as she tugged on the tall blades of grass that covered the inscriptions on her parents' headstones. The work was strangely satisfying, she decided, a split second before she pulled so hard that she was thrown off-balance and onto her backside. Wincing, she scrambled back to her feet and rubbed the bruise she knew was forming there.

Ouch.

Determined not to feel sorry for herself, she leaned forward and gingerly rubbed her fingertips over the small, etched flowers decorating her mom's and dad's headstones. Her parents' monuments were being well cared for, and the surrounding area hadn't required much tidying. Unscrewing her water bottle's lid, Jaycee filled the vases at the foot of the graves, then unwrapped the daisies and red roses she had bought. After placing the flowers in the water, she stepped back to admire them. "There you go, Mom and Dad.

Everything looks perfect now. I hope you like the flowers," she said, patting the memorial's marble angel's wing.

Jaycee took a deep breath of the unseasonably warm breezes before giving the monuments one last lingering look and turning away. Following the church garden's cobblestone pathway, she chose a route that curved around the back of the church. Pushing open a rusty but well-oiled iron gate, she ventured into the oldest part of the cemetery where the tombstones were crumbling and covered with moss. Many of the engravings on them were illegible. A few yards in, she stopped and squinted to read the words on one of the smaller plots. The birth and death dates etched on the crumbling slabs confirmed it was a child's grave and provided a stark reminder of just how dangerous things had been centuries ago for young children.

As she passed more monuments, she noticed that most of the people buried in this part of the cemetery had lived long before her parents or even her grandparents had been born.

"But were you happy?" Jaycee asked aloud, standing in front of one of the more ornately decorated gravesites. "Did you accomplish what you wanted? Did you take chances and chase your dreams?"

Only the sound of birds chirping in the trees answered her questions.

Sighing, she headed back to the exit. After closing the cemetery gate and latching it securely behind her, she made her way back down the uneven walkway to the front of the church. The building sat high above the town on a hill, an imposing tower of gray stone with twin spiral towers and large stained glass windows. Some caring parishioners had obviously been busy, as the cobblestone path leading to the church's beautiful and elaborately carved double entryway doors was edged with colorful mums and other fall foliage. Glancing back to admire it one last time, Jaycee straightened her shoulders and mentally shook off her melancholy before heading across town to the automotive repair shop where Danny had towed her car.

"Here you go," Danny said, handing Jaycee a paper cup filled with cold water. "There's more in the cooler in the back office. Help yourself to as much as you want."

"Thanks. It's like a summer day out there," she said, holding the drink in one hand and using the other to push the hair off the back of her neck. "I can't believe how hot it is for September. I dressed too warmly for such a heat wave."

"You've forgotten how warm the fall can be here." Danny chuckled. "The craziest part is it might snow tomorrow."

Jaycee grinned, remembering from her youth how the temperatures in Larkin Bay had often changed just as dramatically as he suggested. Danny smiled back and returned to work. After pouring herself another cup of water, Jaycee sipped it and looked around the garage, marveling at all the changes since she'd last been here. The lift her car was hoisted up on was shiny and new looking, and the wires that snaked underneath it were attached to a laptop hooked up to another giant machine. The sparkling clean floors were made of some type of shiny epoxy floor treatment that glimmered in the sunshine. Everywhere she looked, there were gleaming surfaces, fresh paint, and state-of-the-art equipment.

She finished her drink and went over to where Danny was working on his computer. Leaning over his shoulder, she tried to decipher what the program was showing. "Hey, Danny? Do you ever dream about car mufflers? Do you wake up exhausted?"

Danny smiled at his computer screen. "Hey, Jaycee? Do you know what happens when a frog's car breaks down?"

"It gets toad!"

The friends laughed compatibly.

"God, those are awful," said Danny.

"That's what makes them so funny," Jaycee declared. She frowned at the squiggly lines and numbers on the computer screen. "Does this really mean anything to you?" she asked. "And why do I have the feeling that it's going to take more than a few dozen cupcakes in payment for you to get my car back in working order again?"

Danny turned to her and chuckled. "I'm sorry it took me so long to get to it."

"That's okay. I haven't needed it."

Danny nodded. "Well, the good news is it can be fixed. The bad news is it's not going to be cheap, even with the healthy family discount I can offer you."

Jaycee grimaced, mentally visualizing her small bank account balance as Danny started rattling off the long list of repairs her car needed. She finally held up her hand to stop him. "While I appreciate all the information, can you just tell me what the total cost would be? I trust that you're going to be fair."

Danny shook his head and quoted her a price that made her wince.

"Yikes. I didn't think my car was even worth that much."

"Oh, it's worth that. And if I were to fix it up and paint it, I could get quite a bit more for it too."

"Really?"

He nodded. "Sure, it's got a solid engine, and the chassis is sound. It's a classic. Why? Were you thinking of selling it? I could get you a decent price for it if you are."

Jaycee gazed at him for a long moment before responding. "Yes, I actually might be," she replied slowly. "But before I do, I'd like you to look at what it would cost to get my mom's old Buick running again. That would get us around town, and it's probably just rusting away in the back garage. We don't need two cars." She shrugged. "Besides, if I'm serious about staying in town, I might as well get rid of everything, so I can't easily run away."

Danny laughed. "Well, I wouldn't want to be responsible for that. But I can take a look at your parents' car and tell you which is the better of the two for you to keep. Although, I wouldn't say no if you wanted to throw in a few cupcakes for my services, either." He cocked his head to one side and grinned at her. "Maybe you really should open a bakery here in town. That's what you always wanted to do, and then that way, I can just buy cupcakes from you. Life is short, and YOLO or whatever the kids say today and just do it."

After delivering that sage piece of advice, Danny turned away to greet another customer. Jaycee frowned after him and shook her head.

Chasing one's dreams seems to be a recurring theme today.

"Does opening a bakery here in Larkin Bay seem like a crazy idea to you?" Jaycee asked Betty later that night as they washed and dried their dinner dishes at the kitchen sink.

"No, not at all. It's what your mother hoped you would do one day. It's what she always wanted to do herself."

Jaycee's mouth dropped open as she put down the plate she was drying and stared at Betty. "Really? Mom wanted to open a bakery?"

"Yes." Betty pulled the plug on the dirty dishwater and turned on the tap to fill it with clean, hot water again. "She loved to bake and knew you did too. She always thought you might return to Larkin Bay once you were done school and open a bakery with her—Jaycee's Bakery."

"She never told me that," Jaycee whispered.

Betty frowned. "How could she? She didn't want you to feel obligated to come back and do anything because of her. It was just a dream—a 'wouldn't it be nice' moment she shared with me."

Jaycee looked up at the ceiling and contemplated how wonderful it would have been to open a bakery with the blessing and help of her mother. "I know some of the costs involved," she said, dragging the back of her hand across her eyes, "but I've never really considered the rest—the permits, the rent, and the cost of the equipment I would need to buy. I just assumed that it was something I couldn't afford."

"Well, I know the town might help you," said Betty, dunking more dishes in the sink. "Larkin Bay's Chamber of Commerce helped arrange a loan at a low-interest rate for Danny to upgrade his garage when he was considering buying it after Old Jake announced he was retiring and Young Jake wasn't interested in it. And I think the money from the house appraisal might be quite substantial, especially when we're done fixing it up."

Jaycee shook her head and stared at the other woman. "I can't believe I'm considering doing this. I'm actually standing here thinking this might be a good idea."

"That's because it is." Betty smiled and handed her another dish to dry and put away.

After the kitchen was tidy, Betty said good night to Chandra and Jaycee and left to spend the night with her daughter and grandchildren. Chandra had disappeared up to her room to do her homework, so Jaycee was alone in the living room, researching the costs of opening a small retail store, when she heard a soft knock on the front door.

"Coming," she called out, scooping up Mew so she wouldn't slip out into the dark night as she headed for the front door.

"Oh, hi," Jaycee said, her voice hitching when she saw it was Jeremy and Bo standing in the glow of the outdoor porch light. "Um, come in," she added, smiling as she held the door open with one foot while keeping a tight grip on Mew.

She motioned for them to follow her into the living room, where she sat down on the couch. Jeremy sat on the edge of the chair across from her while Bo curled up at his feet. Jaycee set the kitten down and they both watched Mew eye the puppy for a long moment before she turned and bolted from the room.

Jaycee laughed. "I don't think Mew has had much experience with dogs."

"Maybe she'll like them better in time."

"Maybe," she replied. She shifted slightly toward him. "I guess you were out for a walk?"

"I was." Jeremy looked at the pile of papers on the table between them. "Am I interrupting something here, though?"

"No, not really. I was just, uh, looking up information online about running a retail business in town," she explained, gesturing toward the open laptop on the coffee table. "I'm thinking about opening a bakery here in Larkin Bay. All my friends seem to think it's a good idea, so I've been researching what things like rent and utilities would cost. I'm trying to put together a business plan so I can approach Larkin Bay's Chamber of Commerce or the town bank to possibly get a small-business loan."

"That sounds exciting." Jeremy smiled at her.

Blushing, Jaycee scooted back in her seat and folded her hands in her lap. "But I shouldn't go on about this so much. I'm sure that's not what you came over to talk about."

"No, seriously, I mean it. That does sound terrific. What you're telling me is really interesting."

"Thank you."

Jeremy shrugged. "I was really just out for a walk with Bo, and I saw your light was on," he said. "So I thought I'd drop in and see if you wanted to go for a run again in the morning. I really enjoyed your company the other day, and Bo did too."

Jaycee sunk back into the sofa cushions and rubbed the scar on her cheek. "That would be great. I'll meet you again at the same spot if that works for you. Eight a.m.?"

"Sounds good." Jeremy smiled and settled back in his seat. "And I really think it's great that you're considering opening a bakery here in Larkin Bay."

Jaycee tried to ignore the warm feeling the happy sprites were creating in the pit of her stomach as she gazed over at him.

"But it also makes me want to catch the arsonist even more now. I don't want your new shop targeted by them."

"That would be terrifying, but I know you'll catch whoever is responsible before that ever becomes a possibility." Reaching out, Jaycee touched his arm to show her sincerity. As her fingertips brushed his skin, a spark jumped between them. She quickly drew her hand back.

Surprised, she gazed at Jeremy, who looked back at her with eyes that suddenly darkened. Jaycee drew in a deep breath and leaned slightly toward him, watching his every move as he got to his feet and stepped around Bo.

Settling on the couch beside Jaycee, he reached over, gently took her face between his hands, and brushed his lips against hers. A soft moan escaped her as she settled back against the couch cushions and pulled him closer. Surfacing a few minutes later from the sensual, hypnotic fog his steadily deepening kisses induced, Jaycee's lips felt swollen, and her breath was hurried.

Her eyes widened.

What am I doing?

Shifting away from Jeremy, Jaycee broke their embrace, but she couldn't tear her gaze from his hooded, questioning look. Finally, she sighed reluctantly and, placing both hands on his chest, pushed him away from her.

Instantly, he was on his feet. Jaycee could see desire had darkened his gray eyes but mixed in was a touch of surprise.

"Well, that was unexpected," she said, trying to sort through the array of feelings that had the sprites in her stomach doing the cha-cha, even as her common sense was telling her she should slow things down.

I just broke up with Tony, and I barely know this man.

"Yeah. Wow. But, um, you need to know—I never do that," Jeremy said and took another step back.

"Do what? Kiss women?" A slow, teasing smile spread across her face as she gazed up at him.

"Well, no, but yes," he said, scrubbing a hand through his hair. "Actually, you're the first woman that I've been close to like this since Marianne died."

"Oh." Jaycee pondered this for a long moment. "Well, it was only a kiss. How did it feel?" Looking away, she straightened up on the couch and ran her tongue over her still sweetly stinging lips.

"Great," he said, and then sighed. "But it was wrong, and I'm sorry."

"Wrong? Really? Well, it's the second time you've done it," she reminded him, giving him a sharp look and then a mischievous smile. "It can't be *that* wrong."

"I know."

Jaycee couldn't help but chuckle at his hangdog expression. "It's fine. And I was right there with you."

Jeremy studied her silently.

She sighed. "But I know what you're trying to say. And, look—I'm not going to lie—you seem like an amazing guy. But if we were to continue down this path, I can't help but feel that I might be rebounding from a terrible relationship. And that's not fair to you."

Jeremy stuffed both hands in the front pockets of his jeans and pressed his lips together. The line between his eyes deepened as he regarded her somberly. "Okay."

Jaycee's hands twisted in her lap. "I just think I need a hot minute to figure out who I am and what I'm doing with my life before I get physical with anyone or even think about another relationship.

I'm sorry. I've just got too much going on right now." Waving her hand, she indicated the house around her and steadfastly ignored the sprites in her stomach demanding that she drag Jeremy back to the couch and continue kissing him until the sun rose. "So, maybe we can agree not to, uh, do that again until we've had a little more time to get to know one another?"

Jeremy's face registered dismay for a split second before he blinked and the expression was replaced with one showing both relief and regret. He quickly moved to sit across from her again. "Sure. We can do that if that's what you want. No more kissing—got it."

"Right, sounds good," Jaycee replied, running her hand across the top of her head to pat her ponytail smooth.

A slight frown creased Jeremy's brow as he tapped one foot. "So, what do you want to do instead?"

Jaycee chuckled, picked up her laptop, and turned the screen toward him. "I think you should sit right here next to me and let me bore you with everything I've been researching on how to open a bakery here in Larkin Bay."

"That sounds good."

"Yeah, I've discovered I'm not supposed to be selling baked goods from my home—that was a revelation."

"That is the law."

She shook her head. "So I just learned. Don't arrest me."

Jeremy grinned but didn't reply.

"And I'm sure I'll be discovering a ton of other new things too," she continued. "So, basically, I want you to just sit right here and tell me how wonderful everything sounds."

She scooted over so Jeremy could fit more comfortably next to her. As he settled beside her, her hand collided with his, causing a current of attraction to sizzle between them again. Jeremy quickly pulled his fingers away.

An amused smile curled Jaycee's lips. "Look at this," she said and, moving her mouse, pulled up a commercial real estate site online that showed several retail properties available for lease in the area. "Some of these look great, but I still want to find a location for the bakery in downtown Larkin Bay if I can."

Jeremy nodded, then leaned back into the faded floral couch cushions. Time flew by as he asked questions to help Jaycee clarify her thoughts and plans. She had almost run all of her ideas by him when he glanced at the time on his phone and stood up. "This is all amazing, and I think it's a fantastic idea, but unfortunately, I can't stick around to hear any more. I really have to get Bo home and into bed. He's still too young to keep off schedule for long," he apologized as he looked down at the slumbering dog.

"Oh, of course," Jaycee said, setting down her laptop and scrambling to her feet. She felt her cheeks heat as she realized she'd been talking nonstop for some time. "I hope I haven't bored you with all this stuff."

Jeremy shook his head. "I wasn't bored at all," he assured her. "It's been fascinating. This is a great idea, and I'm flattered that you shared it with me."

The sprites in Jaycee's stomach swooned at his words as she followed him to the door.

He stopped in the front foyer to shrug on his coat and turned to look down at her. Jaycee sensed that had they not agreed to forgo kissing earlier, they would be doing exactly that right now. She couldn't help but wonder what else a kiss might have led to. Looking up at his half smile, she knew Jeremy's thoughts were going in a similar direction.

Reaching over, he gently ran a fingertip across the scar on her cheek. Jaycee hadn't covered it up with makeup that morning and she was surprised to realize that she didn't feel the least bit self-conscious about him touching it.

"Good night," he whispered.

"Sleep well," she replied as he jogged down the house's front steps with Bo trotting at his side. Humming softly under her breath, she watched him disappear into the shifting fall shadows before returning to the living room.

Opening her laptop again, Jaycee pulled up her Barry Manilow playlist and, while singing along softly to a love song, googled another commercial baking site. Forcing herself to banish Jeremy from her thoughts would be the best course of action, she decided firmly. It didn't matter that being with him caused the happiness sprites to do a cha-cha dance of desire in her stomach. She had too many things to do to even consider getting involved with another man. Chandra and Betty were depending on her right now, and she couldn't let them down. No matter how sexy and almost irresistible Jeremy might be.

Chapter Twelve

Two weeks later, Jaycee sat in one of the dark leather tub chairs in Larkin Bay's town hall lobby. Wiping one clammy hand on her wool skirt, she swallowed hard. Her throat felt like sandpaper, and her head ached behind her eyes. Glancing down at her phone, she reread the email she'd been sent inviting her here today and once again ran through the Chamber of Commerce board members' first names. This was the perfect group to pitch her business plan to. They would be able to determine whether her ideas were feasible and what, if any, support they could offer. Closing her eyes, she forced herself to take a deep, calming breath. The last thing she wanted to do was throw up.

When it was finally her turn to present, she pinned a smile onto her face as she was led into the conference room. Taking the only empty seat, she folded her hands on the table in front of her and flipped open a copy of the folder she had sent each of them.

Mayor April gave her a broad, reassuring smile before standing and turning to the rest of the group. "Jaycee is here today to share with us her plans for opening a bakery in Larkin Bay. Since you've all had a chance to read the business plan she sent us, you already know some of her ideas. I'm sure you're just as interested and excited to hear the rest of her proposal as I am. Thank you for coming today, Jaycee. We're happy you decided to join us."

"Thank you, Mayor April. And thank you, everyone, for coming," Jaycee said. She tried to ignore how hard her knees were shaking as she took her place at the front of the room and presented her plan.

A short round of applause met the end of her talk, and after a brief Q&A session, she shook the hands of everyone around the table, thanked them all for their time, and left. Her plan for a bakery in Larkin Bay was now in the Chamber of Commerce members' hands.

Driving home, she blasted the music from her car speakers at full volume, trying unsuccessfully to drive out the voices in her head that insisted she had failed miserably. She ran up the front steps of her house in despair and threw herself face down on her childhood bed, clutching her old teddy bear close. She cringed and bit down hard on her bottom lip when her cell phone chimed.

Oh no.

She apprehensively pressed the accept button. "Hello?"

"Jaycee," came a pleasant and warm voice over the line, "this is Mayor April. I know you're probably very anxious to hear what we decided, so I won't waste time with pleasantries."

Closing her eyes, Jaycee gripped the phone tighter and held her breath.

"The Larkin Bay Chamber of Commerce was thrilled with your presentation and your plans to open a bakery here in town. We have some ideas we think might help you, but your application has been unanimously approved, and your business plan has also been prequalified for financing."

"Really?" Jaycee's voice shook, causing the mayor to chuckle.

"Yes. I think most of us were already on board after simply reading what you sent us over the weekend. We didn't even need to see your presentation. You did an excellent job, my dear."

"I'm shocked. I don't even know what to say."

"I'm so happy for you." The mayor then mentioned an interest rate and loan amount that caused Jaycee's breath to catch in her throat. It was more than she had requested, and the rate was far better than she could have ever dreamed.

She gasped. "Thank you. Thank you ever so much. You have no idea what this means to me. I am so happy, so grateful."

The mayor laughed. "Congratulations, Jaycee. I can't wait to work with you. I know the bakery will be a wonderful addition to our downtown."

Jaycee tried not to stammer as she thanked the mayor for the news again. She then set up a time to meet with her and her staff to finalize the details of her project.

After disconnecting the call, she threw her teddy bear to one side, leaped to her feet, and screamed in excitement. She couldn't believe it—she would be able to send Chandra to college *and* work in Larkin Bay. And, unbelievably, because of these generous, lovely people, she was going to open her own bakery here, just as she had always dreamed.

The following week, Jaycee sat on a multicolored boardwalk bench watching the seagulls scavenge the bay's beach for food. The sun was muted and the breezes from the water were cool against her cheeks. Stretching her legs out in front of her, she leaned back and closed her eyes as she waited for Richard Marshall. Richard was a commercial property realtor who had promised her he had the key to the perfect retail location for her bakery in Larkin Bay.

Jaycee practiced a few deep, calming yoga breaths and tapped her toes against the wooden boardwalk for a few minutes before finally opening her eyes. She was simply too excited to sit still. Turning around, she studied the empty store with the brightly painted For Lease sign in the window behind her.

The shop was a charming redbrick building with wooden shutters that framed two large bay windows. Gingerbread accents dotted the roofline. Jaycee was already half in love with the space, imagining how gorgeous it would look once renovated to house the bakery she envisioned.

She'd spent endless hours over the last week studying county regulations and making lists of the equipment and insurance she needed, as well as the government labeling requirements she'd have to follow to open her bakery. She had also made detailed notes of what had to be done to meet health and safety standards. Seeing all the information together in one folder on her laptop was a little overwhelming, and more than once, Jaycee had wondered if she was crazy to attempt this.

Scrambling to her feet, she clasped her hands in gleeful anticipation when she finally spied Chandra, accompanied by an older, professionally dressed man, making their way up the sidewalk toward her.

"Jaycee! You're here!" the teen cried, grabbing her arm and spinning her around. "Jaycee, this is Richard Marshall, the real estate agent," she said. "And, Mr. Marshall, this is my best friend in the entire world, my sister, Jaycee."

Richard shook her hand and grinned at her. "It's nice to meet you in person, finally. I met up with your sister on the way over here—she and my son go to school together."

Chandra grabbed Jaycee's hand and squeezed it tightly as Richard pulled a key from his pocket and unlocked the front door. After disabling the shop's alarm system, he stepped back to allow the women to enter the shop before him.

"Well, what are you thinking? Do you like it? Are you excited?" Chandra asked in a hushed but happy tone as she pushed her sister through the door.

Looking over, Jaycee tried to come up with an answer that would satisfy the overexcited teen. She didn't know how to categorize her emotions. Perhaps it was in this small space she would create her vision, a place where she could perfect her skills and use her business acumen to make a name for herself in the baking community.

"I'm so excited—I'm almost speechless," she whispered.

Taking a deep breath, she looked around the empty shop. The floor was pale with dust and the long wall across from where she stood was covered in a brightly painted mural of a mariachi band. It was a far cry from the pastel-colored, sparkling-clean bakery she imagined.

"It's uh, colorful," she blurted out.

Richard nodded. "The Mexican restaurant who rented it for the last few years moved to a bigger space. The owner will repaint it for a new tenant, though. He was just waiting so they could choose a suitable color."

Jaycee nodded slowly and tried to imagine what the place would look like with a fresh coat of light blue paint.

The windows behind her were large and let in an enormous amount of natural light. She could see the back area down a small hallway. It looked spacious and was already laid out as a kitchen. The double doors leading to the alley would be handy for unloading supplies and meant they wouldn't have to traipse through the retail area of the bakery for deliveries. She imagined a long counter along the front with glass cabinets displaying her baked goods. Behind it she would build floor-to-ceiling shelving units.

"I could put a beautiful deep serving counter here and still have tons of room," she murmured.

"You could," Chandra said, moving closer to her. "And just imagine, it might be at that very counter where you glance up and meet the gaze of a handsome stranger. He could be your soulmate and the father of your children! One day I could have adorable nieces and nephews sitting at a counter right here, stealing cookies and kisses and begging to lick clean the bowls of everything you bake!"

Jaycee looked at her sister and rolled her eyes, but she couldn't stop the twitch of a smile.

"Well," Richard said, exchanging an amused look with Jaycee, "I never thought about finding you a space for a bakery for those reasons, but I suppose anything is possible. Can I tell you a few other things about the property as well?"

Jaycee nodded and saw Chandra was now blushing a pretty pink color. Together, the sisters accompanied him around the store, listening closely as he pointed out the ample space for multiple display cases and explained how he thought the kitchen could easily be rearranged to fit the large bakery ovens that Jaycee would need.

Chandra clapped her hands and beamed when the tour was complete. "Don't you think it's perfect? Are we going to open the bakery here?"

"Maybe, but let's get a little more information before we decide. We need to consider a few other things before we sign a lease," replied Jaycee.

After spending more time poking into every corner of the premises and discussing the property's benefits, Jaycee felt her excitement growing as she saw how this space could meet all of the bakery's needs. The steady stream of traffic she had been carefully tracking going by the front window also seemed promising.

She grinned as Chandra excitedly suggested paint colors, possible packaging ideas, and even names for the store. Her enthusiasm was contagious, but Chandra was only considering the creative and fun part of running a bakery. Turning back to Richard, Jaycee tried to ignore the pounding of her heart as she asked him to tell her more about the shop's legal fees, rental agreements, utility costs, and insurance requirements.

Hearing the questions, Chandra stopped dancing through the empty shop and tiptoed over to stand beside her sister.

"Well," said Jaycee when Richard had finished giving her all the information she needed, "I think assuming I can find someone to do the renovations, we've found the perfect physical location for the bakery." Her voice trembled as she said the words.

Chandra threw herself into her sister's arms and gave a whoop of joy at this pronouncement. Jaycee smiled over at her, enjoying the happy dance the sprites were doing in the pit of her stomach, and just barely stopping herself from giving a joyous whoop too.

I'm one step closer to achieving my dream.

Chapter Thirteen

The success of their garage sale was important for several reasons. First, it was a great way to declutter the house and get it into a more presentable condition for the bank to appraise. Second, it would help raise some money that Jaycee planned to stash right into a high-interest savings account for Chandra's college expenses. And finally, it was an excellent way to say goodbye to some of their antiquated things. Little had been done in the house since the accident that had killed their parents and after eight years, it was time to make changes.

Determined to do some serious updating, Jaycee and Chandra had pulled one of their outdated, faded living room couches outside and placed it at the end of the driveway to be taken away. After positioning it near the curb, Jaycee had patted one of its floral cushions fondly and sighed. She felt like she was bidding farewell to an old friend, but she also knew it was time to say goodbye.

"Are you still okay with us getting rid of all these things?" she asked Chandra later that evening as they dusted off some china and kitchen utensils to sell.

"Yep. It makes me a little sad, but honestly, we need to get rid of a lot of stuff if we want to make room for better things."

Jaycee nodded, pleased that her sister shared her positive outlook.

Business was brisk at their garage sale the next day, and the hours flew by. Soon, it was late afternoon and the sisters were gathering up the remaining articles that hadn't sold, placing them in boxes to donate to the town's secondhand shop.

"How many things did you sneak back into the house, deciding you couldn't bear to part with them?" Jaycee asked her sister with a teasing smile.

Chandra blushed. "Not much, just a few stuffed animals and one old Christmas decoration that Mom liked."

Jaycee laughed and hugged her sister.

"How much money did we make?"

"Um, I haven't counted it all yet, but hopefully enough to keep you in college for at least a week."

"Or enough to buy a dishwasher for the bakery?" asked Chandra with a grin.

"You never know," Jaycee said and, with a skip in her step, turned away to fill another empty box.

Jeremy drew back the bat and swung hard, sending the ball flying over the heads of the infield players.

Wow.

Danny pushed back the bill of his Yankees cap and wiped his brow as he turned on the pitcher's mound to admire the hit as the baseball soared over his head. While an outfielder ran to snag it, he shifted his attention to the rest of the diamond. Earlier that year, the town had installed new fencing, freshly sodded the outfields, and painted the bleachers at the park. The small stadium now looked shiny, clean, and welcoming. A loud call brought his attention back to the practice and Danny lobbed another pitch toward Jeremy, who once again hit it out of the infield.

"Okay, I think we all know you can hit now." Danny chuckled under his breath. Placing two fingers in his mouth, he gave a shrill whistle and then waved his hand to signal to his teammates that they should all join him in the dugout.

A few of the guys cheered as they jogged in, and everyone grabbed their water bottles as they took their seats on the benches, where they joked and talked over their past performances on the field. "I think we've had a great practice," Danny announced once the team had finished drinking and gathered in a rough circle around him. "And I think we can all agree based on what we've seen today, we'd love to have Jeremy join our team for the last few weeks of the season. He'd be our one addition to the team for the playoffs and an important part of our team for next year. That is, if he's still in town."

The team applauded his words and were quick to remind Danny that Jeremy, as the team's newest member, was required to buy them all a round of beer.

Grinning, Jeremy pulled his wallet out of his jacket pocket and waved it in the air, acknowledging his acceptance of the suggestion. After everyone gathered their belongings, they made their way as one jostling, chattering group to the local pub.

Sullivan's Place wasn't crowded, and the team was led to a long, scarred wooden table. A server brought over a large tray of frosty, beer-filled mugs, and soon the group was toasting and telling Jeremy what to expect for the playoff games that were just about to start. After they ordered, the talk around the table shifted to the arsonist targeting the town.

"Do the police have any new leads?" Benny, a teacher at Larkin Bay's elementary school, asked Jeremy.

He took a long drink of his beer before answering. "Some. We hope to catch the person or group responsible for the fires soon, but we don't want to rush into any arrests or risk compromising the investigation by moving too fast."

"The quicker the better, I say," grumbled another man who Jeremy recognized as the owner of the dry cleaning business in town. The others around the table nodded in agreement.

Danny frowned and threw an arm over Jeremy's shoulder. "Don't let these numbskulls get to you. We all have perfect faith in you and know that you're doing everything possible to keep Larkin Bay safe. We're happy to help too. Just let us know if there's anything we can do."

"Agreed!" said Benny, tipping his beer bottle's rim toward Jeremy.

He nodded and settled back in his seat as their discussion moved to other topics and they all helped themselves to some food. He smiled at the rest of the team's easy acceptance of his being there and reached for a spicy chicken wing, but below the table, his foot tapped steadily as he wondered if one of these men knew something that could help him find the arsonist.

The large leather satchel slung over Jaycee's shoulder held the year-long lease she had just signed at Richard Marshall's real estate office.

And now, trying to calm the sprites jitterbugging in her stomach, Jaycee was here trying to imagine how her *Jaycee's Bakery* sign would look hanging at the front of the store. Clutching the key, she took a deep breath and pressed a hand against her leg to try and stop her knees from trembling. She'd discovered ever since she started this project that one's hands and knees really did shake when a person was overwhelmed by big emotional and financial decisions. It wasn't just a cliché.

Jaycee used her key to open the door to the empty store. After deactivating the alarm, she set everything she was carrying down and clasped her hands together in front of her. Taking a long look at the dusty countertops, dull wooden floors, and streaky windows, she tried to visualize what the space would look like after the renovations were complete. She had been up late for several nights, sketching and rejecting multiple renovation plans with Lisa via Skype. Jaycee wanted her diagrams to be perfect so she could show the contractor precisely what she wanted done—exactly how she envisioned her dream bakery space.

She looked down at Mew's carrier, where the kitten was already pawing at the bars of the cage, obviously wondering when he would be let free to investigate the unfamiliar smells of this place. Jaycee smiled, watching his nose twitch a mile a minute. Unsnapping the locks on his transporter, she scooped him out, giving him a quick cuddle before she set him down.

"Well, Mew," she said to the curious kitten as he sat at her feet, looking around. "Here we are." Jaycee chewed her bottom lip, debating again if she should laugh with joy or cry tears of terror over the commitment she had just made. "This is the place that's going to take all my time and money for the next few years. So go ahead and look around for a bit and while you're at it, see if you can chase away any mice you might find. We don't want them in here." She watched the kitten crouch down with his long tail and whiskers twitching for a moment before curiosity got the better of his wariness and he scampered off.

Jaycee filled his water bowl and scanned the floor again to be sure there was nothing that could hurt him. Once she was satisfied, she turned her attention to what she had come here to accomplish. Opening her leather pouch, she pulled out her rough bakery design sketches and unrolled them on the counter. After a quick glance at them, she dug to the bottom of her bag and pulled out a roll of tape, a pair of scissors, and a measuring tape. Taking everything to the back corner of the shop, she began laying out long strips of colorful masking tape on the floor, carefully marking out exactly where she wanted the countertops, display counters, and ovens placed in the kitchen.

This mapping of equipment and work areas had been Betty's idea, and Jaycee thought it was brilliant. Time flew by as she marked where she thought all the new equipment would work most efficiently. She was making slow but steady progress when the little bell attached to the front door rang.

Looking up, Jaycee expected to see Chandra charging through the door, but instead, her heart fluttered as Jeremy came in. Putting down her roll of tape, she stood up to greet him. "It's gorgeous!" she declared, smiling with delight as she admired the oversized, hand-painted cookie jar he was holding out to her. "I love it! It's the perfect addition to the bakery. Thank you!"

"You're welcome," he replied, returning her warm greeting with a sexy, dimpled smile that made Jaycee's pulse beat a little faster. "Just remember to put a few peanut butter cookies in it for me."

Jeremy was wearing a long-sleeved shirt rolled up to his elbows and had tucked his hands into the front pockets of his snug-fitting jeans. He looked incredibly handsome, and although Jaycee wanted to keep looking at him, she forced herself to tear her gaze away and focus on the gift he had given her instead.

"You like peanut butter cookies?" she asked him with a teasing smile.

"My favorite. Especially the ones you make."

"I'll have to keep that in mind." As she was admiring the cookie jar, Mew bounced out from the back of the store, and Jeremy kneeled to scoop up the small animal. "Hello, pretty one," he said, scratching her under the chin. "Look at you, growing so fast."

"She *is* getting big," Jaycee acknowledged, blushing as Jeremy turned his attentive gaze back to her. "And thank you again for the cookie jar. I love it. I think for now, however, I'll just stow it in one of the big sinks in the back here so it can't accidentally get knocked over. I don't trust our little friend there around breakable things." She nodded toward the cat, who was now headbutting Jeremy's chin as he cuddled her.

"I wasn't sure what to get someone opening a new bakery. But somehow flowers didn't seem appropriate before you opened, so I went with this instead. I figured you might be able to find a place to display it, or at the very least find a cookie or two to put in it."

Jaycee hugged the jar. "It's a wonderful gift," she said, heading to the back of the shop. "But how did you even know I was here?"

"Oh, well, you told me when we were running together that you'd be signing the lease this afternoon. So when I was driving by and saw the lights on, I figured you were probably already here working on the place."

"Well, you were right. I signed the lease just a few hours ago and came straight over. I couldn't wait to get started on everything," Jaycee said, setting the jar down and turning back to him with a bright smile.

Looking down, Jeremy tilted his head to the side as he studied her work with the tape.

"I was just marking up where I thought everything should go before I meet with the contractor tomorrow," Jaycee explained. Seeing his puzzled look, she quickly elaborated. "At the back here, I've put tape on the floor where I want the counters to be and where I think the large ovens should go." She pointed to another marked-off area. "This taped-off area here shows how big a cupboard I think I'll need for supplies."

"Good idea."

She waved a hand at the drawings and photos she'd pinned to the wall. "What I'm trying to achieve is an old-fashioned feel to the place with lots of chrome and splashes of blue and white that'll make the place seem retro but fun."

Jeremy admired her colorful sketches and nodded appreciatively at what she had outlined.

Pulling open her leather bag, Jaycee showed him a picture of the refurbished antique cash register she was thinking of buying to add to the vintage look she was after.

Even in her excitement over her plans, Jaycee wasn't oblivious to Jeremy's admiring glances. She was just about to show him the design for the layout of the display cases when the bell at the front of the store rang again, this time announcing Chandra's arrival.

The girl tumbled through the door but skidded to a stop when she saw Jeremy. She greeted him, hugged her sister, and scooped up Mew. As she looked around, she gave a little skip of excitement. "This is awesome!" she exclaimed. She placed her phone on the counter and began hopping between the taped-up areas on the floor. "I feel like I know exactly how it's all going to work and what it'll look like now that you've got it all laid out."

Jeremy grinned as he watched Chandra flit through the taped-up areas.

"It is a good way to see how everything will fit together," agreed Jaycee. "So, what do you think? Is there enough room behind the counter to get into the display cases and still be able to turn to the back counter and package up everything? Now that I've laid it all out, the space looks tight." She frowned as she watched Chandra pretend to reach into a display and remove cookies, then turn behind her to wrap them on an imaginary shelf.

"I think it'll be perfect just as you have it," Jeremy said, watching Chandra. "You don't want too much space between the display cases and the counter because the servers will just be wasting extra steps and time."

Jaycee nodded. As they continued to discuss her plans, she discovered Jeremy was very knowledgeable about building code practices and could answer many of the questions she had planned to ask her contractor the next day. Their conversation was interrupted when she heard Chandra's stomach rumble loudly.

"Should we grab some take-out Chinese food as a lease-signing celebration?" Jaycee asked her sister with a smile.

"Please," Chandra replied. "The cafeteria lunch today was gross. I'm starving!"

Jeremy laughed, but before Jaycee could ask him if he wanted to join them, the quiet of the early evening was shattered by flashing lights and the scream of a fire truck's siren as it raced by the bakery's front window. A moment later, the thinner wail of a police car's alarm followed.

Mew scurried over and hid behind Jaycee, his tail twitching in fright at the sounds. She quickly scooped the kitten up to calm him.

Frowning, Jeremy set down the measuring tape he had been tossing from one hand to the other and went to the front of the store to see which way the truck was headed. He stood at the window for a few minutes, then came back scowling.

Jaycee and Chandra exchanged troubled glances.

"It looks like there's another fire close by," Jeremy announced.

"Is it another arson attack?" asked Chandra, going over to the window and rubbing away a circle of dust so she could peer out.

"I don't know yet. It's too early to tell, but I should probably head over there and see what's going on."

Jaycee rubbed the scar on her cheek and tried not to let the thought of an arsonist targeting stores in the area overtake her celebratory mood.

"Don't worry," Jeremy said, seeing Jaycee's troubled look. "The odds of a fire threatening your bakery are fairly remote. The entire Larkin Bay police force and fire department are all over this case."

"The arsonist won't target this place," added Chandra. "I'm sure of it!"

Jaycee felt the jittering sprites in her stomach calm slightly at their reassurances.

"I guess I should probably get back to work," Jeremy said, shooting her a compassionate look. "Try not to worry," he added, and after giving both girls a hurried wave goodbye, he headed out into the night.

Chapter Fourteen

Jaycee was in the kitchen putting all the finishing touches on the platters she was creating when Betty came through the back door. "Okay, I finished clearing out all my things from the downstairs bedroom," she announced.

Jaycee looked over at her and frowned. "You know you didn't have to do that."

"Yes, I did. Honestly, I'm looking forward to having my own little place again."

"Are you sure?"

Betty hugged Jaycee around the waist. "It's time, honey. You're back here full-time, and Chandra is off to college next year. You don't really need me anymore. And I need some space now to do all the projects I've been dreaming about."

"What are you going to do?" Jaycee asked, taking a step back from the counter.

"All sorts of things. A little knitting and biking, to start. I will probably also look for a part-time job. I'd still like to pay back some of the trust money that man took from you girls."

"We won't take it from you. Don't worry about us," Jaycee said, giving a firm nod.

Betty sighed. "Well, I'm also going to spend more time with my grandkids and do some traveling. I can't wait to use my pension to go on a cruise! I've been planning for it all my life. I've never been to the Caribbean, and I can't wait to see if the beach water is really the perfect turquoise blue like it shows in all the travel ads."

Jaycee laughed. "I want lots of pictures."

Betty smiled and, after washing her hands, helped fill the second charcuterie board and put away the rest of the cheese, meat, and crackers they weren't using. Her eyes widened in appreciation as Jaycee pulled some large containers from the fridge, lifting out several types of cookies and squares that she swiftly arranged on a glass platter.

Betty stole a cookie off the tray and took a bite. She closed her eyes in bliss for a moment before smiling at Jaycee. "These are so good. I think they're my favorite."

"You say that about every new thing I make."

"It's true with every new batch, though."

Jaycee laughed.

Betty finished the cookie and wiped her hands on the front of her jeans. "And that's another good reason for me to move back with my daughter. If I stay here and you keep baking, I'm going to fall into a sugar coma one day!"

"Betty!"

"It's true," she protested. "I have no self-control when it comes to your cookies and squares."

Jaycee shook her head, and after checking that everything was now either arranged on the platters or packed away to her liking, she carried the trays into the living room. A moment later, the doorbell rang.

Pulling open the front door, she greeted each of her friends with a hug. "I'm so happy to see you," she exclaimed. "It's been ages since I've been able to have you over." After hanging their coats in the front hall closet, she led them into the living room.

"The place looks great," announced Amanda, the smile on her face turning wistful when she saw a photo of Jaycee's parents on the fireplace mantel before brightening again as she looked around. "It's so nice to get together here. It's just like the good old days," she said, settling down on the sofa and patting the faded arm fondly.

"I'm glad you could all come."

Leaning over, Amanda hugged Jaycee. "Also, you have to talk to Tina. On the way over, she told us she's looking for a used car. They need another one." She raised an eyebrow meaningfully.

"You guys need a second car?" Jaycee exclaimed, looking over at Tina. "I have an extra car. I was just about to put it up for sale!"

"That's what I told her," Amanda said, picking up a napkin from the table and carefully filling it with several sweets from both platters.

"Tell me all about it," demanded Tina as she filled a small plate as well.

"It's my old Honda. But Danny's spent a ton of time painting it, reworking all the electrical, and installing new brakes, so now it's in great shape again."

Tina tilted her head to one side. "So why are you selling it, then?"

"We don't need two cars, and we've still got my mom's old Buick that Chandra and I can use when we need to get around. It's about the same age."

"I sometimes see Chandra driving Betty's car too," said Denise.

Jaycee nodded. "Yup, we also use hers, but now that I'm back, I think Betty is planning on doing a little more traveling and seeing her kids and grandkids more, so we're trying not to rely on her as much."

"That breaks my heart to hear," announced Betty, coming into the room carrying two wooden boards displaying a wide variety of meat and cheeses. After setting them down in front of the women, she perched herself on the edge of a chair next to Jaycee. "You girls are welcome to use my old clunker anytime you need it. You know that."

Jaycee leaned over and hugged her. "We do. And we appreciate it, but we honestly don't need three cars. So if you're interested, Tina, just go down to the shop. Danny's still got it there, and he can tell you everything about it."

"I will, and I'll have Charlie come with me. Thanks, Jaycee," Tina replied with a smile.

Betty visited with the women for a few minutes longer. Just as she was leaving, Jennifer and Noelle, both friends from Jaycee's high school days, arrived, each carrying a bottle of wine. The older woman hugged them both. "It's so nice to see everyone here again," she declared. "You girls are going to have such fun!" She scooped up Mew, who was following her to the door. "Make sure you behave yourselves!" She laughed and kissed the kitten on the head before handing her back to Jaycee and waving goodbye to everyone.

Going into the kitchen to fetch a corkscrew, Jaycee grabbed the Tupperware containers full of baked goods. Settling on the couch between Denise and Amanda, she placed the containers in the middle of the coffee table. "Here," she said. "I'm done making fancy trays with all this stuff. I can't keep up with you guys—you eat too fast. Just help yourselves right out of the storage containers."

Denise grinned and picked up a box of cookies. "This works for me," she declared, placing it in her lap. "And now I have a balanced diet," she joked, using her arms to mime a scale by holding a cookie in one hand and a glass of wine in the other.

The other women rolled their eyes and groaned at her before turning their attention once again to studying the room. "The place is looking great," Jennifer commented. "Have you been doing a lot of work here?"

Jaycee frowned. "Not as much as I would like. I've painted and decluttered, but I still have a ton of work to do." She set down her wineglass on the table in front of her. "I will have to go back to the city soon and move my furniture to replace the stuff in here. This room will look so much better when I do."

"Take down the old curtains too," said Amanda, giving the heavy, dark burgundy drapes around each window some side-eye. "I mean, if you want to. Or at least consider it. They are a nice color but sort of dated. The windows are in good shape and pretty, so if you were just to put up some simple drop curtains or blinds, it would really make a big difference in here."

Jaycee sighed. "Yeah, and the carpeting needs to be taken out and replaced with hardwood too. Cindy from Larkin Bay Realty gave me an entire list of suggestions. Now I just need to find the time and money to put them all into action."

"There'll be plenty of time for that in January," Amanda commented as she helped herself to another cookie. "I always get to my indoor decorating projects when it's cold out. And I'll help you too. I love ripping up old carpet."

"Thanks. I'll need all the help I can get. Just getting everything ready for the bakery to open is taking up all my time."

"How's that going?" asked Noelle.

Jaycee smiled as she looked over at her friend. "Great. I mean, it's a ton of work, but I'm so excited about it. I'm learning a lot, and the members of the Chamber of Commerce have been terrific about giving me advice, and Betty has been helping whenever she can."

"Have you started hiring any staff yet?" asked Noelle.

"Not yet—I was going to wait a little closer to opening. At first, I'll probably have to work all the time as well as do all the baking. I'm on a tight budget."

"You aren't going to need any nighttime help, are you?" Noelle asked. "My brother, Kenny, is a night owl and is looking for work somewhere in town with a night shift. Right now he sleeps all day and stays up all night playing video games. It's driving my parents crazy—he needs a job."

Jaycee looked over at her friend and gave a yip of excitement. "That would be great! Has Kenny ever baked before?"

"He did in the city for a few years at a bread place when he was in college. He's always liked working off hours. I told him to call you, but he's shy. Like a complete introvert. Working nights and alone would be perfect for him. I'll get you guys together if you think you might have something for him."

"I'd love to meet him. I was wondering how I would find someone to cover the early-morning hours. I thought I might have to work them myself at first, but I'd love to talk to him."

Noelle nodded. "I'll call him and have him send you his contact information."

"Thank you. But that's enough about me," Jaycee said firmly. "What's been happening with all of you?"

The women looked at each other and shrugged. "The usual," Amanda replied. "House stuff, work stuff, and for me, baby and husband stuff."

"Yeah, honestly, I thought being a grown-up would be more fun than this," Noelle added, yawning. "It seems like I have even less time to do things now than when I was a kid."

Jaycee laughed and raised her glass. "I hear you. What happened to all the free time and money we were supposed to have? I have less of both now than I did when I was in school."

"I'll drink to that," said Noelle with a grin.

"I don't know if I want to drink to that. But I *do* want to drink, so here's to us!" Amanda declared, raising her glass and smiling as the others reached out and tapped the rims of their glasses against hers.

"It's nice that your sister still has friends in town," Dean said, picking up Chandra's hand and holding it as they left the movie theater and walked through the dimly lit streets of Larkin Bay. "You see what can happen if you stay here?"

Chandra laughed as she swung their joined hands. "Actually, I think everyone who came over tonight went to college after high school and just came back to Larkin Bay afterward. Several of them are still with their high school boyfriends. A couple even married them."

"Oh."

Chandra laughed at the dismay on his face and squeezed his hand a little tighter in hers. "So that's just more proof that if we both go off to college, we can always come back and still be together once we've graduated."

She frowned when she saw Dean looked downcast. "Have you given any more thought to applying?" she asked him.

Dean dropped her hand and increased his pace slightly. Chandra gave a little skip to keep up.

"No, and you know I'm not going to. That's not right for me. Besides, my mom doesn't have the money for me to go. I'm going to stay here and get a job and help her after I graduate. I'd do it right now, but she'd kill me if I dropped out of high school."

"Well, it probably makes sense to finish our diplomas. We've been working on getting them since we were five," she said with a grin.

"It's all just a waste of time."

"I used to think that too, but I've been talking to Mrs. Gunther in the guidance office, and she's been showing me all sorts of programs that don't cost a ton of money. It's worth considering, at least."

"I can learn everything I need to know once I get a job."

"That's true. Apprenticeships are great. Don't be mad. I'm just looking at all my options."

"The options you're looking at mean you're leaving me," he grumbled.

Chandra grabbed his hand again. "Not you. Just the town and just for a few months at a time. You can visit me as much as you want, and I'll come home. Now that Jaycee is opening the bakery here, I'll have to come back all the time to help."

"You're still leaving."

"Aren't you the least bit curious about what the world outside of Larkin Bay is like?"

"Not really."

Chandra sighed. She and Dean had had this conversation many times, and nothing ever seemed to change. She shivered and pulled the front of her jean jacket closed. "Let's go get a burger," she suggested.

"Are you buying?"

Chandra thought about the money she had been hoping to give to Jaycee to help with some of the household expenses. "Sure, I got paid today. Daisy gave me a little bit extra too because the dress shop has been so busy. But we'll have to share. I don't have a lot to spare."

"Sounds like a plan," he replied and, towing her by the hand, turned down the next street and into Larkin Bay's Burger Palace.

The small, wood-paneled diner's red plastic booths were all full, and Chandra and Dean crowded just inside the front entrance while they waited for a table to free up. As she looked around the restaurant, a girl waved at her. Chandra smiled back and tugged free from Dean's hold. Ignoring his annoyed expression, she made her way over to the table.

"Hey, guys, how are you?" she asked, reaching over to steal a french fry off the girl's plate nearest to her.

Willa smacked her hand and frowned. "Hey, yourself. And leave my fries alone."

"I'll give you one off my plate when I get some," Chandra replied. "So, what's going on? What are you guys doing here tonight?"

The three girls looked at each other and shrugged. "Not much," one responded, pointedly turning her back to Chandra and pouring ketchup onto her fries.

Chandra flipped her hair back and swallowed over the hard lump that had suddenly formed in her throat. Not too long ago, had she appeared at their table, her friends would have squealed in delight and immediately made room on the benches so she could join them. Their chilly reception now was hurtful, but she lifted her chin and smiled at them. "Okay, well, we just saw the new Black Panther movie at the theater. You guys should go see it. It's fantastic!"

"Yeah, we know. We went together to see it last week," Lyndsey replied, smiling briefly at Chandra. "Hey, look, there's Kate. Kate! We're over here," she called out.

As Kate approached the table, Chandra turned to greet her. The other girl gave her a shy smile and slid into the booth. As soon as she sat down, all four girls turned to each other and began talking excitedly.

Chandra shifted from one foot to the other as she watched. "Okay, I'll leave you to your food. I think we'll probably get a table soon," she said and tried not to feel hurt when the girls barely glanced her way as she left.

"So did you catch up?" Dean asked, sneering at her.

"Yeah, everyone seems good," she replied.

"Looked like they were shutting you out from here."

Chandra blinked hard. "A little, maybe," she replied. "But I can't really say I blame them. Every time they invite me to do something, you and I always seem to already have plans, so I don't go. I think I've hurt their feelings."

Dean leaned over and kissed her on the temple. "It's okay, babe. You still have me."

"I'll have to text them so we can all get together," Chandra replied, pulling away from him slightly. "Jaycee tells me I'll always need my girlfriends."

Dean shrugged dismissively. "If you want. Doesn't matter to me."

"I do want," Chandra replied and smiled as he kissed her temple again.

"I'm very excited," Jeremy announced.

Jaycee placed a glass bowl on the kitchen counter between them and raised an eyebrow at him while ignoring the cooing sprites in her stomach. "You're excited about baking cookies?"

He nodded from the kitchen doorway. "Yes, but I'm not excited *just* about baking cookies. I'm excited because I'm about to learn the secret ingredients that go into making the best peanut butter cookies in the world."

Jaycee laughed and shook her head. "Don't get too excited. I can't give away all my secrets."

"You can't?"

"Of course not. How would I ever keep you in my life if I didn't have the promise of cookies to keep you coming back?"

"True. That is the only reason I'm here, you know," Jeremy replied with a teasing grin.

Jaycee swatted him with an oven mitt as she turned to preheat the oven.

"The secret to baking great cookies isn't really all that hard," she announced, waving a finger at him playfully.

"It's not?"

"No, you just have to make sure you use fresh ingredients and cook them evenly. It's especially important to use good butter and high-quality flour. You also have to measure everything really carefully. Baking is an exact science."

"They are also best straight out of the oven."

"Some people think so. I personally like them better when they've had a chance to set a bit."

"We should sample them both ways and compare."

"We can do that," she replied, smiling back at him.

A short time later, the first pan of cookies came out of the oven and, after letting them sit for a few minutes, Jaycee used a spatula to place them on a cooling rack.

"My mom used to just take the cookies off the pan and put them right on a plate," Jeremy observed.

"You could do that. But if you use a cooking rack, the air will get underneath and stop them from baking more and prevent them from getting soggy."

"I never knew that."

"That's okay. I'm sure there are a thousand things about arson that I don't know."

"Possibly. That's one thing about my job. Every case is as different as the person committing the crime."

"All cookies are different too. They just have the advantage of not causing a lot of harm to others, unlike the criminals you're after."

"Can I try one now?" Jeremy asked, pointing at a cooling peanut butter cookie.

"Yup, they should be okay. They'll still be a little hot, though, so watch your fingers." She giggled as she watched him pick up a cookie and toss it from one hand to another a few times to cool it enough so he could comfortably eat it.

"Do you still like cookies hot out of the oven?" she asked him.

He nodded, his expression serious. "I do, but I'll have to try another when they're cooled and at least one off of every pan before I can give you my expert opinion on how they taste."

"Fair enough," Jaycee replied, laughing. "I made a lot of dough, though, so I hope you're hungry."

"These are amazing," Jeremy groaned a few minutes later, reaching for another.

Jaycee smiled at him and then gulped hard as she suddenly found herself mesmerized by a cookie crumb caught on his lower lip.

She stepped back so she wouldn't be tempted to reach out and brush it away.

Touching his mouth was as intimate as kissing, wasn't it?

She sighed as she watched him lick the crumbs away, ignoring the sprites dancing in her stomach who were demanding she move closer to him.

"Maybe we should try baking something else next," she said as she looked away. "Do you like chocolate chip cookies too?"

Chapter Fifteen

Jeremy knocked on the front door of his sister's house and grinned when he heard small feet pattering to the door to greet him. "It's Unca Germy," cried his niece, as she launched herself into his arms.

"Lucy!" he called back and swung her high in the air, causing her to scream with delight. After kissing her noisily on the forehead, he set her back on her feet and she grabbed two of his fingers to pull him after her as she went in search of her mother.

"Mama, he's here," she called.

When they finally located Julie, Jeremy's oldest sister, in the kitchen, she turned to greet them both with a smile. "Hello, Uncle Germy," she said.

Jeremy laughed. "Hey you."

"You know, we really need to start correcting her soon. She honestly believes that's your real name."

"There's no hurry. It's sort of cute."

"True," Julie replied, hugging him tightly for a long moment before dropping a kiss on his cheek. "Beer's in the fridge. Help yourself," she added. "Everyone else is out back. Lucy's been watching for you since you're the last to arrive. She likes to make sure everyone is here before she joins the party."

"That's very considerate of you," Jeremy said, patting his niece on her head.

"Where's Bo?" the little girl demanded, putting her hands on her hips and frowning as she stepped to one side and peered behind him.

"He's with all his doggy brothers and sisters for the week, getting in some puppy playtime," Jeremy replied. "He needs it to grow up to be a well-rounded big dog."

"Oh," she frowned and pondered this for a moment. "I'll miss him today," she finally said with a shrug before she raced away to join the rest of the party.

Julie winced as they watched her youngest tumble down the back steps, then scramble back to her feet to join her cousins. Shaking her head, Julie picked up the platters she had been filling and motioned with a head nod that Jeremy should open the back door for her. He quickly grabbed a beer from the fridge, tugged open the door, and, sweeping a hand, indicated she should precede him. Following his sister outside, he ignored her eye roll.

"Oh, look. It is Uncle Germy. You're right, Lucy," said Amber, Jeremy's younger sister, as he joined everyone in the back garden where the rest of the family had gathered. "Hello, stranger," she said and, after closing a fist, punched his upper arm.

"Ow," Jeremy said, returning the greeting but careful not to put too much weight behind his jab. Although his little sister liked to hit him with a decent amount of force, she didn't enjoy receiving it back, so ever since he'd been old enough to restrain himself, he'd stopped punching her back with any actual weight.

"Please don't do that, you two," his mother said, stepping between her two youngest children. "Your impressionable nieces and nephews are watching," she added as she hugged Jeremy.

"Hi, Ma."

"Hello, Jeremy. I'm glad you came. I've missed you," she responded, then turned away to join Lucy, who was calling for help on the swings.

Jeremy took a swig of his beer and looked around the large backyard. By the sizable leaf piles pushed into the corners, he could tell that his brother-in-law had been busy. He smiled, then whooped loudly as one of his nephews launched off a swing into one. It was nice that the unseasonably warm fall temperatures allowed them to fit in one last BBQ for the year, he reflected.

All his brothers-in-law were gathered around a smoking BBQ, and the mouthwatering smell of some type of grilling red meat wafted over to Jeremy. His nieces and nephews were happily occupied by the swing set with their grandmother. Jeremy debated heading directly over to the grill to talk to the guys, but turned instead toward the picnic table where his sisters were gathered. His oldest sister, Julie, after following him out, had deposited the food trays on the table and taken a seat there alongside Jeremy's other three older sisters. As far as he could tell, they were all talking at the same time as they worked their way through some sizable portions from the charcuterie board.

"Hello, Jay girls," he said in greeting. They all huffed together, then studied him for a long moment with an almost motherly concern, as he gave each of them a squeeze on the shoulder and a kiss on the cheek.

Julie, Janet, Jenny, and Jaylyn were tall, dark-haired, finely built, and blessed with thick-lashed green eyes and high, chiseled cheekbones. They all looked enough alike that they'd been constantly confused growing up. Jeremy had referred to all of them as Jay since he'd recognized at about eight years old that they hated it. And now, with the joy only a younger brother could understand, he continued to use the nickname some twenty years later.

"Hey, I'm here too," said Amber, sliding into a seat next to one of her sisters. She was the only member of the family whose name didn't start with the letter *J* and also the only blue-eyed strawberry blonde. She was also five years younger than her sisters, and at least a foot shorter and much curvier. Amber looked exactly like their late father. This was a good thing too, or the family would still be teasing her about how she looked so different from the rest of them.

"I already punched you," Jeremy reminded her, and pivoted away from his sisters before they could start quizzing him on his love life or some other topic he wasn't interested in sharing. Spending time with their husbands and boyfriends talking about sports or the weather seemed a much better option.

"Hey, Jeremy, brother, good to see you," Julie's husband, Adam, said when he reached the grill. "You escaped your sisters' interrogation already?"

Jeremy tipped the top of his beer bottle in greeting to the small group of men gathered there and chuckled. "I did. For the moment at least."

His brother-in-law looked up from the meat he was flipping on the grill. "*For the moment* is right," he said. "Julie's been wondering what you're doing in Larkin Bay and why you haven't been in touch daily. You're in for a grilling, and I don't mean this type," he said, gesturing at the BBQ.

Jeremy rolled his eyes. "Can't wait," he responded.

"Any new arsonist action or arrests in town?"

Jeremy frowned. "No. There was a false alarm the other night—just a faulty smoke detector—but everyone's still on edge."

The other men looked at him sympathetically and then spent the next fifteen minutes huddled around the grill, discussing the current hockey and football seasons, while Adam poked at the chunk of meat he was responsible for on the egg-shaped smoker beside them. After Julie had looked over at them pointedly for what seemed like the hundredth time, her husband shrugged. "Yeah, I think it's finally done, Jules. If you want to get the salads and other sides ready, I'll take this off and slice it up."

"Sounds good," she replied, getting up from the picnic table to bring out the rest of their meal. The other women trailed behind her to help, except Amber, who came over to watch the men take the meat off the spit.

"You're not helping with the table setting?" Jeremy asked with a teasing smile.

"Nope, my contribution today was dessert for the kids, and I'll serve that up later," she said. "Besides, I wanted to talk to you." Her tone was serious as she glanced around to ensure no one was close enough to overhear her.

Jeremy felt his stomach roll with concern as he stepped away from the grill. "Everything okay? What's up?"

Amber tugged on his arm, and he followed her over to the swing set, which had been abandoned by the children once their mothers had called them to come wash their hands for dinner.

"Spill it," Jeremy demanded as he settled onto a swing beside her.

Amber glanced at him, then looked away. "I'm going to quit my job and take some time off to finish writing my book," she blurted out. "And all the Jay sisters and Mom will not like it, so I need your help when I tell them," she said.

Jeremy opened his mouth and closed it again. He stared over at her and considered her request. She was right, their sisters wouldn't like this. They'd immediately worry about how Amber would support herself.

I can help her if she needs it.

He felt his heart warm at the idea of helping Amber achieve a dream he knew she'd had since childhood.

He reached over and gave her a one-armed hug. "I support you," he said before his swing pulled him away from her. "And I'll help you with the others when you tell them too."

"Thank you."

"But are you sure you want to quit your job? I thought you loved managing the gift shop at the zoo."

Amber placed one foot on the ground to steady herself. "I do. But there aren't enough hours in a day to work there and write," she said, frowning. "And I want to take my novel to the next level, which means committing all my time to it, and I can't do that and keep running the gift shop. I mean, there's nothing wrong with that. It's just not what I want to spend all my time doing anymore."

Jeremy nodded. "Can you afford to quit?"

"I think so, for about a year, if I'm careful. And then I can always find another job. Or maybe even see if they'll keep me on part-time at the shop so I can squeeze a few more months' rent out. I still have some of the money I got after Dad died. I had enough scholarships for school, so I didn't blow through all he left me."

Jeremy considered this, then smiled at his younger sister. "Sounds like a good plan, then," he said. Their mother and the rest of the family would soon give her enough reasons this wasn't a good idea—she deserved at least one family member supporting her.

"Okay, I'll try to help when you tell them, but I'll also expect you to help me when they ask about my love life," he said, hopping to his feet and holding out a hand toward her.

Amber nodded and slid off her swing. "Deal," she agreed, and gently punched him on the arm once more.

As she turned away, Amber didn't see the smile fall from her brother's face as he looked around at his family, who were gathering now to eat. He couldn't help but remember how much Marianne had loved getting together with his sisters at these family events. They had all been the best of friends, and if things had been different, his and Marianne's children would probably be here playing with their cousins. Today the thought made him melancholy. But he realized he was not nearly as devastated as he would have been a year ago. A wry smile crossed his face as he thought of Jaycee and wondered exactly what he was going to tell his family about her.

After the family had all eaten, Amber dished out bowls of vanilla and pumpkin-flavored ice cream for the kids to enjoy on a picnic blanket under a large maple tree in the far corner of the yard. She threw several thick blankets over their laps to keep them warm and then returned to the picnic table where all the adults had gathered.

"So, Jeremy," Jenny said above the family chatter. "I hear you're hanging out with someone in Larkin Bay." The talk around the table was silenced as everyone looked at her and then Jeremy.

He picked up his beer and smiled tightly at her. "Just doing my job over there," he replied. Avoiding everyone's gaze, he took a long sip from the bottle.

"But you're seeing someone?" asked his mother, her tone both sad and hopeful.

"I have something to share," Amber interrupted, her voice trembling slightly.

Everyone frowned and looked from Jeremy to her. Settling back in his lawn chair at the head of the table, he shot Amber a grateful look for the change of subject.

After announcing her new life plan, Amber's words were met by silence. Jeremy glanced around at his siblings before getting to his feet to walk over and stand beside her. "That's amazing, Amber," he said, looping an arm around her shoulders and giving her a half hug. "And I can't wait to read the first copy. I also want a dedication," he added.

"Thanks," his sister mumbled back, glancing up and giving him a shaky smile.

Jeremy gave the rest of their family a warning frown. None of them had moved. The men were all looking at Jeremy's sisters, trying to gauge their wife's feelings before responding.

Wimps.

Their mother spoke first. "Are you going to move home, Amber?"

Jeremy smiled sadly at the hopeful note in her voice.

"I mean, you won't have much money and we could put a desk in the dining room to give you a quiet place to work if you like."

Amber smiled. "Thanks, Mom. Maybe one day, but I hope it won't come to that. I've got enough money to keep paying the rent on my place for a few more months, and then hopefully I'll publish something and have more than enough to cover my bills."

Julie frowned and glanced around the table at the rest of her family. "It sounds like an exciting idea, Amber," she said, her eyes sharp as she studied her, making it abundantly clear to everyone she would return to talking about her little sister's announcement later. "But stop distracting us from learning more about the girl Jeremy's running with every morning."

Jeremy blinked and felt his cheeks warm slightly. "Wow, I didn't know my every move was being watched."

"You should know better. It's a very small town."

Jeremy chuckled. "She's only a friend. She's just moved back to Larkin Bay and is opening a bakery. We're compatible in our running styles so she comes with me most mornings to exercise Bo."

"That's it?"

Jeremy felt a silly smile creep across his face. "That's all I'm willing to say for now."

His sisters cooed in chorus and Jeremy felt his face flush.

He turned to Amber. "I'm happy for you, kiddo. I just know you're going to write a bestseller."

Amber laughed. "Well, I doubt that. But I want to try."

Jeremy put an arm around her waist. "Don't worry, kiddo. We won't let you starve."

"Good to know. Thanks, big brother."

The rest of the family murmured in agreement, then looked over at the maple tree as two of the children shouted. Several of Jeremy's sisters groaned as they got to their feet and hurried over to tend to their children.

"Saved by the next generation," Jeremy whispered in Amber's ear as he stepped away.

"They saved you too," she replied with a sly grin, before taking an empty seat at the picnic table to answer the rest of her family's questions about her book and plans.

Jeremy went over to help his mom comfort Lucy. "Lucy, is Grandma making you cry?" he asked the little girl, winking over her head at his mother as they both looked down at her ice cream lying in the leaves.

"Not Grandma," she replied. "It was the ice cream."

Jeremy and his mother smiled as they watched her wipe away her tears and race off to find more dessert. "If only it was always this easy to make things right in our children's worlds as they get older," she commented.

Jeremy saw she was looking over at Amber and reached over to hug her. "She'll be fine," he said. "Besides, who knows? This time next year, we might have a bestselling author in the family. That can't be a bad thing, right?"

"I suppose," his mother answered with a smile. "But it's hard not to worry about all of you. I think your father would approve of Amber's decision, though." She nibbled on her bottom lip for a minute. "And I know when I meet the girl you're seeing, I'll say he'd have liked her too."

"I think that's right," Jeremy agreed. "You don't think it's too soon for me to be dating someone else, do you? To move on?" he asked in a rush.

His mother patted his hand. "No. Of course not. It's been a few years now. And Marianne loved you. She'd hate for you to be alone and she'd want you to be happy."

Raising to her tiptoes, his mother kissed him on the cheek. Jeremy gave her another long hug, then helped her scoop up the spilled ice cream before they returned to the picnic table to join the rest of their family.

Chapter Sixteen

Standing outside the bakery, Jaycee and Amanda studied the sign that Chandra had hung the day before. "It's not straight," Jaycee announced.

"Well, maybe it's a little off," her friend conceded, pulling her coat's collar a little higher around her face.

Jaycee grimaced. "How could my little sister not see this is so crooked?" She placed a small metal level on top of the sign and stepped back so her friend could see that the bubble in it clearly floated off to one side.

"It's not just a little off—it's really, and I mean *really* badly off," Jaycee said, trying not to let any frustration creep into her tone. Amanda was volunteering some of her precious free time to help her today, and Jaycee didn't want to ruin it by complaining about Chandra's lack of carpentry skills.

Amanda tapped one foot while she waited to see what Jaycee would do next. She wasn't surprised when, a moment later, her friend pulled a screwdriver out of her back pocket and started removing the screws that held the bakery's opening hours sign in place.

Amanda smiled. "Where is Chandra today, anyway?"

"I'm not sure. I think she had to study or write a paper or do something for school. She wasn't too clear on what she was up to, but she's spent so much time helping here lately that I was happy to give her some time off, especially after you offered to come in."

Jaycee smiled at her friend, then turned her attention back to the level to ensure the sign was perfectly straight. She had almost finished when a heavy step behind her caused her to startle.

"Do you need some help with that?"

Jaycee bristled at the implied insinuation that she might need a man's help with a simple carpentry job. "No thanks, we're good here," she replied sharply.

Simultaneously, Amanda answered, "Yes, please. I want to get this done. I'm starving, but I'll never get anything to eat if we leave things to Ms. Everything-Must-Be-Perfect here."

Everyone chuckled, and Jaycee turned with a scowl, which she quickly swallowed when she saw Jeremy and Danny were standing next to her friend.

"Um, well, thanks for the offer," she stammered. "To help, I mean. But I'm fine. I'm almost done here too."

After flashing her a quick smile, Jeremy nodded and leaned back against the door frame to watch her work. Beside him, Danny and Amanda bantered good-naturedly about the superior abilities of female carpenters to their male counterparts.

As she concentrated on screwing the sign back into place, Jaycee nipped her lower lip between her teeth. Although Chandra had hung the sign crooked, rehanging it straight was a simple task, even with Jeremy looking toned and sexy in his workout gear, acting as a distraction beside her. Jaycee had just seen him that morning when they'd met up for their run, but his presence now had still started the sprites jitterbugging in her stomach. When she was finished rehanging the sign, she turned to acknowledge his silent but watchful look with a smile. "Hello, stranger. I haven't seen you in a few hours. What brings you by?"

Jeremy shrugged. "I was just playing some pickup basketball at the rec center with my friend here"—he nodded toward Danny, who was still bickering good-naturedly with his wife—"and we came downtown to grab some lunch. Are you ladies free? Can we interest you in joining us?"

"Yes, please! Take us for lunch! I'm starving, and my taskmaster here"—Amanda gestured to Jaycee with a teasing grimace—"won't let me stop working long enough to get anything to eat."

Jaycee rolled her eyes. "Lunch would be nice. But if I come, I'll have to be quick, as I still have a million things I need to get done here this afternoon."

Jeremy nodded and stood back while Jaycee methodically put her tools away in her small tool bag. When she was finished, he followed her into the bakery, where he whistled in appreciation as he admired the freshly painted blue walls and highly polished floors. The new glass display cases at the front of the shop were beautifully illuminated by the sunshine coming through the oversized picture windows. The entire space had an airy and spacious feel.

"The place looks great," he exclaimed, unwinding the scarf from around his neck. "What a difference from the first time I was here!"

"Thank you," Jaycee replied, feeling slightly lightheaded at his unexpected presence and praise. "I'm really thrilled that everything is coming together so quickly."

"And that's because you've worked so hard. You've done a great job," Amanda added firmly.

Jaycee blushed and glanced around proudly.

"Now, let's go get something to eat," Amanda said. "I'm famished and craving a burger."

Jaycee nodded and shooed everyone out the door. After ensuring the bakery was locked up tight and the fire and security alarms were set, she followed her friends down the street to find a place for lunch.

Jeremy smiled as Jaycee gave a joyful shout and stopped to admire the toy store window's holiday display. He was happy she and Amanda had agreed to go to lunch with Danny and him. While he and Jaycee had been running together most mornings, it was difficult to have proper conversations while jogging. Fall had flown by as he'd worked double shifts, and she'd been busy renovating the bakery—hoping to open it in time for the holidays. They hadn't really spent as much time together as he would have liked.

"You haven't told me what you've got planned for Christmas," he said, smiling over at her.

"Well..." she replied, then stopped and frowned as he suddenly lifted a hand and halted. Danny and Amanda stopped too, their expressions puzzled as Jeremy sniffed the air. They looked at one another in confusion.

"What's going on?" Danny asked.

A second later, the bitter smell of smoke filled the air.

"Oh." Amanda reached out and took Danny's hand.

Jaycee's eyes widened in alarm as Jeremy reached over and grabbed her hand, then motioned for the other couple to follow them. They set off at a quick pace, but stopped again when they rounded the next block and saw that the connecting street was hazy with smoke.

"Help!" someone called.

Hearing the plea, the friends all broke into a run, racing through the thickening smoke toward the sound, passing by several stores before skidding to a stop in front of a small antique shop. The heritage stone building didn't seem to be in any imminent danger, but plumes of gray smoke rising from the back of the store made it obvious that if a fire wasn't already burning there, it was at least smoldering.

"What can we do to help?" Jaycee called to a gray-haired woman standing on the sidewalk, holding a small wooden chest.

She was pale, but her voice was steady as she motioned for a car to stop so a man holding a large wooden rocking chair could cross the road. "We're trying to move as much as we can out of the shop. We're not sure what's causing the smoke, but we need to get things out before they're damaged. Anything you can grab and help move would be great. We're putting everything just across the street for now until we come up with a better plan."

"Has anyone called the fire department?" asked Jeremy, pulling his cell phone from his jacket pocket.

"I did," a man carrying a large Ming vase called over. "They should be here any minute."

Nodding, Jeremy tucked his phone away and ran to join his friends as they went into the antique store to help.

After Jeremy and Danny worked together to move a heavy wooden chest of drawers across the street to a safer location, Jeremy looked back at the store and saw that the second-story windows were open.

"Is that an apartment?" he asked the woman, who was directing most of the movement of the store's inventory.

"Yes. I banged on the door but got no reply. I'm pretty sure there's no one up there."

"Does anyone know for sure? Is everyone from the second-floor apartments out?" Jeremy yelled.

His words only received shrugs and concerned looks in reply. After studying the open windows for another few seconds, he turned and ran down the small side alleyway to the back of the building, with Danny following close behind.

At the rear of the store, the two men found a metal and glass-paned door. "This must be the entrance to the upstairs apartment," Jeremy shouted.

He pulled and pushed at the long metal doorknob, grunting in dismay when it didn't budge. "Can anyone hear me?" he yelled while banging on the door's metal frame. "There's a fire in the building! You need to get out!"

Nothing stirred.

"Do you think anyone is still up there?" Danny asked, his forehead creased in concern.

"I don't know, but we need to check. Help me find something that'll break one of the glass panels in the door."

Jeremy hurried to look through the junk piled in and around the trash barrels on the other side of the alley. Danny quickly joined his search, shouting happily when a small, stout pipe fell out of one of the larger garbage bins.

"This might work," he cried, holding it up.

Nodding, Jeremy pulled off his coat and handed it to him. Wrapping the jacket around his arm, Danny swung the iron piece and, after several attempts, broke one of the small glass panels inside the door frame.

"Got it!" he cried. Dropping the pipe, he leaned over and cupping his hands, gave his friend a leg up.

A moment later, Jeremy had pushed the last of the shattered glass out and reached in to unlock the door from the inside. Hopping back down, he pulled the door open, and both men raced up the stairwell.

Across the street from the antique store, Jaycee set a small ornate end table down beside the rest of the shop's inventory. She coughed and wiped her brow with her mitten. The smoke had thickened considerably around them in the short time she and Amanda had been helping move furniture.

"Jaycee? Have you seen the guys? They went around the back of the building to check if anyone was still in the apartments above the store, but I haven't seen them come back." Amanda had a streak of dirt on one cheek, and her mouth was twisted in concern.

Jaycee's eyes widened as she turned and looked up at the building. The sprites in her stomach were whimpering as she grabbed Amanda by the hand and ran with her down the back alley. "Come on," she panted as they ran. "Let's go see where they went. Where the heck are the fire trucks and police, anyway? It seems to be taking them a long time to get here—Larkin Bay isn't that big!"

When they reached the back of the building, the women ran straight to the broken door. They peered in but could only see a hazy layer of smoke obscuring an empty foyer and stairwell.

"Danny? Danny?! Where are you?" Amanda cried. She turned to Jaycee. "What should we do?"

Jaycee frowned. "We're probably supposed to stay here until the firefighters arrive. But I can't just stand around waiting for them when the guys might need help."

Taking a deep breath, she swung open the door and ran inside. Grabbing onto the stair railing, she started up the stairs, feeling Amanda tugging on the hem of her jacket while following close behind. After a few steps, Jaycee stopped and pulled the collar up over her nose and mouth. She crouched down and motioned for her friend to do the same before they continued their climb.

Once upstairs, Jaycee looked up and down the narrow hallway. She hurried toward an open door. "It's about time," she muttered when she heard the faint sirens in the distance growing louder.

"Jeremy? Danny? Where are you?" she called out.

"Jaycee? We're here! We need help. And we haven't got much time!"

The girls raced to the door and were met at the entrance by Jeremy.

"Here," he said, pushing wet cloths into both girl's hands. "Cover your faces and get down." He pushed gently on Jaycee's shoulder and she fell to her knees, where she gratefully gulped in clearer air. Jeremy peered down at her. "Are you okay?"

She nodded.

"Good. Now, I need you and Amanda to take these kids and get out of here. And no matter what happens, don't come back into the building again."

Jaycee gulped hard. Kids? There were *children* in here? She rubbed her eyes to see better through the smoke.

"Just wait for the firefighters to arrive and tell them we're up here," Jeremy commanded as he pushed a whimpering child toward her.

Before he had finished speaking, Jaycee was already reaching for the little girl. Amanda rose to one knee beside her and held out her arms for the other child, who was crying for his mother as she pulled him close.

"Go," Jeremy said firmly as he pushed the four of them back toward the door.

"Where's Danny?" Amanda cried.

"He's here. He'll be coming out right behind you. We just have to help the mother get out," Jeremy replied, turning away.

Jaycee scooped up the crying little girl and tugged on Amanda's jacket. "Come on—we've got to get them out of here!"

Amanda hesitated, looking in the direction Jeremy had gone. A moment later, they heard Danny call out, and she sighed in relief as she wrapped the little boy in her arms and followed Jaycee out of the apartment.

The children hid their faces in the women's necks and Jaycee ignored her straining arms as she swiftly carried the youngster down the back staircase. The smoke thinned out as they descended, and the hot tears streaming down Jaycee's face subsided. When they reached the bottom of the staircase, the women rushed out the open doorway and greedily gulped in the cool, fresh air as they gratefully handed the crying and struggling children to the two firefighters who came up to greet them.

"There are still people up there! They need help!" Jaycee called out, her voice husky with smoke and fear.

Two firefighters raced past her and up the staircase. Another led both women away from the building. A moment later, Amanda and Jaycee were sitting on a gurney in the back of an ambulance with air masks covering their mouths. They watched silently as the paramedic attached a light probe to their fingers.

"We just want to ensure you didn't inhale any smoke," he explained as he pulled out a small tablet to record their vital signs.

Jaycee reached for Amanda's hand and clasped it in hers. Together, they watched wide-eyed through the open back door as the two crying children they had brought out of the building were loaded into another ambulance and driven away.

"Don't worry. I think they're both fine," the paramedic assured them. "They're just being taken to the children's hospital as a precaution. I'd be more worried about the kids if they were lethargic."

As Jaycee tried to catch her breath and will her heart rate back to normal, she watched a police officer help a woman into the back of another emergency vehicle.

"Well, I don't think either of you will require additional treatment," the paramedic informed her a short time later. "Your breathing sounds normal and all your vitals look great."

Jaycee gave him a weak smile.

"The men seem to be fine too, from what I'm hearing on the radio." He nodded toward the crackling box. "And the woman they helped is on her way to the hospital to be reunited with her children."

"That's wonderful," Jaycee croaked out as he removed her mask.

"It is, and you are all *heroes*," he said, patting her shoulder and removing the light probe from her finger. "The family may not have gotten out as quickly without your help." He held her arm as he helped her climb down the vehicle steps and back onto the sidewalk.

A moment later Amanda was by her side and Jaycee took her friend's hand in hers again. Despite the paramedic's words, Jaycee didn't feel like she'd done anything special. She'd just followed the guys into the building. Jeremy was the one who had run in to find the family and had organized everyone so they all got out safely. Shuddering, she considered what could have happened if the men hadn't found the woman and her children.

"Thank you," she whispered to the paramedic.

He nodded.

Amanda tugged her hand free from Jaycee's and went to find her husband.

And Jaycee, her heart full of gratitude, followed her to find Jeremy—the true hero of the day.

Chapter Seventeen

Pacing the edges of the soot-stained sidewalk, Jeremy waited for the fire chief to finish inspecting the antique store.

"Same pattern," Jeremy called over to him.

The officer didn't reply.

Jeremy slapped his clipboard in frustration.

I should have caught the arsonist by now.

He couldn't believe someone had the gall to start a fire in broad daylight when the downtown shops were full of families starting their holiday shopping. The only good news, which he had just received via text, was that the family he had helped escape from the apartment had been released from the hospital and would be fine.

Letting out an exasperated sigh, Jeremy walked away so the fire chief could focus on his work at the back of the shop. Wandering outside the taped-off area, he ran a hand across the stubble on his chin. In some ways, he reflected, the case moving slowly was a good thing because it meant he could stay longer in Larkin Bay. He was enjoying his twice-weekly recreational basketball games, followed by the get-togethers at Sullivan's Place. He really liked many of the other guys he'd met here. Also, a time or two, he'd encountered a set of sparkling dark eyes and a heart-stopping smile during his visits to the pub.

Jaycee.

They might both be too busy to spend a lot of quality time together, but that didn't mean he didn't think about her.

Constantly.

Shaking his head, he forced himself to focus on the task at hand. Skirting the police crime-scene tape, he marched back to where the fire chief was now closing his notebook.

"Well?" Jeremy demanded.

Chief Robertson shrugged. "Off the record?"

Jeremy nodded.

The other man rubbed a hand through his thinning white hair. "Well, I have to agree with ya. The flames followed the same pattern as the last fire and the trouble was started with the same type of gasoline bottles too. Whoever ignited it didn't even come into the store. Still, you'd think someone would have seen them hanging around. Whoever's starting these fires is clever, and that's a problem, as the smart ones are usually more dangerous."

Jeremy scowled and nodded in agreement. "Is there anything else you can tell me?"

"Yep. I found this."

Jeremy felt his lips curve into a smile when he saw a plastic bag containing a half-used matchbook in the fire chief's outstretched hand.

"Where did you find that?"

"Under one of the side windows—right where the fire path starts and where whoever started it left the scene. It hasn't snowed since the fire, so I'm betting there are prints on it. Now all you have to do is figure out who they belong to."

Jeremy grinned broadly as he took the bag. "Thank you! This is great. I'll take this to the lab in the city right now and see what I can find. Even a partial print could be all we need to catch this guy."

"Well, I sure hope you get a clear print from it. I'm tired of meeting up with you and delivering bad news," the other man replied with a chuckle.

Jeremy shook his hand. "I'm tired of it too. But now that we've got this print, let's hope it's all we need to put this arsonist behind bars."

Humming happily to herself, Chandra pulled the envelope of college brochures out of her backpack and placed it in the middle of the kitchen table where it couldn't be missed. After digging through another pocket, she threw away what remained of her lunch and zipped it shut before tossing her bag in the doorway's direction so she would remember to take it upstairs later. Placing a hand on her growling stomach, she sniffed something sweet and headed to the counter to help herself to a handful of the snickerdoodles that Jaycee had left cooling on a wire rack. As she munched on one of the still-warm cookies, she poured herself a glass of milk and sat down at the kitchen table to study the first three chapters of *The Wars*. Chandra liked to read, so she didn't mind doing this homework.

A few minutes later, the screen door banged open. Chandra looked up from her novel as Jaycee came into the room. "Hey," she greeted her sister, then looked away as she felt her cheeks heat.

"Um, these cookies are great, but you didn't bake them for anyone in particular, did you? I kind of got carried away eating them."

Jaycee laughed. "No, it's fine. I was just experimenting with the recipe. I still have to work out the proper ingredient amounts so I can make them in bigger batches. I'll probably bake even more tonight, so it's a good thing you like them. You might be sick of eating them before I'm done."

Chandra drained the rest of the milk from her glass and checked her phone for texts as she reached for another cookie. "I can live with that problem," she replied, grinning.

"What's this?" her sister asked, spying the envelope on the table.

"Oh, just something they asked me to bring home from school." Chandra looked down at her book to hide her excited smile.

Seeing the high school's return address on the envelope, Jaycee shot her a worried look before taking a knife from the kitchen junk drawer and carefully slitting the envelope open. Her eyes widened as a cascade of booklets and application papers with portfolio requirements for some of the best fashion design schools in the country slid into her hands.

Chandra put down her novel and grinned broadly as she watched her sister sift through the envelope's contents.

"Wow! Look at all this stuff. I see you've been talking to Denise. Did she help you pull all this together?"

Swinging her hair back, Chandra's nodded. "Sort of. I've had a few meetings in guidance with her. I also took some tests to figure out what I was good at, and then we talked for a long time about my interests. I even took an aptitude test and a practice SAT, and I did really well!"

Jaycee tilted her head to one side and blinked at her sister. "I'm not surprised."

Chandra shrugged. "Well, I am. Mrs. Gunther said that if I studied just a little harder, I could probably even get the grades I needed to get into some of these places. Can you believe it, Jaycee? I might be smart enough to go to college!" Hopping up from her seat, Chandra pulled out one of the larger glossy booklets from the pile. "I've been looking at this school's website and it looks pretty amazing. Going here to study fashion would be so cool."

Jaycee peered over her sister's shoulder at the book. "It does look great. And of course you're smart enough to go to college. Did you really think you weren't?" Jaycee looked momentarily confused, then frowned. "When do you have to apply by?" she asked. "And do you have everything you need? Should I call Denise and talk to her about this? Do I need to go online and look for more information?"

Chandra sat back down at the table, her eyes glowing as she looked up at her sister. "No, I think I'm okay. All the application deadlines are listed in the back of the books, and the printout here shows when all the testing dates are. I just have to study and work on a portfolio for now, I think."

Jaycee picked up a second brochure and flipped through its pages, trying to remain calm and not show how thrilled she was that her sister was not only showing interest in applying to colleges, but also seemed excited by the idea.

"But..." Chandra slumped in her chair. "It looks great, but it's also four years, and the tuition is a lot. Can we afford it? I mean, I'll get a job to help pay for as much of it as I can. But it's still a ton of money, and I know Betty lost most of Mom and Dad's savings, and you'll need money to finish renovating the bakery..."

"Yes," Jaycee answered firmly, putting the brochure back down on the table. "We may not have everything you need right now, but Denise told me there are many ways to finance college. All you should worry about is studying and putting together the best portfolio you can to get you into the schools you want. I'll take care of the financial part of it. It may be tight, but we'll find the money."

"Okay, but only if you're sure."

"I am. Besides, you know how the pilgrims traveled on the Mayflower?"

Chandra blinked in confusion. "Yes?"

"Then do you know what college students travel on?"

"Oh no. Not another lame joke."

"Scholar-ships."

Chandra groaned.

Jaycee reached over and hugged her sister. "Don't you worry about the money part of this at all," she told her. "By the time you leave for school, the bakery will be up and running, and we'll have plenty of money to pay your tuition fees." And as Jaycee listened to Chandra excitedly plan for her future, she sent a silent prayer to whatever god might be listening that everything she was telling her sister was true.

"Surprise! It's me," called out a sweet-pitched, singsong voice that made the sprites in Jaycee's heart leap with recognition and joy.

"Lisa!" she cried. A smile spread across her face. She climbed off her stool behind the bakery's front counter and ran to greet her friend at the door.

They hugged once before pulling away to grin widely at each other, then fell back into each other's arms again. Jaycee felt a lump rising in her throat. She'd missed Lisa more than she had realized—texting several times a day just didn't make up for seeing her friend in person.

"You're here! This is so amazing. I'm so happy to see you! I never thought they'd let you leave the bakery to come and spend time with me so soon!"

"How could they stop me?" Lisa asked with a shrug. "Since you left, they haven't found anyone to replace you. Tony has Rhonda coming in to work out front and serve customers every day so he can help in the kitchen. But she can't be on her feet all day, being pregnant and all, so it's not going well. That leaves me as the only competent full-time employee, and I wanted to see you, so I simply told them I was taking a week off." Lisa set her bag down on the counter. "They weren't thrilled, but they really couldn't say no, either. Last night, Michael helped me throw everything you'd left in your apartment into the back of a rental van, and here I am!"

Jaycee hugged her friend again. "I'm so happy you're here! And you brought all my stuff too? I can't believe it!"

"Yep, at least all that would fit in the back of the truck is here. The rest is in the bin, and you owe me two hundred bucks for that. But I also found someone to sublet your apartment, which should more than offset it. Now you are officially moved out of the big city and stuck here in Larkin Bay. So I hope you love this place as much as you say you do."

Stretching, Lisa reached over to massage the tight muscles in the small of her back while she looked curiously around the bakery. "So this is it? This is the place you're leaving me and the bright lights of the big city for?"

"It is," Jaycee replied. She was momentarily at a loss for words while she considered the enormity of what her friend had done for her. Swallowing back the grateful tears she knew would embarrass them both, she grabbed Lisa's hand and proudly started showing her around the bakery.

"I loved the old flooring, so I just had it refinished, and I think it turned out pretty nice," she said, flipping over some of the thick paper protecting the newly refinished wooden floors so her friend could admire them.

Lisa squatted down and ran a hand over the dark, shiny varnish. "They're beautiful, and the color is perfect. It should hold up great with all the foot traffic you're going to get."

"I hope so," Jaycee said. After carefully smoothing down the protective covering again, she led her friend to the back of the shop, where she introduced her to the carpenters who were busy putting the last of the custom-built cabinetry and cupboards in place. After complimenting the men on their work, both women paused to admire the state-of-the-art commercial ovens that had just been delivered that morning.

"Gorgeous!" trilled Lisa as she opened one door to peek inside.

Jaycee grinned and nodded. Since Lisa had helped her plan most of the bakery's layout via Skype, her friend was already familiar with a lot of what Jaycee was showing her. Having also worked as a baker for almost a decade, Lisa was well-versed in what was needed in a professional kitchen.

"Everything looks great. You've pulled it all together really quickly too. It's very impressive."

"There was so much to think about." Jaycee sighed and sat back down on a counter stool. "I'm sure I've missed a thousand things."

Lisa shrugged. "It all looks well in hand so far, and I'm here for at least a week, so we can go over everything together. As a team, we made Tony and Rhonda's bakery successful. We'll have this place running as smoothly or even better than their shop in no time at all."

"I hope so."

"We will. And honestly, Tony deserves whatever happens. Rhonda is miserable being pregnant, and it's kind of fun watching her take it out on him. I've been looking around the city for a better position. When I leave, they're going to be up the creek. Karma will get him in the end—you'll see."

Jaycee chuckled at her friend's pronouncement, her smile broadening when she realized she didn't even feel a pang of emotion hearing about Tony.

After sharing more of her ideas for finishing the bakery with her friend, she saw Lisa was yawning.

"That's enough for today," she declared. "Let's get you out of here. You've had a long drive and need to rest."

After bidding good night to the carpenters and grabbing her things, Jaycee followed Lisa out front to her parking spot and happily hopped into the van's passenger seat to show her friend the way home.

After pulling into Jaycee's driveway, Lisa strode around to the back of the rental truck to wrestle with the padlock on its sliding door.

When she finally got it unlocked, she pushed it open and hauled out two potted plants, which she handed to Jaycee.

"What are these?"

Lisa grinned. "These are to replace the ones you gave me to look after when you left. The other two were only with me for about two weeks before they turned yellow and all their leaves fell off."

Jaycee gave a loud laugh.

"What can I say? I'm a baker, not a florist!"

Still giggling, Jaycee held out both of the small plants and admired them. "That's hilarious. You didn't have to replace them, though. I would have understood. Still, these are beautiful, thank you."

Inside, Jaycee found a sunny place for both of the pots before hurrying back out to help her friend unload the rest of her belongings from the van.

When Chandra and Dean arrived home from school a few minutes later, Jaycee offered some hasty introductions before the teens started helping unpack the van's contents.

The four were making quick progress when a pickup truck driving past slowed down and did a U-turn. A moment later, it parked against the curb, and Danny and Jeremy climbed out of the cab. "Do you need help?" Danny called out.

"If you have the time, that would be great," Jaycee answered, coming down the front steps, her heart fluttering happily when she saw Jeremy.

The two men climbed into the back of the van and together helped carry the last of the van's bulkier contents inside.

Later, as they swept out the empty van together, Lisa and Jaycee watched the men maneuver a few pieces of the family's decades-old furniture out of the house and into the garage to be picked up by a charity truck. Studying the men, Lisa noted Jeremy's lack of a wedding ring and raised one eyebrow at Jaycee.

Jaycee felt heat stain her cheeks at the unasked question.

"You've turned all pink! That's so cute! And Jeremy is kind of adorable, so what's going on between the two of you?" Lisa asked, leaning on her broom and smiling at her friend.

"Nothing! I mean, I know he's good-looking, and he's smart and easy to talk to, but we're both so busy with work that nothing's happening between us. We do run together most mornings, though, so I'm getting to know a little about him. He's really pretty great." She turned to watch Jeremy for a moment and sighed. "And look how hard he's working with Danny. He's a good guy, and he's been a great friend. I guess I might have been interested and had a bit of a silly crush on him when I first moved home, but I've had to focus on getting the house sorted, the bakery open, and Chandra ready to apply to college. I just don't have any time for a boyfriend right now."

Lisa nodded "Uh-huh."

"What?"

She rolled her eyes. "Nothing. I just don't believe a word you're saying."

Jaycee sputtered but didn't answer, leaving Lisa laughing as she returned to her sweeping.

Chapter Eighteen

The following day, after the painters had finished their work, Jaycee was left alone to admire her bakery.

The space, she decided, even if she was more than slightly biased, looked beautiful. The new paint job, display cabinets, and hardwood floors made the shop pretty and functional. She couldn't wait to clean and stock it so she could show it off to everyone in town.

A small bell chimed at the front of the store and Jaycee hurried to meet Larkin Bay's fire chief, who was there to complete the bakery's fire code compliance inspection. Forcing herself to relax while greeting him, she reassured herself silently that since everything had been completed strictly to code, she had nothing to worry about. Besides, even if something was wrong, she still had over a week before the bakery was scheduled to open to fix it.

After showing the chief the storage area where the alarm systems were kept, Jaycee left him to do his inspection. She smiled when she heard him grunt in approval when he saw the alarms were wired directly to the local fire station. It had been an added expense, but Jaycee knew she would save the money many times over if a fire ever started.

"Well," said the chief after he had finished his meticulous scrutiny, "everything looks good. I'll just fill out your inspection certificate, and then you're all set to open as far as the Larkin Bay Fire Department is concerned."

After filling out and signing the required paperwork, he handed the documentation to Jaycee with a grin. "I'll be dropping in as soon as you open. My sweet tooth and I are both looking forward to having a bakery here in town," he said, patting his ample tummy.

"Thank you. I'm excited too," she replied. "But I was wondering..." she added, her smile fading. "Do you know anything about the arsonist? Has he been caught yet? And is it true that the same person has been setting all the fires like the town newspaper is reporting?"

He shook his head. "It looks like they are. But try not to worry. Everyone is working hard on the case. We'll catch whoever is responsible soon."

"I hope so. It's just so awful, especially for all the retail stores that have been affected."

"Yep. It's not fair at all. So we're asking everyone to keep their eyes open for any suspicious activity in the area and to contact us if they see anything that might help us catch this guy."

"Do the police have any new leads?" she asked. She had asked Jeremy the same question that morning during their run, but his reply had been vague.

"A few. We've had a couple of reports about a young person lurking by some of the locations shortly before the fires were reported. The police have stepped up their foot patrols in the area too, so that should help catch him, or at least maybe slow him down. We're also hoping that all the publicity we're giving the case might just scare the arsonist off altogether."

"If I see anything suspicious at all, I'll call it in right away."

"That would be great," the chief said, giving her a reassuring pat on the forearm. "But try not to worry. We should catch this guy soon."

After bidding the fire chief good night, Jaycee locked the door behind him. She studied her fire compliance certificate and smiled. Passing this inspection might seem like a small thing to anyone else, but it was another important step toward getting the bakery open, and that made her want to join the sprites in her stomach in a happy jig.

As Jaycee stared at the few clothes left hanging in straight, neat rows in her closet, she sighed. She didn't know why she was having such a hard time deciding what to wear. Seeing Jeremy tonight wasn't a date. So there was no reason for her indecisiveness. They were simply two friends going out together because the antique store fire had spoiled their previous plans to have a meal together.

Jaycee had been surprised when Jeremy had asked her after their Monday morning run if she would have dinner with him. She hadn't been expecting the invitation.

Frowning, she threw a tank top into the middle of her bed, pulled a pair of jeans to the top of the pile, and tossed a white cotton blouse beside it. She studied the jumbled heap of clothes for a long moment, then shrugged and turned toward the door.

"Chandra! Come and help me! I need something to make me look better than normal. I mean, make me look like who I am, but, uh, better." She groaned and tapped the side of her head with an open palm. "Oh crap. I don't know what I need. Therapy probably." She raised her voice again, hoping her plea was carrying across the hallway that separated their rooms. "Chandra? Please come help me!"

The teen appeared in Jaycee's bedroom doorway a few seconds later, yawning widely. Approaching the bed, she studied the pile of clothes, then looked at her sister questioningly.

"Help me figure out what to wear tonight," Jaycee begged. "Something that makes me look nice but doesn't look like I tried too hard."

Chandra stretched and then nodded as if the request made perfect sense. "Ok, where are you going? Do you want formal, casual, or in-between?"

"In-between. I don't know where we're going, but there aren't many places that require formal dress around Larkin Bay, so I think I should lean heavily toward the casual option. But still nice."

She bit back a sound of protest as Chandra started digging through her clothes, pushing most of them onto the floor.

"You should just throw out most of these," she muttered.

"What?"

"Nothing," the girl replied, finally pulling out a pair of dark skinny jeans and a lightweight cream-colored sweater from the pile. Going over to Jaycee's small walk-in closet, she returned with a belt. Placing her selections on the bed, the teen studied them for a moment, then nodded and went over to the dresser, where she found a bracelet and small felted handbag and tossed them onto the bed as well. Leaving the room, she reappeared a few minutes later with a set of wedge-heeled booties and a soft white-and-cream-striped scarf.

"There you are. You should be good to go now," she stated.

Jaycee looked from the outfit spread out on her bed to her sister in admiration. "Wow, that was fast. No wonder you want to study fashion. You're a natural."

Chandra shrugged at the compliment and, after giving her sister instructions on how to properly wrinkle and smooth her skinny jeans after she pulled them on, she turned to leave the room so Jaycee could get dressed.

"Come back in five minutes and help me with my hair and make-up!" Jaycee called after her. Chandra waved her hand in what Jaycee hoped was agreement before she disappeared out the door.

"You look beautiful," Jeremy exclaimed when he picked up Jaycee later that evening. His eyes glowed with appreciation as they made their way down the front steps of her house together.

Jaycee felt her cheeks color. "Why, thank you," she replied, twisting her fingers through her scarf. "You look pretty dashing yourself," she added, admiring his dark jeans and the lightweight navy sweater that was peeking out from under his open winter coat.

He chuckled and reached out to take her hand as they started off toward Pepos, the pretty little Italian restaurant nestled by Larkin Bay's town pier.

"Do you think it's going to snow tonight?" he asked, looking up at the sky.

"Maybe. It's warmed up a little. It never snows when it's really cold."

"I love the fresh smell in the air before we get the first snowfall of the year."

Jaycee nodded as she looked up at the slowly darkening sky. "Me too. The leaves might all be down, but I can see the stars starting to come out. I doubt we'll get snow tonight if there's no clouds. Soon, though."

This is nice. Date-like too.

Jeremy smiled at her as he swung their linked hands between them. "That'll be good. There's less crime when it snows."

"Really? I didn't know that. You must know all sorts of interesting things like that. Did you always want to be a police investigator?"

"Yep. My father was in the force his entire career, and the guys he worked with were like family to my sisters and me. When my dad was killed, they helped my mom keep an eye on all of us."

"You were lucky to have them."

"Yeah, the force back then looked after their own. It's different now, especially in the bigger cities where the men can't possibly all know each other. But here in Larkin Bay, like in Harlen where I grew up, the police unit is still small, and you can tell there's a strong sense of unity. It's important."

"I didn't realize you grew up so close to here."

"I did. Harlen's a good place. A few of my sisters still live there and there's still a great sense of community."

"It's like that here too, and it's been like that for a while. When my parents died, it seemed like the entire town dropped by with food for us. I was in such a state of shock at the time that I didn't realize how special that was. The community also helped Betty with Chandra after I left, and I never fully appreciated how much everyone did until I came back."

"It's amazing all the things we take for granted when we're young."

They continued walking in comfortable silence down the moonlit street for a few more blocks before Jeremy spoke again. "It's nice being out with you like this."

"I'm enjoying it too. I must admit, though, I was a little surprised when you asked to get together tonight. I thought maybe all I was to you was a morning running partner." She felt color flood her cheeks at how direct she was being and was happy that the streetlights were dim so Jeremy wouldn't be able to see it.

He looked down at their clasped hands. "I've always thought of you as more than that. It's just..."

"Just what?"

Jeremy shrugged. "Well, I really haven't gone out at all since Marianne died. And I know we talked about being too busy to date, but seeing you every morning and not really being able to talk to you because we're running got me thinking that I'd like to spend more time with you. Get to know you better."

It's a date!

The sprites in Jaycee's stomach got up and danced at this realization, then paused in surprise when she heard the rumble of raised voices ahead.

The moon had moved behind the single cloud overhead, but in the shadows of the dim street lighting, she could just make out the shapes of a group of young men who were arguing. Slowing her steps, she moved a half step closer to Jeremy.

His jaw tightened, and he clasped her hand tighter as they got closer. "Good evening, boys. How are you all doing tonight?" Jeremy asked the teens.

Jaycee studied the group of five teenage boys standing with their feet planted apart and their hands curled into fists. Two blocked the sidewalk while three others stood on the running path. She recognized Chandra's boyfriend, Dean, and another boy from Larkin Bay among them.

"We're fine," snarled one of them. Jaycee remembered him from their cookout and thought his name was Ryan. Glancing over at her, he nodded in recognition. "We were just discussing a few things, that's all."

"You're the new cop in town, aren't you?" asked another boy.

"I am," Jeremy replied calmly. "I'm not on duty tonight, though, just out walking to dinner with a pretty woman."

At the mention of the police, the temperature of the discussion between the boys lowered substantially. Whatever the teens were arguing about, they obviously didn't want the authorities involved.

Jaycee felt Jeremy's hold on her hand relax.

"But there's no need to bother the police tonight, from what I can see," he continued. "Besides, Jaycee and I were just talking about how a small town like Larkin Bay takes care of its own. So if there is ever anything we can do to help you boys, just let us know."

The teens had shuffled farther away from each other while Jeremy addressed them, but Jaycee could see they were still eyeing each other warily. She gave them all what she hoped was a warm but confident smile and nodded to confirm Jeremy's words.

After bidding the teens good night, she and Jeremy continued on their way. They had only gone a few steps when one of the boys called out after them. "Have you caught that arsonist yet?"

Jeremy raised his eyebrows and turned on his heel, dropping Jaycee's hand. "The arsonist? No, why? Do you know something about them?"

Ryan and Dean had slipped back into their usual teenage slouch, but upon hearing the other boy's question, they straightened up, crossed their arms over their chests, and drew their shoulders back.

Interesting, thought Jaycee. She could tell by Jeremy's slight shift in position that he thought so too.

"Everyone knows," replied the teen. He stepped back as Ryan slipped a hand into his jacket pocket.

"Everyone knows what?" asked Jeremy, his tone relaxed but his gaze steady on the boy.

Does Ryan have a weapon hidden in his jacket pocket?

Jaycee moved closer to Jeremy and squeezed his forearm.

"Nothing," laughed the other boy, who was also watching the Ryan's movements. "Everyone knows nothing, I guess. And what do I care? Burn down the whole town—I don't live here."

Turning away, he addressed two of the boys. "Let's get out of here before we get in trouble for just existing. There's got to be something better to do than standing around here arguing with these stupid arson lovers."

The other teens sneered back and followed him to an older-model sports car parked at the curb. After much jostling between them for seats, they finally got in and slammed the doors shut.

Jeremy watched the car squeal its tires while pulling away and slowly turned back to Ryan and Dean, who were now studying the pavement at their feet.

"Well, that was interesting."

The teens remained silent.

"Jaycee and I are late for our reservation at Pepos," he finally said. "But I'm working all week here and I'll be doing patrols around town, or if not that, just doing paperwork at the police station. If you think you might have something to share with me about the arson investigation or just want to talk about anything else that might be bothering you, I should be easy to find."

Jeremy turned to Jaycee and subtly motioned in the direction they were going so she would precede him down the sidewalk toward the restaurant.

"What do you think that was all about?" she asked him quietly as he held the door to Pepos open a few minutes later.

"About what the boys said?" he asked.

At her nod, he was silent for a long moment.

"Well, my guess is they know more about the arsonist investigation than they want to share right now. But that's not too unusual. Teens dislike authoritative figures, and besides their parents, there isn't anyone who shouts *authority* louder than a police officer in, or out, of uniform."

Jaycee frowned. "I think you're right. They seem like nice kids, and Ryan and Dean are Chandra's friends. I'd hate to discover that one of them is involved in something as terrible as arson."

Jeremy smiled at her, but she couldn't help but notice that the expression didn't quite reach his eyes. After they had followed the hostess to their table and settled into their seats, Jeremy reached over and grabbed Jaycee's hand to give it a gentle squeeze. "It's all going to be fine," he said. "The kids will tell us what they know when they're ready."

"I just hope it's before the arsonist does any more damage."

Jeremy let go of her hand and sighed. "Me too," he replied. "Me too."

Chapter Nineteen

"I think it's cool that Jaycee's going out to dinner tonight with Jeremy," Chandra said, picking up the fork beside her plate and waving it at Lisa. "He seems okay too, like decent even. Do you think she really likes him?"

Lisa sat down at the kitchen table across from her and took a large spoonful of the homemade spicy chicken macaroni and cheese from the dish in the middle of the table. She placed it on her plate alongside a serving of tossed salad. "I do," she replied, shaking the vinaigrette bottle and pouring some of it onto her greens. "But from what Jaycee tells me, he's still grieving over his wife, so she's not sure he's ready for a new relationship yet. Honestly, your sister has the worst luck with men."

They ate in silence for a few minutes, then Lisa pulled one of the colorful college brochures that was lying on the kitchen table toward her. She flipped it open and studied it for a few minutes, then looked up and smiled at Chandra. "So this is what you want to do at college? Study fashion design?"

Chandra shrugged. "I think so, but I'm not really sure. I mean, I would like to learn more about it, but since Betty lost all the money that Mom and Dad left for my tuition, I'm not sure we can afford it."

"Oh?"

"Yeah, I know Jaycee wants me to go, and she says she'll find the money somehow, but I don't want to take what she needs for the bakery, either." Chandra toyed with the pasta on her plate for a moment. "Honestly, I don't know what to do. It might be best if I just stayed here and worked at the shop with Jaycee."

Lisa frowned. "Best? Well, maybe in some ways, but I doubt Jaycee'll let you do that. All she talks about is you going to college."

"But what if I don't want to go?"

Lisa raised one eyebrow. "Really? You don't want to study fashion and makeup and stuff and get out of Larkin Bay for at least a little while to see what things are like in the rest of the world? You're almost eighteen, and you've lived in this small town all your life." She sat back and studied the teen intently. "I don't believe you."

Chandra flushed and looked down at her dinner plate. "Well, maybe I do. But if we can't afford it or if it means Jaycee is going to have to give up opening the bakery—"

"I promise you, that will not happen," Lisa interrupted. "There are scholarships and loans and all sorts of things you can apply for to get money to go to school. Besides, the bakery is almost ready to open, and it's going to be wildly successful whether you go to college or not."

"You really think so?" Chandra looked equal parts hopeful and skeptical as she asked the question.

"I know so. Don't worry about that at all." Lisa pulled another of the catalogs toward her. "Now, which college looks the most interesting? I know nothing about fashion, but I can help you sort out what needs to be done to apply."

Chandra gazed at Lisa, then pressed her lips firmly together as she dragged an oversized course calendar out from the bottom of the pile and handed it to her. "This program looks amazing. But it's really tough to get into, so I doubt they'll even accept me."

"Well, you'll never know if you don't try," said Lisa, pushing their dishes to one side. After handing Chandra a pen and notepad, she flipped open the brochure and started to read it aloud, helping Chandra create a list of what she needed to do to apply to the college program of her dreams.

As Jeremy and Jaycee walked home from the restaurant, he kicked a pile of leaves into the air, then stopped to watch them fall. "We have the whole downtown to ourselves," he observed.

The night was crisp and cool, but with her scarf and a wool jacket, Jaycee felt warm and cozy. She was humming happily under her breath as she walked. The wine they'd had with dinner had left her relaxed, and she pressed herself closer to Jeremy's side. Glancing down, he slipped his arm around her shoulder. He was taller than she was, even in her boots, but he was also considerate in his stride, so she didn't feel rushed to keep up with him.

As they meandered through the moonlit streets of downtown Larkin Bay, they saw no one. Jaycee placed a hand on her stomach as the sprites there gave a happy cheer. She sighed softly. "I guess we really do have the whole place to ourselves," she said. "And this might be the last time we don't have snow on the ground for a while too."

Dropping Jeremy's hand, she gave him a mischievous smile, then stepping away, picked up a large handful of leaves. With a happy giggle, she turned and tossed them at him.

Jeremy grinned and swatted the falling red and gold leaves away. "Where I come from, we don't fight with leaves. We have snowball fights," he laughed.

"Same idea, I think," Jaycee replied. Quickly stepping to one side, she scooped up another armful of the crisp, dry leaves and tossed them at him.

She moved fast, but Jeremy was taller, and in a few long strides, he quickly caught up with her and showered her with a colorful cascade of fragrant leaves in return.

Scooping, throwing, and racing away from each other, both managed a few direct hits until finally, giggling uncontrollably, Jaycee held up both hands. "Truce!" she exclaimed. "I give up! I don't know how you are with snow, but you're pretty good in a leaf fight!"

Jeremy dropped the pile of leaves he was holding and clasped both hands triumphantly over his head before reaching over to help her pick off some leaves that were stuck in her hair and on her coat. "You forget," he explained, stepping closer to her and loosening a particularly stubborn leaf caught in her curls, "I have five sisters, so I am a pro at competitions with women."

Jaycee gasped and looked up at him, placing both hands on her hips in mock outrage. "I am absolutely certain that there are many things you can't beat your sisters at."

Jeremy's smile widened, and his eyes twinkled. "Definitely," he agreed, "but none that I'm admitting to you, at least not tonight."

Grinning, Jaycee turned away and continued walking toward home. Jeremy quickened his step to catch up. When he reached her, he pulled her hand into his, and drew her close to his side again.

She looked up at him. "Tell me more about yourself."

"What do you want to know?"

"Well, you have a large family. I think that's nice. I only have one sister and my parents both died years ago."

"You have lots of friends, though."

"I do. It's almost the same, my chosen family and all that, but I'd love to have had lots of siblings too."

"Sometimes it's great, but it can be annoying too."

She laughed and swatted at him. "You like it."

Jeremy grinned. "Most of the time."

"I think I'd really like to be a part of a large family." Jaycee stared at him for a long moment and then frowned and glanced away before returning her gaze to meet his. "Should we talk about Marianne? I mean, we're here together and laughing and holding hands. Are you okay with all of this? I know it must be hard. She was your wife and your first love, after all. I don't want you to feel like you're betraying her memory or anything like that by being here with me..." Jaycee's words trailed off as she stepped away from him. "I also want to make sure you're not getting yourself into something you're not ready for." She paused again before continuing in a trembling voice. "I know from experience that grieving can take a really long time."

Jeremy stopped and studied the street ahead of him for a long moment before pulling Jaycee back into his arms. In the still night, she could clearly hear the steady beat of his heart as she stared up at him.

"There was a time after Marianne died when I was sure I wouldn't ever want to be close to another woman again. But that seems to have changed since I've been spending time with you. I still love Marianne, and I know she will always have a special place in my heart. But I also know she'd want me to be happy. And I know she'd have liked you..."

Jaycee nodded, feeling her eyes well up with emotion over all Marianne and Jeremy had lost. Leaning on his chest, she inhaled his lemony cologne and sighed as she closed her eyes. After a moment, he gently lifted her chin with one finger.

"What else do you want to know?" he asked, gazing into her eyes.

Nothing. I want you to kiss me.

The sprites in her stomach were doing a tap dance of desire. Jaycee swallowed hard as she remembered their agreement not to start anything.

Why did I ever think that was a good idea?

She struggled to focus her thoughts and come up with a question less fraught with emotion. "Um. Well, what's your favorite thing to do when you're not working as an arson investigator or running?"

Jeremy chuckled. "I like lots of things. I like to read—I especially like mystery novels. I like to play sports; I'm a huge Boston Red Sox fan, but I like other things too."

"Oh, like what?" asked Jaycee. Her eyelids fluttered shut as he dipped his head down toward her.

"Things like this," he whispered, kissing her gently on the lips.

Jaycee breathed out slowly, savoring the moment. He tasted lovely, a mix of fall cider and mint chapstick and another taste that was sweet and warm and uniquely him. She parted her lips, and Jeremy, recognizing the sign of consent, pulled her closer.

After a few minutes, Jaycee smiled against his mouth and drew back slightly. "I guess we've decided to ditch the no-kissing rule?"

Jeremy gave a low laugh before kissing her again.

Jaycee rolled over in bed and grabbed her phone off the side table the next morning. She sighed happily when she saw a text had already arrived from Jeremy. He was working all day, so wouldn't be able to see her until later that evening when they planned to get together for a run and share some takeout.

She groaned and tugged her quilt up closer to her chin. Lisa was leaving to drive back to the city today, and Jaycee needed to see her off. She also planned to head over to the bakery to continue cleaning and disinfecting. Still, she decided, sitting up in bed and stretching, it was very nice to wake up to a text letting her know that someone as gorgeous and kind as Jeremy was thinking about her.

After shooting off a quick reply to him, she threw back the covers, eager to get ready for the day ahead.

Jaycee helped Lisa load her things into her rental car and gave her friend a long hug. "I'm going to miss you," she declared.

"Well, I'm glad to hear that, but you look far too happy for me to believe it," Lisa teased.

Her grin broadened as Jaycee showed her Jeremy's text and filled her in on their date.

"I am happy," Jaycee admitted with a sigh. "I honestly feel like a giddy schoolgirl today. I am desperately smitten."

"Well, it's good to be, uh, smitten? Is that the word you used? At least at the beginning of a relationship. Hell, *I'd* like to be smitten.

All the guys I meet in the city are definitely not worth being smitten over!"

Both women laughed. "We'll find you someone nice soon if that's what you want," Jaycee said, giving Lisa another long hug goodbye.

"Maybe. We'll just have to wait and see what the fates have in store. But whatever happens, I'll miss you, my friend," she replied. "It's been such a great week. Thank you for the movies and the meals you made me and for letting me muck around with all your bakery plans."

"Are you kidding me?" Jaycee stepped back and raised both hands. "Thank *you*! I had so much fun. And thanks for all your help with the bakery too. I'd have gotten nothing right if it wasn't for you."

"True. It'd be a mess," Lisa said, tossing her hair.

Jaycee giggled at her friend's teasing and slammed the driver's side door shut.

"Text me," she demanded as Lisa rolled down the window and started the car.

"Okay."

"Something funny."

Lisa frowned. "I will. But also, in all seriousness, promise me you'll stop worrying so much. Everything in the bakery looks great, and I'm just a phone call or text away if you need me."

"I know. I just got used to you being here. I liked it," Jaycee said and forced a smile to her lips as her friend pulled out of the driveway and honked the horn twice in farewell before driving away.

While perusing the bookcase in his living room, Jeremy pulled out the only cookbook from the small load of belongings he'd had shipped to his Larkin Bay apartment. After flipping it open, he saw that one page was so well-read that the book fell open to it in his hands.

Smiling sadly, he realized he was looking down at Marianne's well-loved spaghetti sauce recipe. He sighed while remembering how his young wife would spend what seemed like forever in the grocery store picking up, squeezing, and then rejecting many fine-looking tomatoes until she found exactly the right ones for her sauce. In the silliest ways, she had been a perfectionist, and he had loved her little quirks because they had made her the unique and lovable person she had been.

As he read through the directions, Jeremy smiled at the memories they inspired. After a few minutes, he also noticed how this recipe was similar to what he had seen Jaycee prepare the night before. She and Jeremy had seen each other a few times since their dinner out, and last night, she had made spaghetti for him, Betty, and Chandra.

His smile brightened as he recalled how she had slapped his hand away when he had tried to dip a spoon into the pot to taste her sauce.

"Not yet," Jaycee had cried, "it's not done, and you can't taste the magic until it's properly simmered!"

The rest of the night, Jeremy had teased her about the magic in her sauce, and she had responded to his banter by good-naturedly pestering him right back about the state of his Boston baseball cap. He had worn the hat throughout the dinner she had carefully prepared, claiming that the Red Sox would lose next season's opening game if he took it off.

He'd enjoyed every minute they'd spent together.

Closing the cookbook slowly, he placed it back on the bookshelf. He smiled and laughed a lot whenever he was around Jaycee.

Marianne, he decided, would have liked that—she would have liked that a lot.

Chapter Twenty

"Thanks for letting me have my friends sleep over tonight," Chandra said to her sister.

Jaycee nodded as she wiped the top of the TV with a dust cloth. "I'm glad you invited them," she replied, turning to straighten the cushions on the couch while Chandra used a small handheld vacuum to suck up the cat hair stuck to its arms. "Betty told me they used to be here all the time, and she was actually a little worried because she hasn't seen them as much lately. I hope it's not because of me that they're not coming around."

"No." Chandra bit her bottom lip. "I think it's because I've been spending so much time with Dean, honestly. I don't think they like him much."

Jaycee frowned over at her sister. "They don't like him, or they don't like you not having as much free time to spend with them?"

"Honestly, both, I think."

"Huh." Jaycee picked up a pile of magazines off the floor and stacked them on the coffee table before sitting on the edge of the couch. Picking up a throw pillow, she placed it in her lap, her fingers twisting through its tassels.

Chandra turned off the vacuum. "I'm not sure how it all happened, actually. I just know when I was out with him, I saw the group of girls who used to be my best friends, but when I went over to talk to them, I didn't feel welcome anymore."

"Oh?"

"Yeah, and it made me sad but angry too, you know? So I thought I should have them over and talk about it. We used to be really close and go everywhere together. I just want it to be like that again. I mean, I want to be close to them but date Dean too. I want us all to be friends."

Jaycee frowned. "It's hard to juggle these things sometimes. But I think talking to them about how you're feeling is a good way to start. You know what they say, boyfriends come and go, but girlfriends are forever."

Chandra looked away.

Jaycee gentled her tone. "I bet their feelings have just been hurt. I think it's great that you're going to let them know they're important to you, and that you miss them."

Chandra blinked hard and looked back at her sister. "I really *do* miss them."

Jaycee got to her feet and punched the pillow she had been holding back into shape before setting it down. "Well, make sure you tell *them* that."

Chandra pursed her lips but didn't reply.

Jaycee sighed. "You finish up in here. I'm going to go and make some Hello Dolly bars and then clean up the kitchen."

"Yum." A small smile crept across Chandra's face.

"Yeah, I hope so. Make sure you bring the girls in when they get here so I can use them as taste testers."

Chandra grinned. "I think they'll like that."

"Good. It'll be interesting to see what they think, and I'm going to need lots of practice before I open the bakery, so invite them over as much as you want."

"I'm happy to taste test everything I can. I'm sure all my friends will be too."

"Perfect." Jaycee laughed and the sisters exchanged a quick grin before each turned away to get on with their tasks.

An hour later, Chandra's girlfriends arrived and Lyndsy and Willa flopped down on pillows on the floor of Chandra's bedroom. Sharing TikToks and magazine articles, they watched Chandra do Rachel's hair and makeup at her desk in the corner of the room.

Lyndsey was lying on her back, holding a magazine in the air above her head while flipping through its pages. "I can't believe what they dress these models in," she said. "Why can't they just put them in normal clothes?"

"I think it's like art, made just for admiring—not real life. If you want to see stuff we can actually wear, you need to watch TikToks and look at the girls on there that get free stuff," Willa said.

Lyndsey flipped over and frowned. "I wonder how they get it all? I mean, they get tons of expensive stuff for nothing just so they'll talk about it for thirty seconds. Can you even imagine how cool that would be?"

"You could probably get things, Chandy," Rachel declared, looking up from the magazine in her lap and shaking her head to make the curls Chandra was creating bounce. "I mean, you've been suggesting clothes and makeup for all of us since we were little kids. I bet the product people would love you using their stuff and showing it off to everyone."

Chandra squinted and studied Rachel's hair in the mirror she'd propped up on the desk. She shrugged. "I *was* thinking about doing a few makeover videos for my college portfolios."

"You should!" exclaimed Lyndsey.

"I don't know. I'd probably look all clumsy and weird in them. I don't think I'm very good in front of a camera."

Willa struggled to a sitting position from her nest of pillows on the floor and shook her head. "That's not true. We did that Shakespeare recording for English class and you were great. The best in it by far. Everyone said so. You're just too hard on yourself."

"All you need is some practice. I think you'd be great too. And think how cool it would be to get free stuff," Rachel added.

Chandra shook her head. "Nah, you have to be a natural, and that's not me."

Willa got to her feet. "Let's try. You can finish styling Rachel, and I'll record you doing it on my phone." She frowned and looked around the bedroom. "Do you have a floor lamp anywhere? We need more light. And let's pull the desk away from the wall so I can walk around you and get a full panoramic view of what you're doing."

Rachel's hands fluttered to her cheeks. "Not me! Not like this. I won't look good on camera at all." Her mouth pulled down in a pout.

"You're perfect," Willa said, placing both hands on her hips. "Everyone wants to see real people being made up to look beautiful and you always look great when Chandra is done." She turned to leave the room. "I'm going to find a lamp."

A few minutes later, the other girls had dragged the desk to the middle of the room and covered it with a sheet. Betty appeared while they were setting up and stood in the doorway, watching with a smile as Chandra put together some clothing options for Rachel on the bed to wear while filming.

"I can't wait to see how you look," Betty exclaimed, beaming at them.

Once Rachel had changed her clothes, she donned a faded floral robe to act as a cape. After she had taken her seat in the desk chair again, the living room lamp Willa had lugged upstairs was plugged in and adjusted to shine on Chandra. Before they began taping, Betty hugged each of the girls. "I've missed seeing all of you," she exclaimed. "I'm so glad you're all here together tonight."

The girls glanced at each other for a long moment before Willa shrugged and hugged Betty back. "We're all glad to be here again too. I hear you're spending more time with the grandkids, Betty. Is it weird not living here now?" she asked.

Betty shook her head and smiled. "No, it's time I went my own way. Besides, I see Chandra and Jaycee all the time. I enjoy having my place and my own little garden again too. I'm so blessed my daughter is letting me rent the condo she owns. It's much easier to look after than this big place," she said, beaming at them all.

"I can understand that," Willa said. Tilting her head to one side, she smiled as she looked back at Betty. "Chandra, why don't you do a makeover on Betty too, once you're done with Rachel? I bet there are tons of people on TikTok who'd love to see someone as pretty as her on there."

Betty laughed. "Oh, no. I'm not doing anything like that. You girls have fun, though. I'm going to help Jaycee bake her squares. That's much more my speed."

"You're not going to stream this live, are you?" asked Rachel, shifting on the desk chair and holding up one hand to block some of the light from the lamp shining in her eyes.

"No. Don't worry. I'll just make a video that we can edit and upload later. You can see it before we share it," replied Willa with a grin. She took a step back and held up her phone. "Okay, Chandra, start explaining what you're doing and don't worry about what you say too much. We'll edit out anything that makes you sound stupid later."

Chandra looked over at her with wide eyes. Opening and closing her mouth, she gulped, then took a deep breath and picked up a hairbrush. After holding it in the air for a long moment, she began brushing Rachel's hair and talking.

Chandra and her friends thundered down the stairs, causing Jaycee and Betty to smile at each other over the pans of squares they had just finished cutting in the kitchen. "Perfect timing," Jaycee declared, and the other woman nodded in agreement.

Jaycee placed the last of the baked goods onto a platter before turning away to get a jug of milk from the refrigerator and a set of glasses from the cupboard behind her.

"Hello, we hear you need tasters!" Willa declared, charging into the kitchen, closely followed by the other girls. "And you should see the video we did of Chandra. She was fantastic. And look at how good Rachel looks!"

Jaycee smiled at the group of young women, happy to see all the teens were smiling and that Willa was still the beautiful, talkative girl that she remembered from when she had babysat her and her younger brother.

"Show me," Jaycee demanded.

A moment later, the video was pulled up and the entire group gathered around to watch the clip of Chandra styling Rachel's hair and makeup. "After we're done helping you here, we're going to tape some more footage of Chandra helping Rachel choose an outfit for a date or something."

"That sounds great."

"Yeah, Rachel is fantastic at editing this stuff. When she's done, I'll put it all up on Chandra's new TikTok account on Monday morning. We just need to come up with a name for it."

"Why are you waiting until Monday?" asked Betty, motioning for the girls to sit down at the kitchen island. Once they were settled, she placed milk glasses and a plate in front of each of them.

"Most TikTok users access the app daily, but they are on there mostly in the morning and later at night," answered Rachel matter-of-factly as she took a seat and picked up a glass. "So it's best when you're starting a new account to post then so you get as many people as you can to see it."

"Makes sense," said Jaycee. "Remind me to hire you when I'm trying to grow the social media accounts for the bakery."

Rachel nodded. "I'd be happy to help. I think working with social marketing apps is really interesting. You can use them to reach lots of people—it'd be a great way to drum up business for your shop."

Jaycee smiled at her serious expression. "That's good to know. I'd love to hear more. But right now, I need a different type of help. I've made two different magic bars. I need you to taste one of each and see if you can tell me what the differences are. Then I want to know which one you like better." She smacked Chandra's hand as the teen reached out. "Hey, let your friends go first," she admonished, waving a playful finger at her.

Chandra blushed. "Hurry then, everyone—I'm hungry," she said, sitting back in her chair.

A short time later, the friends had tasted the squares, drank the milk, and discussed the pros and cons of both recipes. "Well, that wasn't a lot of help," Jaycee said to Betty after the girls had trooped back upstairs. "They liked everything. And it was equally split between them as to which one I should sell."

"So do the simpler one for the first few months and see how that goes. You can always add the second bar to your offerings later."

"Sounds like a good plan," Jaycee replied as she packed up a small container of treats to pass on to Jeremy when she saw him the next morning. "It'll be so much easier when I can do the baking in my own shop."

"It won't be long now," Betty said, giving her a long hug. "Soon, your dream will be a reality."

Jaycee smiled as the sprites gave a happy cheer and cartwheeled in her stomach.

I can't wait!

Chapter Twenty-One

"Mom? Are you okay? What's going on?" Jeremy took the front steps of his sister's house two at a time as he tried to determine from his mother's expression how bad things were. He could see her brow was furrowed, and she was picking at the cuff of her sweater while peering out at him from behind the screen door.

"Jenny told me I needed to come over quickly and then wouldn't answer any of my texts or pick up my calls. What's going on? I came as soon as I could," he said as he came to a stop just outside the screen door.

His mother sighed and pushed open the door. Stepping out, she let the screen swing closed behind her and met him on the top flagstone step. Placing one finger on her lips, she glanced over her shoulder and made a soft shushing sound. "It's okay, Jeremy. Nothing's wrong. The girls just wanted you to come over for a visit."

Jeremy stared at his mother. "What? Why? Nothing's wrong?"

His mother blushed. "Well, they don't seem to think you spend enough time with the family. But that said, I also don't think they should be scaring you. I told them just to call you, not to do this."

He blinked. "What are you talking about? Is everything okay?"

"Everything's fine, love. Just come in and let's have a quick visit, okay?" She reached behind her to open the screen door and waved for him to follow her inside.

Jeremy frowned and didn't move. "What's going on, Ma?"

"Nothing. Your sisters just wanted you to come by and spend time with us, that's all."

Jeremy pondered this for a minute, then sighed. "They've got someone here they want me to meet, don't they?"

His mother flushed. "Well, they do have a nice girl visiting. She's a friend of Jaylyn's, and she seems very nice. I don't know much about her, though."

"Mom, I told all of you that when I'm ready to date someone, I'll find them myself.

"Well, since you've brought no one around, I guess your sisters thought they'd help. I don't think they believed you when you mentioned that girl you run with. And they just want you to be happy. They worry about you being all alone."

Jeremy closed his eyes for a second and then retreated back down the front steps.

"Jeremy." His mother's voice was pleading. He paused and looked back to see she was holding out one hand.

He sighed heavily. "Oh, all right. I'll come in. But don't expect me to be nice."

She pursed her lips and frowned. "I don't expect it, Jeremiah. I *know* you'll be nice."

Jeremy sighed and glared at his mother's back as he followed her into the house.

He was tired. The drive from Larkin Bay would usually only take him forty minutes, but it had taken considerably longer today because of the heavy rain that was changing to slush and snow. The commute had also been unpleasant because he'd been worried the whole way that something was seriously wrong. His expression must have reflected his displeasure, as his mother bit her lip and didn't meet his eye as he stalked past her.

Heading straight into the living room, where he heard voices, Jeremy shoved both hands in his uniform pants' front pockets and tried to arrange a more pleasant expression on his face. Whoever this girl was that his family wanted him to meet, it wasn't her fault that he'd been brought here under false pretenses. Maybe she had been too. Stopping in the doorway to his sister's living room, he leaned against the door frame and tapped one foot as he looked around.

Jaylyn sat in one corner of the room, conversing with a woman he didn't know on the sofa. Jenny was hovering to one side.

"Hi," said Amber, hurrying past him from the kitchen and sliding into a chair on the far side of the room. Jeremy shot a glare at her, knowing she had taken this position so she could see not only him but also her sisters. Once she was settled, she peered over her glass of water and a faint smile crept across her lips as she winked at him. He scowled back. Even if she had nothing to do with this, he was annoyed at her for not calling to warn him about it.

She has no right to look so entertained.

Their silent interaction caught the attention of Jenny, who turned and narrowed her eyes for a second while studying Amber. She then slowly turned and focused her gaze on Jeremy. A predatory expression crept across her face, and he groaned quietly as she hurried over to him.

"Hey, little brother," she cooed. "Thanks for dropping in."

"Really, Jenny? Did I have a choice?" he asked quietly. "I thought there was a problem—like something serious had happened to one of you or Mom. And you know what, Jenn? I'm kind of annoyed right now. There is a lot of work I need to get done today and it's serious stuff. I don't have time for a tea party with my sisters." He sighed and gentled his tone. "So just tell me straight out. Is everything okay?"

His sister flushed and dropped her eyes to study her shoes.

"Jenn?"

She sighed, then took his hand and towed him over to where a pretty brunette was talking to Jaylyn. The two women broke off their conversation, and tilted their heads to one side as they looked up.

"Hi? Everything okay?" Jaylyn asked, her forehead scrunching as she frowned at her siblings. "Jeremy, have you met my friend Darcy before? She had the room next to mine in college."

He nodded curtly. "Hello."

Jaylyn frowned at his tone. "Darcy's staying with me for a few days while she looks for a place to live. She just took a job in the city but likes the small-town life, so is planning on working remotely."

Darcy smiled. "Nice to meet you, Jeremy. I didn't realize Jaylyn had a brother."

"The one and only. We have many sisters in this family," he answered quickly. "But I just stopped by for a minute to pick up some things from Julie. I have to get back to work. It's nice to meet you, Darcy."

She smiled and nodded up at him.

"You should get Darcy's number, Jeremy. She's single and doesn't know anyone here in town. I thought it would be nice if you showed her around," Jenny blurted out.

Jeremy sighed. "Oh. Well, I'd be happy to help in any way I can, but I'm sort of seeing someone, so it's not really appropriate." He immediately smacked himself on the forehead when he realized what he had said.

"What?" Jenny exclaimed and grabbed his arm.

"Who?" demanded Julie.

"Since when?" Jaylyn asked, setting her wineglass down on the table in front of her with a bang.

"This is so great," Amber declared as she got up from her seat and clapped both hands. "Tell us all about her."

Jeremy felt the blood rush to his face. "There's nothing to tell."

Julie's eyes narrowed as she studied her brother. "I don't believe you."

"Well, she's really terrific. And I've already told you a bit about her. She's the woman I run with. And for now, that's all I'm willing to share. And so, since everyone seems to be well here, I'll be on my way. I have work to do," he said, giving Jenny a pointed look.

She blushed.

"Why don't you sit and stay for a bit, Jeremy," his mother said, touching his arm. "I'd love to catch up."

"Sorry, Mom. Maybe next week," he said, giving her a quick hug before turning back to Darcy, who had been watching the conversation playing out in front of her with an entertained expression. "Nice to meet you, Darcy. I'm sure I'll see you again."

"Thank you. You too. And hopefully you'll cause a stir the next time too. It's fun to watch," she replied, giving him a small wave along with an amused smile before he turned away and hurried out the door.

Looking up at the dark sky, Jeremy sniffed the damp air around him. He was happy to see the thick gray clouds were moving out. He'd had enough of driving in this damp weather. Pulling his coat a little tighter against the chill in the air, he started toward his car. He'd only gotten partway back when he heard footsteps hurrying down the steps behind him.

"Jeremy, wait up for a second." He turned and frowned when he saw Amber was following him.

He glanced at his phone to check the time. "What's up, Amber? I have a lot to do today."

She reached out and gently punched his arm. "Hey, don't be mad at me. I had nothing to do with this. When they demanded I come over, I actually thought they were trying to set *me* up with someone. They do it all the time, you know. I was actually kind of relieved that it was you for a change."

Jeremy chuckled. "Really? That's awful. I only came over because I thought something had happened to Mom."

Amber grinned. "Yeah, but in their defense, I don't think they realized that's what you were thinking until you arrived. Which is kind of stupid because what else would make you rush here like that? I'm sure they all feel guilty now."

Jeremy frowned and glanced back at the house. "Well, they probably should, even though part of me doesn't want them to."

"Fair enough. But I'm still happy to hear that you're seeing someone."

Jeremy shifted his weight from one foot to the other. "Thank you. Like I said, it's early going still. But I really like her."

"That's so great."

"Yeah. How's your book going?"

Amber laughed at the obvious change of subject. "Good. It's early going with it too." The smile on her face faded. "But tell me something. How did you know you were ready to start seeing someone again?"

Jeremy sighed and looked down at his little sister. Amber had broken up with her high school sweetheart the year before, a young man she had dated for years. They had even gotten engaged and then she'd surprised her family a few weeks later when she'd suddenly announced she had ended the relationship.

"I don't really know. It just sort of happened. I met her, and there was a spark between us. Different from what I had with Marianne, but a pull nonetheless. She's nice too, and hardworking and a good person. I think you'll all like her."

Amber smiled up at him, but her eyes were sad. "She sounds wonderful. Maybe one day that'll happen to me too."

"It will. When the time is right."

"I hope so. And you know, Marianne would be happy that you met someone you liked. Dad would have been too." A silence stretched out between them as they both contemplated the truth of her statement.

"Yeah, I guess. But it's just hard too, you know?"

"I can understand that. But Marianne also loved you enough that she'd want you to find someone else and be happy."

Jeremy reached over and hugged his sister, but didn't reply.

Amber smiled at him. "Well, I should go back in there and eavesdrop on all the plans they're making to find out who this mystery woman is that you're dating. The good news is this might stop them from focusing on me quitting my job and writing my book for a few hours."

Jeremy grimaced. "Glad to have helped. But let me know what they're planning so I can set up a counter-offensive."

Amber grinned. "Maybe, big brother, but all this insider information is gonna cost you."

"I don't doubt that at all," he replied and, after punching her lightly on the arm, headed back to his car with a lighter step. It felt good to tell his family about Jaycee. Getting behind the wheel, he whistled happily and wondered what she was doing and if he should call her now or wait until he got home. He smiled as he realized he suddenly had a powerful craving for peanut butter cookies.

Chapter Twenty-Two

Jaycee opened the front door and immediately stepped back, her eyes wide when she saw who was standing on her front porch.

"Rhonda?" she exclaimed, her voice high with surprise as she stared at the other woman.

"Hi, Jaycee," she replied. "Yeah, it's me. Uh, is it okay if I come in? I want to talk to you." She then grimaced and touched her rounded belly. "And is it possible to use your bathroom? I really need to pee. This baby has been jumping on my bladder for the last hour, and I'm ready to pop."

"Oh, sure," Jaycee replied, fumbling for a second with the door latch, then holding the screen open. Waving down the hallway, she flattened herself against the wall so the other woman could fit in the narrow space alongside her. "The bathroom is just down the hall there. Help yourself," she said. She bit her bottom lip as she watched Rhonda waddle away.

A few minutes later, Rhonda reappeared in the hallway, looking far more comfortable. "Can I get you anything? Tea or water?" Jaycee asked. Rhonda had gained some weight since she had last seen her, not surprising since she was pregnant, but she also had gray shadows under her eyes and lines around her mouth that Jaycee was positive hadn't been there a few months prior.

"Tea would be great, thank you. I won't stay long. I just wanted to talk to you for a few minutes," she replied with a grateful smile. Jaycee motioned to the living room, where Rhonda immediately sank into a chair and put her feet up on the footstool in front of her. She sighed in relief as she shrugged off her coat.

Jaycee hurried back to the kitchen, put fresh water in the kettle, and filled a small platter with an assortment of cookies and squares. Once the tray was complete, she smoothed her hair back in its ponytail and reminded herself that Rhonda was no longer her boss. If she started being nasty, Jaycee could just kick her out. Fixing a pleasant expression on her face, she picked up the tray and lifted her chin before heading back into the living room.

After setting the platter down on the coffee table, she looked over at Rhonda. "The tea will be a few more minutes," she told her, handing her an empty plate and napkin. "But help yourself to a few cookies."

Rhonda struggled to raise herself forward. She nodded as she looked at the desserts in front of her. "This looks lovely, thank you," she replied.

"I hope you find something you like."

"I'm sure it's all wonderful," Rhonda said, popping a cookie in her mouth. She set down her plate and looked around the room. "You have a lovely place. It's so homey."

Jaycee bit back a laugh. She couldn't help but smile as she looked over at Rhonda's couture maternity dress and considered how it contrasted with the pretty but inexpensive velvet armchair she was sitting in. "Thank you. I grew up in this house. I've been trying to move the decorating up into the twenty-first century, but it takes a lot of time to get things the way one wants, and we're on a bit of a tight budget."

She then motioned for her guest to stay seated as she went back into the kitchen and finished making a pot of tea. When she returned, she settled into a chair across from Rhonda, poured out two cups of the herbal mixture, and handed one to her guest.

Rhonda sighed and closed her eyes. Holding her warm teacup close, she curled back into the chair. "This is really comfortable," she said. "Fits into the small of my back perfectly."

Jaycee smiled over the rim of her teacup. "Well, stay there for as long as you like; I'm sure the baby won't mind. You could even have a nap."

Rhonda's eyes snapped open at her remark. "You're being so nice, and honestly, you have no reason to be. I wasn't always that pleasant to you." A blush rose to her cheeks. "I'm sorry for that."

Jaycee nodded slowly. "That's okay. It seems like a long time ago now."

"It really does."

They both drank their tea in silence for a moment.

"Aren't you wondering why I'm here?" Rhonda finally asked.

Jaycee shrugged and leaned over to straighten the pile of napkins on the table in front of her. "A little, maybe, but I thought you'd tell me when you'd had more time to rest. I'm not in any hurry. You've apologized and, looking back, most of the heartache I experienced in the city was because of Tony, not anything you did. Honestly, I see you as the injured party here too, not just me."

Rhonda's face fell. "So he did have an affair with you?"

Jaycee bit her lip before responding. "An affair? No, I wouldn't call it that. I mean, neither of us were married." She grimaced as she looked down at the napkin she was holding. "At least, I wasn't. I only found out later how much he was lying to me."

"How long were you two seeing each other?"

Jaycee met her gaze steadily. "Just over a year. And I honestly thought it was an exclusive relationship. It was a bit of a shock to learn you were pregnant and he was the father."

Rhonda nodded. "It was a bit of a shock to me to find out that he was seeing you too. We weren't dating for very long before I got pregnant." She blushed. "I guess I should have figured it out, though. He never wanted to talk about our relationship at work and never introduced me to any of his friends." She frowned. "And now I've just discovered that while I've been busy planning our wedding, he's been seeing another woman too."

Jaycee's hand flew to cover her mouth, causing the napkin and cookies she had been holding to tumble to the floor. "Really?" She looked at Rhonda with wide eyes, her mouth twisting in distress.

No matter how much she hadn't liked Rhonda, no one deserved this.

"I'm so sorry."

Rhonda looked up at the ceiling and blinked her eyes rapidly. "Thank you. And thank you for being so kind."

"How can I help?"

Rhonda shook her head. "Truthfully? You can't. I was just looking for you to confirm what Lisa had told me. Funny, I'd never really liked her, but she's been a good person and a lot of help over the last few days. No one else seemed to want to tell me what Tony was up to, but she told me as soon as she found out about his other girlfriend. It was hard to hear, but better to know before the wedding, especially because of the baby, you know?"

Jaycee nodded. "I think you should stay here tonight. All of this is a shock, and you shouldn't drive back; you must be exhausted."

"Thank you. But it's okay. I had my sister drive up with me. She's booked us a room at a hotel in Ellenville and then we're going to spend a few days with family in the area. It's really pretty here."

"You're not alone, then?"

"No, I had to bring Marge to help with the drive and get her away from Tony. She was threatening to kill him." A shaky smile passed over her lips. "She's waiting outside in the car."

Jaycee got to her feet and waved to Rhonda to stay seated as she hurried out the front door and down the front steps toward her car. Her step hitched and her heart fluttered happily when she saw Jeremy was standing at the driver's side window talking to the woman sitting inside.

"Hello," Jaycee said to Marge before kissing Jeremy on the cheek. "It's nice to see you again so soon," she said to him and ran a finger quickly down the buttons of his coat before turning back to the car window.

"Hi, Marge? I'm Jaycee. Please come into the house. I didn't realize you were out here or I would have invited you in sooner. Rhonda is having some tea. Can I get you some too, or maybe something stronger?" She turned back to Jeremy. "Is your mom okay? I didn't realize you were back from your visit. That was quick. Do you want to come in too? It's cold out here."

Marge looked at them both for a long moment before shrugging and opening her car door. "I'd be happy to get out of this car for a bit." She frowned. "Is Rhonda okay?" she asked.

Jaycee nodded. "She's fine. A little upset by what I had to tell her, but other than that, I think she's okay. Go on in. She's in the living room."

As Rhonda's sister hurried up the stairs into the house, Jeremy drew Jaycee into a hug. "What's that all about?" he asked, rubbing her arms to keep her warm.

"Oh, you remember Tony? This is just more consequences of his idiocy." She waved a hand in the air. "I'm fine, though. I just feel sorry for all the other women involved with him."

"Maybe I'll come back later, then, after they're gone," Jeremy said, looking up at the house with a troubled frown.

Jaycee nodded. "Probably not a bad idea. Maybe I'll take them out to dinner and then call you? They've got a hotel room but Rhonda looks really tired, so I doubt they'll be staying out late."

"Sounds good," Jeremy replied, pulling her close and bringing his lips to hers for a long moment. "Unless you need me, then I can stay."

Jaycee sighed and wrapped her arms around his neck. "I'm beginning to feel like I'll always need you," she replied. "And as much as I'd rather be with you tonight, I think I maybe need to help Rhonda sort a few things out. I'll call you later."

Jeremy smiled at her and trailed one finger down her cheek. "You need me? No, I need you. And maybe later, when you're all done here, we can talk more about how we want to manage that."

"I think that's an excellent idea," Jaycee replied and kissed him again. He held her tightly for a long moment before she pulled away. Giving her a regretful smile, Jeremy made his way over to his car. When he reached the driver's side door, he looked back and waved. Jaycee blew him a kiss and watched him drive away before turning and hurrying back into the house, realizing that even though he'd just left, she already missed him.

Chapter Twenty-Three

Jaycee bolted upright in bed as the shrill ringtone of her phone sounded. Fumbling on the bedside table to find it, she glanced at her alarm clock and struggled to take in the time. It was just after three o'clock in the morning.

Who would call me at this hour?

Locating her shrieking phone, she glanced at the call display and pressed the accept button.

"Hello?"

"Jaycee?"

"Yes?" Jaycee's tone reflected her bewilderment. She sat up in bed and shook her head to clear it. "Betty? What is it? What's wrong? Are you okay?"

"Well, no, not really. I mean, *I* am," came the quivering reply. "And I don't mean to alarm you unnecessarily, but I thought I should tell you what's happening."

"Okay?" Jaycee frowned and rubbed her eyes.

"Billy, my son—you know how he sometimes volunteers for the Larkin Bay Fire Department? Just a few minutes ago, he got a call to help tonight because there's a fire. And it's a big one."

Jaycee gasped.

"And, hon? It's on Lake Street. Jaycee, I think your bakery might be on fire!"

Later, Jaycee couldn't remember how she ended the conversation. She assumed she had thanked Betty and disconnected the call, but afterward, all she could recall was hearing one word.

Fire.

Her bakery was on fire.

She reached for the clothes she'd worn the day before that were folded over the back of her desk chair and threw them on as quickly as she could. Running from her bedroom, she hesitated only for a moment in the hallway before going down the stairs, deciding not to stop and wake Chandra until she knew exactly what was going on. Grabbing her bag, she slammed the front door closed behind her and, cursing the fact that she had left the car with Danny overnight to install winter tires, started running through the silent, empty streets toward her bakery.

After a few blocks, she slowed her pace long enough to fumble through her handbag and dig out her cell phone. Forcing herself to take deep breaths, she choked back her panic and stabbed out Jeremy's number, only to be immediately connected to his voicemail.

She moaned in frustration, then quickly clicked Amanda's number. It took three tries before her sleepy friend finally picked up the phone.

"It might not be the bakery. Don't panic yet," her friend responded calmly to the fear in Jaycee's voice.

"Do you really think so?" Jaycee's tone was hopeful as she pressed the phone closer to her cheek and hurried down a dark side street toward her shop.

"Let's find out. I'm going to get in the car right now, and I'll meet you there. Try not to do anything rash, and please, be careful. I'll be there as quick as I can."

As tears clogged her throat, Jaycee shook her head in agreement.

"Jaycee?" Amanda said sharply. "Do you hear me? I'm coming, and it's going to be okay. Just hold on until I get there."

"Okay."

Jaycee disconnected the call and fought back more tears as she increased her pace, skidding to a stop when she reached Larkin Bay's usually tranquil Main Street.

She raised a hand to cover her mouth at what she saw. Flashing lights and police cars were parked parallel across the intersections, effectively closing off any access to the downtown area. Talking her way around the first barricade, she moved quickly down the next street before being stopped again by the police officer at the next blockade.

"I'm sorry, I know you're worried, but it just isn't safe to go any further," the officer told her with an apologetic frown.

Jaycee nodded and pulled the bulky jacket she was wearing a little closer as she stepped to one side of the cruiser. A few minutes later, when the police officer was busy speaking with another pedestrian, she ducked down and slipped by the police car to continue her journey.

When she reached the end of the street, she turned the corner and stumbled to a stop. The night sky was lit up by the portable spotlights the police had set up, and the street buzzed with the crackle of fire and the frantic work of the volunteer firefighters. As the smell of smoke and burning debris assaulted her nose and ears, Jaycee instinctively raised her hands to cover them.

Firefighters and police were everywhere. Some were busy unrolling hoses and hooking them up to hydrants, while others were dousing the buildings with fire-retardant foam. The library, pharmacy, and art gallery glowed eerily under the thick white protective covering. Looking down, Jaycee tried to lessen the impact of the smell and heat but was blinded momentarily when the wind turned and thick smoke filled the air. Knuckling away tears, she crouched down and slowly crept around the corner of Main and Lake Street. As she moved toward her store, she prayed silently that it had been spared. She'd only moved a short distance when another uniformed police officer appeared from the haze and grabbed her roughly by the arm.

"Hey there!" he shouted. "You can't go that way. What are you even doing here? This is a restricted area. I need you to evacuate up the street to a safer location."

"But I need to get to Lake Street," Jaycee pleaded, peering up at him. "I'm the owner of the new bakery that's ready to open just around the corner. I have to see what's happening and find out if I can save anything!"

The officer frowned at her sympathetically but replied in a no-nonsense tone, "I'm sorry. I know you're worried, but I just can't let you go any further. It really isn't safe, and you're not even supposed to be here. This entire area was cleared of all nonessential personnel hours ago."

He gripped her arm tightly as he firmly escorted her back the way she had come, finally delivering her to a relieved Amanda, who gave a thankful cry when she saw Jaycee. "I'm sorry we weren't here sooner," she cried. "But we needed to wait for Danny's parents to come and stay with the baby. He didn't want me coming down here alone, and I didn't think it was safe to bring her."

Jaycee nodded and pressed her lips into a firm line to ensure she maintained control.

Amanda sighed. "It'll be okay, hon," she said, reaching over to hug her friend. A moment later, a gust of wind brought the smell of ash and smoke wafting over them, causing Amanda to wrinkle her nose in distaste while Jaycee rubbed her burning eyes.

"Are you okay?" asked Danny. He and the policeman looked over at the women in concern.

"I'm fine," Jaycee sputtered out. "But have you heard anything yet? Is the fire under control?"

"Not yet," the police officer replied grimly. "I'm hearing that it's spreading the fastest near the park right now. So, many of the stores by the lake where your bakery is located, so far at least, haven't been too badly affected. Did you have a good sprinkler system installed yet?"

Jaycee nodded.

"Well, that should help minimize the damage to your shop. But sprinkler systems can flood businesses too."

Their conversation was interrupted as some garbled instructions came through on the police radio. Scowling, the police officer confirmed he understood the orders and, after placing his radio into his belt's holster, turned back to address the friends. "Now, I'm afraid I must ask you to move further up the street," he said. "I've been ordered to close off this area."

"But—"

The police officer took in Jaycee's tearful expression and gentled his tone. "I'm sorry about your bakery. And I'm sorry I can't let you get closer to see it, but right now, it just isn't safe."

Amanda squeezed Jaycee's hand reassuringly.

"I think we should leave," Danny announced, pulling his wife closer to him when he saw she was shivering from the cold. "We can keep vigil at my garage; it's not far from here."

Amanda nodded her agreement. "At least there I can make us some fresh, hot coffee and we'll have a warm place to wait while the firefighters take care of things out here." She looked over at Jaycee hopefully.

"I can also turn on the TV, and we can see what's being reported there," Danny added.

Jaycee looked in the direction of her bakery, then sighed heavily and hung her head as she allowed Amanda to take her by the arm and lead her away.

After a short walk, they arrived at Danny's garage. Amanda immediately dragged Jaycee into the customer lounge and made her sit on the small leather couch in the corner of the room.

"You two try to warm up. I'll see what I can find on the news about the fire. I'm sure the local station will be doing a live broadcast," Danny said as he searched for the remote.

Amanda picked up a throw and wrapped it around Jaycee's shoulders. After turning up the room's thermostat, she started the small coffee maker in the corner kitchenette and, a short time later, had poured them all mugs of strong black coffee. Handing one to Jaycee and then to her husband, Amanda sat down between them and the three friends watched in silence as a firefighter on the news station described what was being done to keep the blaze under control. When he had finished his report, the reporter announced she would be interviewing a police officer working at the scene next. Jaycee gasped as the camera panned out and Jeremy appeared next to the woman.

What's he doing there?

Jaycee's hand flew to cover her mouth as her heart sank.

"Oh no! I can't believe that Jeremy has already been called in to investigate. That means this was arson again, doesn't it?" Amanda cried, echoing Jaycee's thoughts.

Frowning, Danny picked up the remote and tapped the volume button a few times to turn up the sound.

"Not necessarily. He could just be helping out with the investigation."

"You think so?"

Danny shrugged as he looked over at Jaycee. "Yeah, it's probably too early for anyone to know whether this fire was caused by arson. Let's just listen to what's being reported, and then I'll see if I can reach him on his phone. Maybe he can tell us more."

"I've been texting him. He's not responding."

Danny shot her a compassionate look. "He's probably really busy."

On the TV, the journalist doing the interview was standing close to Jeremy, her slight frame almost tucked under his chin as she flashed a bright smile up at him and asked for his assessment of the situation. Jaycee felt a jolt of yearning, followed by a wail of jealousy from the sprites in her stomach. But, she reminded herself, both the pretty young reporter and Jeremy were just doing their jobs, and in the middle of this calamity, she could hardly be petty enough to worry about who was standing close to whom. Shaking her head, she pushed aside her feelings and focused on what they were saying.

"I was out supporting the local foot patrol officers when I smelled smoke and called the Larkin Bay Fire Department," Jeremy stated, running a hand through his hair and looking straight at the camera.

Jeremy reported the fire?

Jaycee's eyes widened, and she leaned forward to see what else she could learn. She sighed when she saw how his strong shoulders were slumped in fatigue.

"Can you tell me if any of the local businesses' fire sprinklers were activated?" the reporter asked.

He shrugged. "I don't know yet. They may have been. It's simply too soon in the investigation to know for sure. But I can tell you that many of the shops had early-warning fire systems, and these will hopefully help minimize the damage."

Jaycee nodded, remembering how she had just spent thousands of dollars installing fire sprinklers in the bakery. If what Jeremy told the reporter was true, then maybe the systems she had bought *would* be helping.

"Arson is a scary and heartbreaking crime," Jeremy was saying. "I'm in Larkin Bay to work with the police department to catch the criminals responsible for it. I can't tell you too much about this fire yet, but I can assure you that we will continue to hunt down anyone who threatens this town. We won't let an arsonist destroy Larkin Bay."

As the journalist signed off, there was a long panning shot that stopped for a moment on Jeremy's troubled expression before moving on to show thick black smoke billowing out from behind darkened storefronts on Lake Street. The pictures stopped just short of showing Jaycee's bakery, but she knew, as tears trickled down her cheeks, that she had to prepare herself to accept the worst.

Everything I've been working for is probably gone.

Chapter Twenty-Four

Jaycee's yawn was wide and her steps were heavy as she pulled herself up her home's front porch stairs. She'd been up most of the night, but still knew very little about the state of her bakery. Both she and Danny had tried to contact Jeremy, but he'd only sent a quick text in response, letting them know he was okay and would be in touch soon.

She had gone back to the police blockade closest to her bakery but wasn't permitted past. "Please call as soon as it's safe for me to check on things," Jaycee had begged the officers securing the area. After extracting from them a solemn promise that they would, she'd finally allowed Danny to drive her home.

Unlocking the front door to her house, Jaycee let herself in and was surprised when she saw the kitchen was tidy, the drapes in the living room were still drawn tightly closed, and the pillows on the couch were plumped and perfectly set in place. After such an emotionally charged night, it didn't seem fitting that her house wouldn't reflect the turmoil she had gone through, but everything looked disturbingly normal.

Making her way upstairs to her room, she paused for a moment at the door to the second-floor bathroom that she and Chandra shared. Frowning, she picked up the heap of clothes lying just inside the doorway alongside a wet towel. Her sister had obviously gotten up, showered, and gone out during the night as well.

"These smell like smoke, Mew," Jaycee said to the kitten, who had crept up the stairs behind her. "Actually, they smell exactly like my clothes and hair," she added, returning the cat's unblinking stare. Chandra had not only left home, but by the smell of things, she'd been downtown somewhere near the fire too.

Jaycee dropped the items back on the floor, startled as the door to her sister's room was flung open behind her. Chandra's eyes immediately shot to the pile of smoky clothes at Jaycee's feet, and she blushed.

Knotting the hem of her sleep shirt in one hand, she looked up and met Jaycee's expectant gaze. "I'm sorry," she exclaimed. "But when I got the texts that there was a fire downtown and you weren't here, I went out to try and find you! Everything is such a mess, and I had no idea where you were. I didn't know what to do! Are you okay? Have you seen the bakery? Is everything still there?"

Jaycee shook her head and looked down at the clothes at her feet. "I don't know. I couldn't get close enough to see and, honestly, I'm exhausted, so I finally just came home." She sighed, picked up a towel from the floor, and placed it on a hook behind the door. Raising the cuff of her coat to her nose, she made a face as she sniffed it. "Everything stinks," she said, her tone mournful.

Chandra nodded and started to gather her things from the bathroom floor. "I know. Give me your stuff, and I'll throw it all in the wash along with mine," she offered. She then dropped everything into a heap again as she looked over at Jaycee with a frown. "Unless you're going back down there again soon, then maybe I shouldn't bother."

Jaycee shook her head. "No, not right away, anyway. I'll try to get back to the bakery again in a few hours after I've gotten some sleep, though. You should go back to bed too, especially if you want to come with me later. It's going to be a long and tiring day." Stepping around her sister, Jaycee left the bathroom and headed for her bedroom. Stopping in the doorway, she looked back at the teen. "And please, don't even consider going downtown without me. It's not safe."

After Chandra's nod of confirmation, Jaycee turned away and went into her bedroom. A moment later, she had stripped off everything she was wearing, crawled under the covers of her bed, and immediately fallen into an exhausted sleep.

Despite Jeremy's best efforts, it was not until three days later that Jaycee was finally allowed back on Lake Street. And even then, she could only view her bakery from across the road, held back from even the temptation of peeking through a window by police tape and the watchful eyes of two hired security guards. She gave a sigh of relief, however, when she saw that although the brick around the front window and door to her store was blackened, the shop's walls were still standing.

"I'm so sorry," Jeremy said as he held her close, staring at the bakery while he moved his hand across her back in small, comforting circles.

Jaycee clung to him for a long moment. "I just can't believe this," she whispered, waving a hand at the destruction.

"I can't, either. I'm so so sorry," he repeated. "I should have caught the arsonist long ago, then none of this would have happened."

Jaycee looked over at him and then up and down the shuttered street. "It's not your fault," she said slowly. "It's no one's fault but whoever started the fire. Do you know yet if it's arson?"

"Not yet," Jeremy replied, leaning over to kiss her on the forehead as he gathered her close against his chest. "But I'm doing everything I can to discover exactly what happened. As soon as I have something concrete that I can share with you, I will."

"I believe you," she replied and, leaning against him, closed her eyes to block out the surrounding devastation, trying instead to focus only on the comfort she found being close to him.

For another week, no one other than the police and the insurance investigators were allowed near the fire scene. "This has been the most nerve-racking week of my life," she announced for what was possibly the hundredth time to a patient and sympathetic Lisa, who had been calling daily to check in and see how Jaycee was holding up.

"I'm doing my best to keep myself busy, but I can't seem to think about anything but the bakery. I spend all my time worrying about how hard it's going to be to repair everything." She waved her hand in frustration while pacing the perimeter of the room. "But until I can get in to see how bad the damage actually is, I have no idea what I should even be worrying about!"

"I can't even imagine. I'm sorry, Jay. But hang in there—it might not be as bad as you think.

"You really think so?"

There was a long pause on the other end of the line. "I do. Things will be fine," her friend reassured her in a firm tone.

Finally, as Jaycee waited for the authorities to finish their work, she decided to channel all her pent-up energy and frustration into doing some home improvements. By focusing on updating her family home, she found not only something positive to work on, but also discovered her spirits rose just a little with each task she completed.

She started by scrubbing the house from top to bottom. She then painted the living room and rearranged the furniture that Lisa had brought from the city. Spending an afternoon washing the main-floor windows and throwing out the decades-old heavy drapery led to the pleasant discovery that the bright winter sunshine reflecting off the snow and streaming through the glass made the room seem much bigger and brighter.

Jeremy popped by to see her most evenings, but other than letting her know it looked like the fire had been started intentionally at multiple locations, he had little new information to share. While Jaycee welcomed his visits, they were brief and she couldn't help but notice that as the days went by, the gray circles under his eyes grew wider.

"Are you getting enough sleep?" she asked him one night while they took a short walk together with Bo.

"I'm trying," he replied, a smile creeping across his lips at her concerned tone. "But I must admit, I'm having a hard time falling asleep. I always do when I'm close to the end of a case."

"End?" Jaycee asked. Her eyes were wide as she stared up at him.

"I hope so."

"Me too."

A week after the fire, Jaycee was outside scraping ice from the sidewalk when a small, sporty red car pulled into the driveway and beeped its horn. She removed her gloves and looked up from her shoveling to stare at the car and its driver in disbelief.

"Lisa?" she called, running to the driveway. "Is that really you? What are you doing here?"

"It sounded like you needed me," her friend replied with a shrug of her shoulders as she unwound her long limbs and climbed out of the driver's seat.

Jaycee embraced her, a grin lighting up her face even as she fought back tears. "I do need you! I always need you. But how did you ever get away from Tony and Rhonda again so soon?"

"I quit."

Jaycee stepped back and stared at her friend with wide eyes. "You quit?" she repeated in disbelief.

"Yep. I have a little money saved, and there are plenty of jobs in the bakery business whenever I'm ready to go back to the city, so I thought I'd just come out this way and help you for a bit," Lisa replied with a grin. "Besides, it wasn't any fun there without you. And now that Rhonda's gone, Tony is just barely holding things together. I would have left before the holiday rush anyway, and so you needing me now just encouraged me to give my notice a little sooner."

"I'm so glad you did," Jaycee said and, after shoving her mittens in her coat pockets, she grabbed two suitcases from her friend's trunk and led the way inside.

JAYCEE'S BAKERY

Finally, after a full week of anxious waiting, the highly anticipated day arrived, and Jaycee and her friends were allowed to accompany the fire chief to see the inside of the bakery. A tentative smile slipped from Jaycee's face, and her steps slowed as the group got closer. Dropping Jeremy's hand, she placed a hand on her stomach, attempting to calm the jitterbugging sprites there.

From a distance, the storefront had looked quite good. The building was standing and the bakery sign still swung above the door. The hopeful chatter between everyone died, however, when they reached the doorway. Jaycee's newly installed oversized front window was covered in black soot and had a jagged crack down the middle. The storefront trim and several bricks were also blackened, and many were split from the fire's heat.

Everyone was quiet as Jeremy cleared the snow from the sill and opened the front door. After giving Jaycee a long, worried look, he hugged her quickly, then stepped back so she could step inside.

She gasped and lifted one hand to cover her mouth as she looked around her bakery. Jeremy had told her what to expect. But seeing it herself was still a shock.

The water from the fire sprinkler system had doused and flooded the entire space. The heat of the fire had bent beams, and most of the ceiling plaster and several feet of unidentifiable piping now lay on the floor, obstructing a large section of the front entrance. Her once-beautiful granite front counter was scorched and covered with debris, and the hallway to the kitchen was filled with rubble where an interior wall had fallen, blocking access through it completely.

"I know it's hard to see it like this," the fire chief said to Jaycee, wincing at her stunned expression. "But honestly, there is some good news. The engineers have found almost no structural damage to the property, so once this mess is cleaned out, you should be able to get the walls and the site rebuilt in fairly short order."

Huddled next to her, Chandra reached over and clutched Jaycee's arm as they both gazed around in disbelief.

"There were several fires lit that night. And unfortunately, many stores further down the street haven't fared quite as well, and we've had to condemn them. They'll have to be demolished and rebuilt from the ground up," the officer continued grimly. "You're also lucky you're renting, as the brunt of the cost of restoring should be absorbed by the property owner's insurance."

"But what if the landlord doesn't want to rebuild?" Jaycee whispered, her voice trembling. Jeremy reached over and drew her close to his side. She slumped against him for a moment before straightening and clearing her throat. "I mean, he doesn't have to, does he?" she asked, turning to Chief Robertson. "We could have just lost everything."

Richard, her real estate agent, was quick to reassure her. "That isn't going to happen, Jaycee. I've already talked to the landlord, and he's committed to rebuilding. In fact, he instructed me to see if you're willing to work with a contractor right away so the bakery can be put back together quickly."

"Really?"

Richard nodded. "The owner doesn't want you to go looking for another space. Although if you want to, after what you've seen today, I'm sure he'd understand."

"That's wonderful news," Jaycee whispered as she shifted her gaze to Lisa, who was also surveying the damage but looked more thoughtful than troubled.

"Did the owner say how long he thinks it would take to get everything cleaned up so we can start rebuilding?"

"They're hoping to get on it right away," Richard replied. "The first group the landlord has organized to come in will be here tomorrow. That will be the recovery crew—they'll move out all the unsalvageable debris and start on the cleanup. When they're done, you should be able to get back in and at least walk around the space a little easier so we can sort out what to do next."

"Well, it seems like I've been waiting forever just to see this," Jaycee said with a sigh. "I guess I can wait a few more days to see where we are after everything is cleaned up."

"Do the police or the fire department have any idea what started the fires yet?" Lisa asked, kicking aside some debris on the floor to try and peer farther into the kitchen.

"Not yet," Jeremy replied, "but it's looking like the fires *were* deliberately set. Someone seems to be targeting all the retail properties in Larkin Bay, but we don't know why. It's frustrating because it just makes no sense. But don't worry, we'll figure it out."

Jaycee sighed and looked at her friends. "Maybe I should give up on the whole idea of having my own bakery and just go back to the city and find another job," she said.

Lisa reached over to place a hand on Jaycee's arm. "No," she said firmly. "You're not going back to working for someone else—slaving a million hours a day and letting them take advantage of your talent. And you're not running away from Larkin Bay, either, especially since I just got here!"

Both Chandra and Jeremy nodded.

After a long moment, Jaycee nodded slowly too, but even though she knew she should be wholeheartedly agreeing with Lisa, it was hard to do after seeing the destruction all around her. She sighed and looked over at Jeremy, who was silently watching her.

He didn't smile, but held her gaze steadily, then stepped forward and drew her close to him. "Everything is going to be okay," he whispered.

Jaycee took a deep breath. "Okay," she said, straightening her shoulders and ignoring the jittering sprites in her stomach. "I guess I just have to take a leap of faith and believe we're going to be able to fix this." She looked over at Richard. "Do I need to contact the landlord and tell him I'd like to continue renting the space once it's cleaned up and safe, or is that something you should do?"

He smiled. "I'll do it," he replied. "I'd be happy to do it, and the landlord will be thrilled too. He enjoyed knowing a bakery was opening here. He'll probably call you himself soon, but with all the insurance claims, things are a little busy for him right now."

"That's understandable."

Jaycee quickly took in Chandra's and Lisa's nods of approval before letting herself collapse into Jeremy's comforting embrace. Breathing in the lemony clean smell of his sweater, Jaycee felt stronger and cautiously reassured that with her friends and Jeremy by her side, she could do whatever was necessary to rebuild the bakery—and her dream.

Chapter Twenty-Five

After checking in with the police officers doing the late-night patrol of Larkin Bay's deserted Lake Street, Jeremy returned home to pick up Bo so he could walk the area himself. The security guard looked up from his phone momentarily to acknowledge him as Jeremy opened the gate in the temporary fencing. Picking his way carefully through the debris that still littered the streets, he led the dog up onto the recently cleaned sidewalks, and soon they were standing in front of Jaycee's Bakery. "Sit, boy," Jeremy commanded Bo, who looked up at him and wagged his tail but didn't take a seat.

A smile smoothed out some of Jeremy's worry lines. "Okay, then just stand there, or whatever you want to do—that concrete patch looks safe enough," he said to the dog. Turning to the window, he pulled up a sleeve to cover his hand and rubbed away the soot covering the only undamaged window of the shop.

Using the light from his phone's flashlight, he studied the devastation inside again, then put it away and clasped his hands into angry fists.

Bo whimpered.

"It's okay, boy," Jeremy said, giving the dog a pat on the head and pulling him closer to his side.

Jaycee's Bakery was a mess of fallen beams, soggy drywall, and warped wooden floors. Jeremy frowned as he remembered how shattered Jaycee had looked that morning when she had seen everything. Looking down at Bo, he sighed. He still didn't quite understand how Jaycee didn't blame him for the fire that had destroyed her bakery. They both knew if he'd caught the arsonist sooner, she wouldn't have lost everything, but she didn't seem to blame him at all and for that, he was grateful.

When Jeremy turned the corner at the end of the street and reached the boardwalk, Bo gave a happy yip and lengthened his stride as he spied the lakefront and the seagulls huddled on the shore together against the cold. Jeremy unclipped his leash and let the dog wade in the waves at the lake's edge. After watching the dog shiver but not leave the water, Jeremy shook his head and called him back to his side.

"Don't be such a goofball," he scolded gently. "It's too cold for swimming."

Snapping the leash back on Bo's collar, he looked down as his phone vibrated in his hand. He looked at the call display for a long minute before he picked it up. "Hi, Danny," he said.

"Hey, buddy, we missed you at basketball tonight. All the guys and I assumed you were busy with work, but I wanted to call and check that everything was okay."

Jeremy sighed. "Yeah, thanks. I'm good. Sorry I missed meeting up with everyone. I've had a lot going on."

Danny's tone was sympathetic. "Not a problem. Is there anything we can do to help with the investigation or the cleanup?"

Jeremy watched Bo dig in the sand for a few moments while considering Danny's question. "No, not yet at least. But thanks for offering," he finally replied.

"Always happy to help if I can. Don't forget we have another time slot to play pickup this Saturday. We'd love to have you there, but understand if you can't make it."

"Yeah, thanks. I'll see what I can do."

"Sounds good. Later, then."

"Yeah, later." Jeremy disconnected the call and put his phone back in the front pocket of his jeans. It was nice of Danny to call and try to help. Unfortunately, there was very little he could do. There was very little *anyone* could do until Jeremy caught the arsonist. He looked down at Bo.

"Do you want to visit Jaycee?" he asked the dog, smiling when he got a tail wag in response. "It might not be too late. I'll text her and see if she's still up." With a lighter step, Jeremy walked Bo along the boardwalk toward her house and realized he was smiling.

The time he had spent with Jaycee lately had made all his concerns about falling in love again disappear. She was caring, supportive, and kind. He enjoyed her company, and it seemed every day he was learning something new about her that made him care for her even more.

And she makes excellent peanut butter cookies.

Giving a loud laugh at the unexpected thought, he pulled Bo closer and sent her a text.

Lisa placed her laptop on the battered kitchen table and took a seat across from Jaycee. "So how about we split the list in two? I'll look for what's available online to replace the equipment you lost, and you look over the financial stuff and let me know what the insurance will cover. I'll start by making a list of what the bakery can't do without," she suggested.

Jaycee looked over at her friend and nodded. They had time to fill while they waited for the restoration and demolition crew to finish their work at the bakery, but there was still a lot that needed to be organized for the rebuild. "I hate looking at spreadsheets at the best of times," she moaned. "Trying to figure out how to redo all this should be easy, though. At least, I hope so. I tried to keep good notes the first time I pulled it all together."

Lisa shot her a look of sympathy across the table and then booted up her laptop and pulled her cell phone over so she could start contacting vendors to see if any had refurbished bakery equipment they could buy to replace what had been destroyed by the fire.

After an hour of activity, Jaycee put her head down on her folded arms and groaned. Lisa clicked off her phone and looked over with a concerned frown.

"It's no use," Jaycee said, peering up at her friend. "Even if we can get all the equipment manufacturers to wait for their payments until the insurance money is paid out, I'm still not going to have enough money to repurchase everything we need." She shook her head. "I also have to hold some money back so Chandra and I have something to live on until I can open the bakery and take a salary again."

"Oh."

"And I can't ask Larkin Bay's Chamber of Commerce for more help. They've halted the payments on my loan for now, but I really don't want to take on any more debt."

Lisa stood up and walked over to the far side of the table. Looking over Jaycee's shoulder, she squinted at the spreadsheet.

"Exactly how much money do you need?" she asked after studying the numbers for a few minutes.

"Almost ten thousand dollars."

"Oh, well, I have that. I'll lend it to you."

Jaycee's jaw dropped, and her eyes grew wide as she turned in her seat to look up at her friend. "You have ten thousand dollars to loan me?" she asked incredulously. "Since when? You've always lived paycheck to paycheck, like me."

Lisa sat back down at the kitchen table and grinned. "Well, I did, but that doesn't mean I didn't have some money put away too. My parents made sure I was well set up when I went away to school."

"Are you kidding me?"

Lisa shrugged. "No. Mom and Dad didn't believe me when I said I was making a decent salary, and they didn't want me to starve, so they've been pretty generous over the years. I've also done a little bit of investing, so I've got quite a nice little nest egg put away."

She settled back in her seat across from Jaycee and put her elbows on the table. Holding her chin in her hands, she gave her friend a half smile. "I'd be happy to loan you what you need to rebuild the bakery, but actually, what I'd rather do is buy in as a partner."

"Really? You'd consider being my partner?"

"Of course, just a minor one, though," laughed Lisa, "if you want me, that is. We were always a great team, and I like Larkin Bay enough to try living here for a while."

Jaycee pushed back her chair and tackled her friend across the table in a hug. "You'd really stay here and work with me and help rebuild the bakery?" she asked.

Lisa smiled. "Sure. Besides, if it doesn't work out, you can always buy me out."

"This is wonderful!"

"I think so too, and since I intend to help make this bakery a roaring success, I should tell you I plan on charging you a lot more than this ten grand when you want my share back one day."

"It's a deal!" cried Jaycee happily, sticking out her hand, and the two women grinned broadly at each other as they shook hands, then hugged again to seal their agreement.

Later that evening, Jaycee heard a soft knock at the door and smiled when she saw Jeremy on her front porch.

His expression was glum as he stepped just inside the door, and he waved away her invitation to come farther into the house and sit down. Standing in the foyer, he shifted his weight from one foot to the other as the dim overhead chandelier threw shadows over him. Jaycee reached up and kissed him, but her smile of welcome quickly changed to a puzzled look of concern as he pulled back. Jeremy's brow was furrowed, and the gray shadows under his eyes were highlighted by small lines around their corners.

She reached out and touched him lightly on the arm. "What's happened?" she asked. "You look like you've just lost your best friend..."

Jeremy closed his eyes briefly and then cleared his throat. "I'm actually here professionally," he told her.

"Oh?" She stepped back and blinked up at him. She frowned when she saw a flash of remorse cross his features as they both watched Bo curl up at his feet.

"We got a break in the case," he told her, not meeting her gaze. "A few weeks ago at the antique store fire, we found a matchbook, and it had a fingerprint on it. I just got the results back as Bo and I were walking over."

"But, that's wonderful," said Lisa, coming up behind Jaycee. "I mean, isn't it?" she asked. "Now you can arrest the arsonist, and we can all stop worrying about more fires. That's great news, right?"

She looked in confusion from Jeremy's sad expression to Jaycee's worried one.

"Who's here? What's going on?" asked Chandra, coming down the stairs and squeezing into the foyer to join the conversation.

"There's been a break in the arson case," Jaycee informed her. "The police think they know who's been starting the fires."

"Well, we don't know for sure that the arsonist is definitely the one whose fingerprint we found. We just have a match, and so tomorrow, the police will need to speak to them..." said Jeremy.

"Who is it?" interrupted Lisa. "Anyone we know? Can you tell us?"

"Well, that's sort of why I'm here," Jeremy said, shifting his glance between the three women uncomfortably. "I wanted to tell you before the police came and, um, talked to you about it."

"Talked to us? Why would they want to talk to us?"

Jeremy sighed heavily and looked over at Chandra, who now had tears rolling silently down her pale cheeks.

Jaycee followed his gaze, and, frowning, pulled the teen closer to her. "Chandy? What's wrong? Jeremy, what are you trying to tell us?"

He hesitated for a long moment, then cleared his throat. "The fingerprints we found on the matchbook are the same as the ones the police have on file for Chandra. Your parents gave them to the school in case she ever went missing as a child," he said dully.

"What?" exclaimed Lisa.

"But I don't understand. Chandra has nothing to do with a matchbook or the arsonist. Do you, Chandy?" Jaycee looked from Jeremy to her sister, her face twisting in disbelief. "You can't honestly believe Chandra had anything to do with the fire that destroyed my bakery. That just makes no sense, Jeremy."

He nodded sadly. "I thought you'd feel that way," he replied. "But I wanted to warn you that someone from the unit will be coming over tomorrow to talk to you."

Jaycee felt heat rise to her face. Lisa reached for her, but as the other two women watched in stunned silence, Jaycee strode past Jeremy, pushed open the front door, and motioned that he should leave.

"Stop," cried Chandra as she saw him give Jaycee a pain-filled look.

"No, Chandra, just hush," Jaycee demanded. "We need to figure this out, and Jeremy can't be a part of that. He's a police officer—he'll have to report anything you say."

Chandra reached out and grabbed Jeremy by the arm. "There's nothing to figure out, Jaycee. You don't understand. He's right! Jeremy is telling you the truth. It was me. I'm the arsonist!"

After Chandra had blurted out her confession, she ran up the stairs and the sound of her door slamming reverberated throughout the house.

Jaycee turned to go after her but was restrained by Lisa's gentle hold on her arm.

"Just leave her alone for a minute, hon."

"But did you hear what she just said? She can't be saying things like that. I need to go talk some sense into her."

"She's upset. You need to give her some space for a few minutes. If you go after her right now, she's just going to push back at you and you're both going to say things you don't mean. Trust me, I went through this a million times with my mother."

This can't be happening.

Jaycee straightened. "I know she's not the one starting the fires," she said firmly, then looked over at Lisa. "Do you think it's possible she's the arsonist?"

Her friend shrugged. "Honestly? No. But her fingerprints are on the matchbook, so she knows, or at least she's been in contact recently with whoever is."

"I can't believe this is happening," Jaycee said. She reached for Jeremy, but then stopped herself and stepped back to wrap her arms tightly around her stomach to try and calm the frightened sprites there. Her eyes filled with tears.

Lisa pressed her lips together. "Well, believe it or not, we have to deal with it and try to sort out exactly what's going on. Preferably"—she nodded at Jeremy—"before the police show up tomorrow."

"It won't be me but another group who specializes in dealing with troubled youth," Jeremy said.

"Chandra is not troubled," Jaycee whispered. She put her hands on her hips and her eyes were sad as she looked over at him. "But I think we're done here for tonight. I need some time to sort this out and talk to her."

He nodded.

"I'm sorry," she whispered to Jeremy.

He nodded once more, grasped Bo's leash, and left.

Chapter Twenty-Six

The next morning, Jaycee paused outside Chandra's bedroom when she heard the unmistakable sound of crying. Music was playing loudly to muffle it, but the sound was undeniable. She tapped on the door. "Chandra, is everything okay?" Not receiving a reply, she pushed open the door and went inside.

Chandra was lying face down on her bed, sniffling into her pillow.

"Hey, what's going on?" Jaycee asked softly, going over to sit on the edge of the mattress. She rubbed her sister's shoulder, causing her to pull away and crush the pillow around her face to further muffle her sobs.

Jaycee looked around the room and sighed at the clothes, books, and stuffed toys she saw strewn everywhere. Forcing herself to look away from the mess, Jaycee continued rubbing Chandra's back while waiting for her to calm down.

After a few minutes, the girl rolled over and looked up at her. Her eyes were puffy, and her cheeks mottled. "I didn't start the fires. I'm not an arsonist. I would never have done anything to hurt the bakery."

"I know, you told me that last night and I believe you," Jaycee replied. "But what you didn't tell me was why you said you were."

Chandra gathered more pillows into a pile next to her before sitting up. "I don't know. I just *think* I know who's doing it, but I don't know how to tell them to stop or get them help without making things an even bigger mess."

"What? Chandy..."

Her sister shook her head vehemently. "No, Jaycee. I can't tell you or anyone. Not now, anyway. But I would have if I'd known the bakery would get destroyed. You have to believe me. I would never have let that happen."

Jaycee got to her feet and placed her hands on her hips. She stared down at Chandra. "Do you honestly think you know who's been starting the fires? Who is it, Chandy? You have to tell the police if you know!"

Her sister sat up straighter and pulled back. "I can't tell them, Jaycee! I don't know for sure who it is. I only have my suspicions. Without proof, I can't accuse anyone."

"Chandra!"

"No! What if I'm wrong? This could ruin their life! It happens all the time. People are accused, and they're innocent, but the accusations, they like, taint them forever."

Jaycee chewed her bottom lip for a second and glared down at her sister. "Who is it?" she demanded again.

Chandra shut her eyes. "I can't tell you."

"What did they do to make you suspect them, then? Can you at least tell me that?"

Chandra gazed out her bedroom window for a long moment before looking back at her. "I know where the matchbook came from." Her voice was soft as she said the words. She glanced up quickly at Jaycee before looking down at her hands.

"Well, that makes sense. Your fingerprints *are* on it," Jaycee said. Taking a deep breath, she forced herself to gentle her tone. "But do you know who used it to light the fires, Chandy? Because if you do, you need to tell the police that much, at least."

The teen put her head in her hands. "I know. I know. And I will. I just have to figure out what to tell everyone without causing even more trouble."

"Just tell the police the truth!"

"No. Don't you see? Just because I know where the matches are from doesn't mean the person who had them is the arsonist. Anyone could have taken them! My friend wouldn't have wanted to hurt anyone! They're not like that."

Jaycee looked over at her sister and swallowed hard. "But they did hurt people, Chandra. They've hurt many people by destroying their livelihoods and homes. And now they've hurt *you* by involving you in this mess."

Chandra wiped a hand across her eyes.

Jaycee folded her arms. "You need to come downstairs right now and tell everything you suspect to the police. You know that, right?"

Chandra didn't move.

Jaycee sat down on the edge of the bed again, picked up her sister's hand, and tried to warm it by rubbing it between her palms. "There is a police counselor down in our living room right now talking with Lisa and Betty. So if you can't tell Jeremy, at least tell *her*. She'll make sure whoever it is gets the help they need."

Chandra stared at her, then sighed. Finally, she pushed the pillows beside her onto the floor and climbed out of bed. Walking over to her dresser, she looked at herself in the mirror and nodded. "Okay, just give me a minute to wash my face, and then I'll come down," she said.

Jaycee pressed her lips together tightly. "Chandy..."

"I'll do it, Jaycee. Just go—I'll be there in a minute."

Jaycee nodded slowly. Looking at her sister, she paused momentarily and reflected on how much older Chandra suddenly looked.

Mom and Dad, I've never missed you as much as I do right now.

A few minutes later, Chandra crept downstairs and found two police officers sitting in the living room talking to Jaycee, Betty, and Lisa. Everyone looked up as she entered the room but not before she had stopped in the shadows of the doorway long enough to hear the phrases—problem-solving skills, anger management, communication skills, aggression replacement training, and cognitive restructuring—being spoken in grave, hushed tones.

Chandra shuddered. She had to put a stop to this. They couldn't send her away. Besides, she wasn't the one that needed help.

"I'm sorry. I lied," she announced, stopping in the middle of the room to draw back her shoulders and raise her chin as she faced everyone. Her voice trembled. "It wasn't me that set the fires. I just can't tell you who I suspect did, as I don't have any proof. When Jeremy came to tell us about it, I panicked because I was so surprised and I lied. I'm sorry," she repeated, looking directly over at the officers. Her eyes filled with tears.

Jaycee got up from the couch and came over to hug her. "I believe you," she said. "I never thought it was you, even when you said it was. But, Chandra, you have to tell us who you suspect the arsonist is, even if you don't have any proof. We need to get this person help. They have to stop lighting fires before someone gets hurt."

Chandra shook her head as she stepped away, watching as the police officers and Lisa frowned and exchanged a long look.

Jaycee took her sister's hand. "It's okay. I've got you," she said. "But I hope whoever you're protecting is worth it," she murmured. "Because they're putting us *both* through a lot."

Chandra blinked hard and didn't reply.

I'm not going to cry...

"So you just left?" Amber's eyes were wide in disbelief as she looked over at Jeremy. "She was upset because you warned her about some trouble Chandra might be in, and you just vamoosed?"

"Of course I did. She asked me to. I had just accused her beloved sister of a terrible crime and she didn't want to see me anymore. What else was I supposed to do?"

"Well, my first thought is that you could have stayed and comforted her."

Jeremy stared at her. "But what if her sister *is* the arsonist?"

"All the more reason for you to support her. She's going to need you more than ever if it's true."

He pressed his lips together but didn't respond.

"I thought you really liked her?"

He blinked. "I did. I mean, I do like her. A lot. But I'm also investigating the case, Amber. Me being with her right now is a conflict of interest."

Amber frowned. "Do you really think her sister's involved?"

"I have no idea. She could be."

"You said that she admitted to it, though, right?"

Jeremy shook his head. "She admitted to knowing something about the evidence. The officer who met with her earlier today told me Chandra's pulled back on her claim of actually being the arsonist."

Amber pondered this for a moment. "You obviously don't believe she's telling the truth, though."

"I have to consider all the facts."

"What happens next?"

He shrugged. "With Jaycee? Nothing."

"Really? That's so sad." Amber's eyes were wide.

He shook his head slowly. "I know. But we can't be together until I sort this out."

"So, what are you going to do?"

Jeremy sighed heavily. "The only thing I can do. I'm going to find out what's really going on. I'm going to talk to Chandra."

Déjà vu.

Jaycee couldn't stop repeating the phrase to herself.

Running a weary hand across her brow, she pondered her fascination with the expression for a minute before returning to the mechanical wiping required to sanitize the smooth granite counter in front of her. Whistling under her breath, she stretched her entire body along the slab and repeatedly pulled back and forth, carefully making sure she reached each edge and corner. Her arm muscles were screaming out in protest. This was the fourth time she'd scrubbed the countertop that evening, and she was starting to think her pectoralis muscles were detaching themselves from her arms with every swipe she took.

And as much as she tried not to dwell on it, she couldn't help but think about how she had given multiple scrubbings to an identical-looking countertop, one just as pretty and silky smooth as this one, just weeks ago. But she'd never even gotten to roll out a single pie crust on it before it had been shattered by falling debris from the fire.

Shaking her head to dismiss the memory, Jaycee instead sang along with the Barry Manilow playlist on her iPhone and tried to quiet the sprites in her stomach that were worrying about another fire occurring.

A few minutes later, the bell on the front door jingled, and she looked up from her work and managed a weary smile as Amanda entered the bakery pulling a wagon behind her that held a warmly bundled Ava.

"Hey, hon," said Amanda, dropping the cart handle and hugging Jaycee. "What are you doing all hunched up over your counter?" Turning back to the wagon, she untied Ava from her wrappings and held the baby up so her daughter could look around the bakery.

"Just cleaning," Jaycee replied, arching back to roll out the knots that had formed between her shoulder blades. "One can't be too careful with making this place sanitary. I do, however, seem to be obsessing over it today. Even though everything looks spick-and-span, I can't help but give it one more good scrubbing."

Amanda hefted Ava higher in her arms and slowly walked around the bakery, admiring the sparkling windows, new flooring, and shiny countertops. "Everything looks amazing. Good enough that I'm scared to put this one down, as she might muck it up," she replied, kissing Ava's cheek. "And usually, when we're out shopping, I'm afraid to let her walk around because I think she'll pick up some weird disease from all the filth."

Jaycee wiped her brow and nodded in relief. "That's good to hear. I'm hoping that this is the last time I'll have to scrub this counter so thoroughly before using it. Lisa and I will be here baking tomorrow if everything goes according to plan. I'm really looking forward to actually using the space and welcoming everyone to it with a big opening party."

Amanda wrinkled her nose in sympathy. "How are you holding up?" she asked. "Not being able to see Jeremy, and getting this place pulled back together is a lot. I've been worried about you, and your texts have been few and far between."

Jaycee looked over at her friend and grimaced. She didn't want to talk about Jeremy—she missed him too much—so she'd carefully packed away all the emotions attached to him to revisit in the future.

"I've seen a little of him. He walks his dog past the house most evenings and I wave from the window or the porch and he waves back."

Amanda raised a hand to her mouth. "That's so sad!"

"It is what it is for now," Jaycee replied. "And honestly, I've just been keeping myself busy by focusing on this place." Cocking her head to one side, she steadfastly ignored the brooding sprites in her stomach and instead reflected on all the purchasing, demolition, and rebuilding that she'd just completed. She'd poured in her blood, sweat, and tears to return the bakery to the place where it was right now, ready to open again. So what was she feeling?

Proud?

She nodded her head firmly. Yes, she felt that and so much more too. She'd been through some challenges, but she also had—with a lot of help and support from Lisa and all her friends—done it. The bakery had been rebuilt and was now almost ready to serve customers.

Jaycee gave her friend a half smile. "I'm okay, I guess. But honestly, it just makes me feel sick whenever I remember that this is exactly where the bakery was before the fire destroyed it."

"I can't even imagine," Amanda replied, her eyes widening in sympathy. "But how is Chandra doing? Is she any more willing to talk to you about the arsonist and what she knows about them yet?"

"She's not named anyone. Not to me, at least. But she's spoken with the police and school counselors a few times. I just can't figure out what she's so afraid of."

"Wow. I'm surprised they've let it go this long. According to the local papers, there have been no arrests, and although there have been no more fires, everyone is still talking about it and worrying."

Jaycee nodded, then cooed as she took a grumbling Ava from Amanda and waltzed her around the bakery to stop her from fussing. "I know. The police have been great about not pushing her, but they also seem to believe her when she says she didn't set the fires. I think the problem is, they don't have enough proof to arrest anyone yet." She stopped dancing for a minute and clutched Ava closer as she looked over at Amanda. "I've left her at home today, working on her college applications."

"That's nice."

Jaycee nodded. "Yeah, but while part of me thinks it will be great for her to get out of Larkin Bay and be on her own, this whole mess has also made me wonder if maybe she's not quite mature enough to handle leaving home yet, either. I honestly don't know how to help her."

"What are all the school and police counselors recommending?"

"They're all saying to just be patient and supportive. They think she's going to tell me everything in her own time."

Amanda tilted her head to one side. Reaching over, she took her daughter from Jaycee's arms. "What's your gut telling you?" she asked.

Jaycee shrugged. "It's telling me she's going to tell me something soon," she said with a sad smile. "But maybe that's just wishful thinking. Everyone seems to think that whatever she knows, she's not sharing it because she's either been threatened or she's afraid she might make things worse."

Amanda nodded and gave her friend a sympathetic smile. Jaycee shrugged in return and then studied her clean counter once more, too afraid to voice what both women were thinking.

What could Chandra possibly know that would make things worse than they already are?

"Hey, Chandra! Wait up!" Dean's call echoed loudly down the quiet side street, and Chandra turned quickly when she heard it.

"Hey, Dean," she replied and accepted his kiss, pulling away before it went on for too long.

"What's wrong?" he asked, frowning at her.

She shrugged. "Nothing. I guess I'm just in a funny mood today. I'm not feeling all that well."

"You never seem to feel well these days," the boy grumbled. "What's up with that?"

"Nothing."

Dean fell into step beside her as she turned to continue walking home.

"Maybe you're spending too much time working on all those TikToks with Willa and everybody. You've done more than enough for a college application now, haven't you?" he asked. "I never see you anymore."

Chandra gave him a small smile and stuffed her mittened hands into her coat pockets. "But I like doing them. They're fun. And soon all my girlfriends and I are going to be off to college, and so we won't be able to do them together anymore. I'm trying to spend as much time with them as I can, while I can."

Dean's brow wrinkled. "So, what's going on, then? You're not still worried about the arsonist, are you? I mean, there haven't been any more fires, so I think that's all over with."

She glanced over at him. "How do you know that?" she asked.

He studied her. "Well, there's been no talk of them, anyway. I mean, if there'd been any more, I'm sure we would have heard about it and it would have been all over the news. It was all everyone was talking about for a while."

"True."

Dean pulled her hand out of her pocket and clasped it in his. They continued the rest of their walk to Chandra's house in silence.

When they reached the pathway, Chandra pulled her hand out of his and looked up at him. "Hey, Dean, I've been thinking maybe it would be a good idea for you and I to take a break."

His eyes widened. "A break? What are you talking about? Where's this coming from?"

She shrugged. "I don't know. I've been thinking about it for a while. There was the whole thing with people thinking I was somehow mixed up with the town fires and now with the school year ending and me trying to get ready for college and you staying here, us dating just doesn't seem to make as much sense as it used to."

His eyes widened. "You're breaking up with me?"

"Yeah, I think I am," Chandra said, blinking in surprise at her words. "We can still be friends, though, I mean, if you want."

Dean's mouth fell open as he stared at her in hurt disbelief.

Chandra gave a sharp nod of her head and let out a long breath that fogged in the cold between them. "I'll always be around if you need something. Or ever want to talk about anything."

His mouth twisted into an angry snarl as he stepped back. "I won't," he retorted.

"Okay," she replied. "And sorry," she added before turning away, hoping he couldn't see she was wiping away tears as she hurried up the front walkway.

Chapter Twenty-Seven

Finally, the signs were rehung, the new stoves were warm, and even the sun was shining. The bakery was ready to open.

Standing behind the front counter, Jaycee took a deep breath and tried to calm the sprites dancing in her stomach. She squeezed her hands together and couldn't help but give a little skip of excitement as she admired the bakery's glistening, glass-covered displays, all of which were fully stocked with the tempting cookies and squares she and Lisa had made.

Walking to the front of the store, she stopped for a minute to run one finger around the edge of the framed photograph of her parents that she had hung there. They were both laughing and smiling with their arms tightly entwined around each other. "I did it, Mom," she whispered as she looked at it, "for both of us."

With a sad smile, she caressed her parents' wedding bands that she now wore on a chain around her neck, then turned to bounce her fingers off the keys of the shiny antique cash register she had bought. Thankfully, the modernized piece had not arrived before the fire had gutted the original bakery, and she had shed happy tears of relief when it had been delivered to the house a week later. It was perfect for the store, and Jaycee was still grateful every time she admired it for the silly shipping error that had delayed it just long enough so it hadn't been damaged by the fire.

Her smile expanded when she checked on the front window displays that she and Lisa had carefully filled with balloons and freshly decorated cookies late the night before. Several people were admiring them, and others were peeking through the windows to see if the bakery was open.

A moment later, a light tapping at the door alerted her that Lisa had arrived, and Jaycee hurried over to let her friend in. She greeted her with a hug.

"I can't believe it's the bakery's opening day! I'm so excited," Lisa said, returning the embrace. "I can't wait to see what everyone thinks of this place. I know they are going to love everything," she continued, hanging up her coat on a hook before donning a pretty blue-and-white-checkered apron. "But I'm still super excited!"

"I hope so," replied Jaycee, who had followed her to the back office. "My fingers are crossed anyway," she added. After taking a quick look in the mirror to assure herself that she was tidy, she returned to the front of the bakery. Pulling out paper cups from behind the counter, she quickly began separating and lining them up so they were ready to fill with the dark roast coffee they had decided to serve their early-morning customers.

Lisa busied herself with starting the coffee brewing and Jaycee hovered around her friend, watching her work for a few minutes before drifting back to the windows at the front of the bakery. She glanced at her watch and although they were not supposed to officially open for business yet, a small group of people were already gathered around the door.

She gave Lisa a questioning look, and after receiving an answering nod, Jaycee flipped over the small, hand-painted sign in the window so it read, "Welcome," and swung the door to the bakery open wide.

"Good morning!" she sang out to the people standing there. Her smile broadened as she propped open the door to let in an early-spring breeze, and a few people slipped by her to venture inside.

"I have coffee here if anyone would like a free cup to sample," Lisa announced as Jaycee followed the customers back into the bakery. Sliding behind the counter, she started filling their blue-and-white-striped boxes with muffins and cookies while answering questions about who she was, what ingredients were used in the baked goods she was selling, and how long she had been a baker.

The morning flew by, and it wasn't until almost noon that there was enough of a lull that Jaycee felt comfortable leaving Lisa and Betty on their own serving customers. She headed to the back of the bakery to tend to some administrative work and was busy at her desk when she was interrupted by a soft tap on her office door. She looked up from her laptop and her eyes widened when she saw Jeremy standing in the doorway.

This must be what people feel when they say their hearts skip a beat.

Pushing back her chair, she stood up and bit her lip, struggling with how to greet him. "Hey, stranger," she finally blurted out, and then winced when she realized it sounded slightly accusatory.

Jaycee hadn't seen or heard much from Jeremy since he'd dropped by to warn her that the police had identified the fingerprints on the matchbook. She understood they couldn't be close while he was investigating the case, but being apart had still been painful.

"How are you?" she quickly added, keeping her tone friendly, hoping this would lighten the unease between them. Before he could reply, one of the kitchen timers went off. Scooting around him, Jaycee rushed toward the ovens in the adjoining room and, after tugging on large, fire-retardant mitts, began pulling sweet-smelling, crusty French baguettes out of the oven. She was glad to have this brief reprieve and took a deep breath to settle the jittering sprites in her stomach. When she had finished transferring the bread onto mesh cooling racks, she turned to face him again.

"So," she said.

Jeremy silently held out a large pottery cookie jar. Jaycee took it from him with shaking hands. It was a twin of the one he had given her months before. The one that had been destroyed by the fire the arsonist had set.

She swallowed hard. "Thank you," she said. As their gazes met, her mouth went dry and her knees wobbled under her long, white apron.

"I wanted to drop by to see how things are going," Jeremy said, giving her a smile that didn't quite reach his eyes but still made the sprites in Jaycee's stomach sigh in sad unison. "And to give you this…" He waved his hand at the jar she was now hugging. "And, of course, to say congratulations."

"It's beautiful. Thank you again," Jaycee replied. "And everything seems to be going great so far. We've been swamped this morning, but I'm going to see how the rest of the day goes before I get too excited. Usually in a bakery, the afternoon business is slower."

"Oh?" Jeremy asked, tilting his head and looking over at her with interest.

She nodded. "Yeah, but we've prepared some sandwiches and stuffed croissants to try to attract the lunchtime office crowd, so I'm hoping those will bring in some noontime sales once people learn we have them." She abruptly stopped talking and blushed when she realized she was speaking very quickly.

Jeremy smiled at her.

"But I'm glad you dropped by," Jaycee added. She reached up and rubbed a finger across her scar and paused for a long moment, looking up through her lashes at him before adding, "I've missed you."

Jeremy frowned. "I know. It's been hard on me, too, not being able to see you because of Chandra's involvement in the investigation."

"Does the fact that you're here now mean she's not involved anymore?" Jaycee's eyes grew wide. "Have you discovered who the arsonist is?"

"As soon as I have them arrested, you'll be among the first to know," Jeremy replied, running a hand through his hair. "But I admire Chandra for leading us in the right direction without betraying a confidence. You should be proud of her."

"I am," replied Jaycee, "but I also have no idea what you're talking about."

Jeremy shook his head but didn't meet her gaze. "I'm sorry, but I can't tell you any more than that right now. But I can tell you that as of this morning, Chandra is no longer a suspect."

Jaycee took a step toward him, but something in his expression stopped her from throwing herself into his arms.

"Why don't you look happy about it?" she asked.

Jeremy shifted his weight from one foot to another. "I am. Of course I am. But I still feel awful that you lost all this"—his hand waved at the surrounding walls—"and it was all because I didn't catch the arsonist sooner."

Jaycee frowned at his words and reached for his arm. "Jeremy, the fire wasn't your fault. There was nothing that you could have done to prevent it. And we're fine. I mean, look around you. Everything here is as good or perhaps even better than it was before all that happened."

Jeremy stared at her but didn't reply.

"Neither of the fires, the one that destroyed my bakery nor the one that killed Marianne, were your fault," she continued, her voice soft and certain. "There was nothing you could have done to stop them." Clenching her hands, she moved closer, gazing up into his face as she struggled to find the words she hoped would convince him she was speaking the truth. Words that would help him release some of the pain he was carrying.

Jeremy blinked down at her, and Jaycee could see in his eyes that hope was warring with doubt and guilt.

"Can you please at least try to believe me?" she asked softly, taking both of his hands in hers and pulling him closer.

Jeremy shrugged and looked away.

She gently placed his hands on her waist.

He sighed and finally tightened the embrace. "I've missed you too," he whispered into her hair. "A lot."

Standing in silence, Jaycee turned her head against his chest and closed her eyes as she felt him slowly relax against her. The sprites in her stomach cooed and demanded that she stay like this forever, but after a few minutes, the continual ringing of the entrance bell and the rise in volume at the front of the store couldn't be ignored.

She stepped back, reluctantly pulling away from his warmth to peek through the slats of the swinging door, and saw that a long line of people were waiting to be served.

After shooting Jeremy an apologetic look, she straightened her apron and smoothed her hair. Raising a hand to push the door open to return to the front of the bakery, she paused and looked back at him.

Is he okay? Are we okay?

Jeremy returned her searching look with a nod and a smile. But it didn't quite reach his eyes, leaving Jaycee to return to work wondering if just too much had happened between them, and too much time had passed for them to go back to how things were.

It was the end of the day, and Jaycee was just considering hanging the bakery's closed sign on the door when Amanda came through it, pushing little Ava in her stroller. A few minutes later, Danny and Chandra arrived as well.

"Hi," Jaycee said, grinning at the group. "Welcome to my bakery."

"Happy to be here," Amanda exclaimed.

"And so are we!" added Denise, coming in, followed by Jennifer and Tina.

"We brought champagne," Amanda announced.

"But she can't open it until the bakery is closed," Danny said, taking the bottle from his wife and tucking it behind the counter. He rolled his eyes when he saw her pout. "And they can't close yet. We need to buy a few things first."

"Oh, true. I want cookies," Amanda said, hurrying over to stand in front of the glass display counter.

"Well, we'll sell you what we have left," said Lisa, coming out from the back to greet everyone. "But you should really come back tomorrow. We'll be here in just a few hours to start baking again, so everything will be fresh in the morning."

"We can do both," said Jennifer, peering over Amanda's shoulder. "But I want the last of the chocolate chip cookies. Amanda likes snickerdoodles, so she can have those."

"But I want chocolate chip cookies too," Amanda wailed. Jaycee laughed and, using a pair of tongs, picked up a single chocolate chip cookie from the display case and handed it to her friend.

"Hey!" Jennifer protested with a grin.

"Wow," Chandra said, studying the empty cases and shelves. "You guys must have been really busy today. Almost everything is gone!"

"We *were* busy," said Betty, her tone smug. "But it was so much fun too!" She then busied herself packing up everyone's orders.

Lisa grinned at the small crowd gathered at the front of the display cases. After checking the time on her phone, she saw it was a few minutes past the time they had posted to close, so she headed to the door, flipped over the sign, and turned the lock.

"We did it," she crowed, shooting a broad smile at Jaycee. "We made it through the first day!"

"Woo-hoo!" replied Jaycee, laughing.

"Let's celebrate," Danny said. He retrieved the champagne from behind the counter and popped it open.

Chandra switched the bakery music to something more upbeat, inspiring Denise and Jennifer to join hands and begin dancing in front of the display cabinets. A moment later, Chandra, Tina, and Betty joined them.

Jaycee smiled as she watched Danny scoop up Ava and join hands with Amanda so the small family could all dance together too.

Jeremy should be here.

Jaycee shook away the sudden pang of longing the thought produced and, walking over to Lisa, handed her a paper cup of champagne.

"Here's to the bakery!" she announced.

"I'll drink to that!" Lisa replied with a smile. She then pulled Jaycee out onto the impromptu dance floor so together with their friends, they could all celebrate the opening of Jaycee's Bakery.

Chapter Twenty-Eight

As temperatures warmed over the next few days, business at Jaycee's Bakery grew brisker. The first week's profits were so good, Jaycee started feeling cautiously optimistic that she might be able to pay back the Chamber of Commerce quicker than she had originally planned. Tonight, however, she didn't want to think about debt—tonight was a night for celebration.

"Jaycee!" A shout from the doorway jolted her from her musings, and she looked up and grinned as Kara entered the bakery's kitchen. She laughed in delight and let herself be engulfed in a floral-scented hug as a massive bouquet was thrust into her arms.

"Thank you! These are beautiful," she said to her friend, stepping back to hold up the stems to both admire them and smell the sweet aroma of their blossoms.

"Well, you can't be surprised that I brought flowers," laughed Kara, who, as the owner of Larkin Bay's garden center, was well-versed in decorative bouquets. "I would have brought you a spring arrangement to go outside the front entrance, but since you've already had the remarkable good taste to order one already from me, these will have to do as my congratulatory gift instead."

Jaycee smiled and took another long moment to admire the bouquet and exclaim over its blue, white, and green foliage that perfectly complimented the bakery's color scheme. Kara then took the flowers back from her and started opening cupboard doors in her usual fast-paced, take-control fashion. "Point me to where I can find a vase. I'll put these in water for you and find a fabulous place to display them while you go and mingle with the rest of your guests," she said, raising an eyebrow and tilting her head toward the half-open door.

Jaycee nodded, acknowledging the implied suggestion of her friend's statement. "You're right. I should be out there with everyone. And you'll find a vase in the supply closet in the back," she directed her friend.

After washing her hands, Jaycee quickly finished filling more trays with hors d'oeuvres, and a few minutes later, they each picked up a platter and headed out to the front, where they were greeted with hugs and cheers.

Tonight's festivities were Jaycee and Lisa's way of thanking everyone who had helped make their dream of opening the bakery a reality. They had hired a very talented local string quartet to come in and play music while they served wine, champagne, and appetizers to their guests. Under the balloon arches and twinkle lights they had used to decorate, Jaycee smiled broadly at the celebratory scene all around her as she was hugged and congratulated by all her friends.

An hour later, she took a step back from the festivities and frowned sadly when she realized one person was missing.

Jeremy.

She sighed and rubbed the scar on her cheek. Jeremy had sent her a text to thank her for the invitation to tonight's party and had promised he would be there, but he hadn't made an appearance yet.

She shook her head to stop herself from thinking about him and forced a pleasant expression onto her face as the local contractor who had installed the bakery's wooden floors approached her. "My floors look great, but I might just like the cupcakes you make better," he joked, causing Jaycee to laugh aloud before turning in surprise as Amanda hugged her from behind.

"Everyone wants to know if you made all the appetizers. And they also want to know if you're selling them. Are you? I don't think you are, but if you aren't, you should, because they are fabulous," her friend interrupted.

Jaycee grinned at the tipsy praise. "Thank you. I'm glad everyone likes them. I guess we could consider putting hors d'oeuvres on the bakery's menu. But I don't want to rush into adding anything else too fast. We're busy enough as it is."

Betty joined them and nodded in agreement. "The bakery is doing just fine," she scolded Amanda. "Now, you leave Jaycee alone. Go and enjoy the party. You can be sure I'll let everyone know when we expand what we're offering."

Amanda rolled her eyes. "I was just trying to help!" she declared with a smile. "But okay, then, I'll just go and find more delectable things to sample."

"I'll help you," the contractor said with a grin.

"You both do that," replied Jaycee, holding up a hand to hide a yawn. She then smiled as she watched them each snag a flute of champagne from one of the server's silver platters before heading over to where Lisa and Chandra were refilling the appetizer trays.

"You're tired," said Betty, frowning over at her. "We need to figure out a better schedule for the bakery so you can take a few days off and catch up on your sleep."

Jaycee nodded. "We all need more time off. You and Lisa have been working almost as many hours as I have this week."

Betty patted her arm gently. "Were you planning on opening any later tomorrow morning or at the very least letting Lisa and I do the first shift on our own?" she asked. "If we get the morning pastries ready tonight, Kenny can put them in the oven along with the bread loaves when he comes in later. Lisa has a key to open, and I can come in earlier so you can sleep in a bit if you like."

Jaycee nodded thoughtfully. It was a good plan. She needed to get more rest, and that, she decided, would start the very next day.

"Yes, I think I'll do that," she said, to Betty's delight. "I'll talk to Lisa in a few minutes and make sure she's okay with it. And tomorrow, when we get a quiet moment, we'll also make up a schedule with more days off for all of us. We'll hire more counter help for out front too."

Betty clapped her hands together. "I'm so glad. You can't keep working as hard as you have been and run a successful business, you know. You need to take a break and come at it fresh if you want things to keep going well."

Jaycee nodded and, smiling at what the dancing sprites in her stomach were telling her was another excellent decision, looked around the crowded bakery to make sure she hadn't missed Jeremy coming in. When she didn't see him, she sighed softly and forced a smile to her lips as she joined her friends to enjoy the party.

It was well after midnight when the celebration started wrapping up. Jaycee thanked the musicians and serving staff before waving them off and returning to her friends.

"You should go home now too, Jaycee," insisted Amanda. "You've had a long day—you must be exhausted."

"I'm fine," she replied. "And if I just stay a little longer, I can get the danishes ready for the breakfast rush tomorrow and then I won't have to come in as early. I've already sent Lisa home. She's offered to cover for me in the morning. And Chandra has offered to stay and keep me company tonight."

"Are you sure?"

"Honestly, I'm looking forward to spending time alone with her. After all, everyone knows a late night at the bakery is the perfect way to bond with family," she said with a laugh.

"Okay, but you *do* need to hire more help and take some time off," grumbled Amanda as she hugged Jaycee good-night. Turning, she quickly pulled Lindsey, Willa, and Rachel away from Chandra's side and firmly led everyone out the door, leaving the sisters alone so they could get on with their work.

"It was a wonderful party," said Chandra, whirling around in a circle and watching her full skirt billow out below her apron. "The only thing missing was dancing."

Jaycee laughed. "Dancing? That would definitely have added more life to the festivities. I just don't know how we would have fit in a dance floor for that many people." Retreating to the back of the store, a smile played around her lips as she recalled all the good wishes and praise she had received that evening.

Tying on a clean apron, Jaycee took a roll of pastry off the counter and rolled it flat. After she had cut it into squares, she passed the trays over to Chandra, who quickly filled each one with fresh fruit, then topped them with cinnamon and butter before pressing each closed. They were making extra since tomorrow was Saturday and many of the bakery's customers would be their neighbors stopping in for a treat to go with their morning coffee.

"So tell me who you talked to tonight," Jaycee said to Chandra.

"Just about everyone, really. And they were all really nice. I didn't know what to expect after the whole arson thing, but no one mentioned it at all."

"That's good."

The women continued to work in silence for a few minutes before Jaycee bit her bottom lip and looked over at her sister. "So you still don't want to tell me anything about it?" she asked.

Chandra kept her eyes on her work. "I can't. I don't have any actual proof. Just my suspicions, and those aren't reason enough to accuse someone of being a pyromaniac or, at least, that's what Jeremy told me."

"Oh, so you've talked to him about it?" Jaycee asked, carefully keeping her tone light as she looked over at Chandra in surprise.

Her sister nodded without looking up. "Of course. I had to tell someone what I suspected so they could keep an eye on things. If the arsonist is who I suspect it is, then Jeremy should be able to find the proof and arrest them. That's his job." She carefully set another pastry on the baking sheet in front of her. "I think that's why he didn't come tonight; he wanted to keep a watch on the suspect instead."

"Hmmm," replied Jaycee. She stopped rolling out the dough and sighed softly, at a loss for what to say next. She supposed she should be happy that Chandra had confided in Jeremy, but her feelings were still hurt by his absence tonight.

"I wrapped up the peanut butter cookies you made for him. They're in the pantry, so you can drop them off tomorrow."

Jaycee glanced over at her sister but didn't respond.

The women quickly finished their preparations and finally Jaycee covered the trays and pushed the carts holding them into the refrigerator, where they would stay fresh until Kenny came in to bake them later that morning. As she exited the large walk-in cooler, a movement out the back window of the bakery caught her attention. Frowning, she glanced at the oven clocks and saw that it was just past one o'clock in the morning.

Who would be in the back alley at this late hour?

All the shopkeepers in the area would have locked up their stores and gone home long ago. Closing the heavy refrigerator door, she turned off the overhead lights, pitching the kitchen into darkness so she could better see who was outside.

A moment later, Chandra crept up next to her and slipped an arm around her waist. "What are you looking at? Raccoons? I've seen a few of them foraging now that it's warmer. I even saw a brown rabbit hopping through the park last week."

"Might be," Jaycee replied slowly. "Whatever I saw was big, though, and it was skulking around the garbage bins."

Chandra shrugged and left her sister's side, yawning as she headed into the back office to gather up their coats and her backpack. Jaycee didn't follow but stayed looking out the window a little longer. When her eyes finally adjusted to the darkness of the dimly lit alley, a hand fluttered to her mouth as she realized there was a darkly dressed man crouched between the oversized garbage dumpsters near the bakery's back entrance.

Frowning, she reached into her large apron pocket to pull out her cell phone to call the police.

Could this be the arsonist who almost destroyed my bakery?

"Damn." She cursed softly under her breath when she realized her phone wasn't in her pocket and turned to run into the office where she had left it. She stopped when she saw the man outside get to his feet.

Jaycee's hands were shaking as she untied the bright white apron she was wearing and let it fall to the ground. She knew if she dashed to grab her phone right now, she would risk losing sight of him.

Holding her breath for a long moment, she tried to ignore the sprites jitterbugging in alarm in her stomach. "Okay, plan B," she murmured, moving toward the alleyway door and sliding the lock open. She would just slip outside and watch him, she decided. Once she saw which way he was headed, she would come back, get her phone, and call the police to let them know what she had seen.

Quietly, she opened the back door to the bakery and stepped out into the alley. Taking a deep breath, she forced herself not to think about all the terrifying things that could happen to her out here alone in the dark.

She jumped as a familiar presence crept up behind her, then quickly pulled Chandra close to her side. "What's going on?" her sister whispered as she dropped a coat across Jaycee's shoulders. "What did you see?"

Forcing herself to stay calm, Jaycee gestured for her to keep quiet and pointed at the man she was watching. Chandra gasped, then raised a hand to cover her mouth as she followed her sister into the alleyway. The stranger was headed toward Main Street, and Jaycee was careful to stay a good distance back, darting behind trees and buildings to stay hidden in their shadows. A few minutes later, she and Chandra crept closer as he headed off onto one of Larkin Bay's quiet side streets.

"Surely he won't try to start a fire where people are sleeping!" Jaycee hissed, giving her sister a fearful glance.

Chandra looked back at her with wide eyes and shook her head. "I don't think so?" she replied, her tone uncertain.

"Do you have your phone? Call 911."

"Not yet," Chandra whispered in return. "Trust me, let's wait another few minutes."

Jaycee frowned at her in confusion but was stopped from arguing further as the man increased his pace, forcing them to move faster too. Synchronizing their steps, the sisters followed him as he ran through residential streets where mature trees shared space with basketball hoops along the boulevard. Jaycee shuddered as she envisioned parents and children sleeping peacefully in their homes while danger lurked in their usual peaceful streets. Tugging on Chandra's arm, she increased her pace again, closing the distance between them and the man.

When the stranger suddenly stopped, Jaycee pulled her sister behind her and stepped behind a thick pine tree. They watched as the man unscrewed the top of the can he had been carrying, took a picture with his phone and then poured a small amount of its contents onto the pavement before carefully closing and setting the tin down.

Jaycee gagged as the unmistakable smell of gasoline wafted toward her.

This has to be the arsonist!

"No!" she cried and, rushing from her hiding spot, kicked the tin out of the man's reach. It gave a loud ringing sound as it bounced on the pavement.

"Help! Chandy, call the police!" she yelled as she ran back to her sister so they could run away together. But the man moved quicker and grabbed her by the arm, pinning her to his side. "Stop! Let me go!" she cried out in fright, clawing at his hand.

"No!" Chandra cried.

Jaycee continued to struggle against his hold, but he was much bigger than she was, and seconds later, knocked off-balance from their struggle, they both fell to the pavement. The man groaned as he pulled her tightly against him, taking the brunt of the fall. Jaycee gasped as his hand came down to her mouth in another attempt to silence her.

Turning her head to one side, she bit down as hard as she could.

He let out a strangled cry, pushed her away from him, and quickly threw back the hood of his sweatshirt so she could finally see his face. Pain-filled eyes looked down at her, and with a sickening jolt in the pit of her stomach, Jaycee realized she was staring up at Jeremy.

Chapter Twenty-Nine

Jeremy!

Jaycee's eyes widened in shock. She watched in disbelief as he sat up and cursed quietly under his breath, holding the finger she had bitten.

She scrambled back to her feet and held both hands out in front of her as she backed away. "What's going on?" she demanded, trying not to let her voice tremble. "What are you doing out here with gasoline? And why were you hiding in the bakery alley?" Her hands fluttered as she drew farther back. "Jeremy! It's not you lighting the fires, is it?"

She stilled when, instead of hearing an apology or explanation from him, he instead made an angry slashing gesture across his mouth, motioning for her and Chandra, who had crept up quietly behind her, to be silent. "No," he hissed. Shocked, Jaycee opened her mouth to protest, but he stepped forward and pressed his hurt finger against her lips, holding it there for a long moment. "The arsonist is just ahead of us," he whispered. "I've been following him. I was just confirming what was in the container."

Jaycee stepped back in surprise, bumping into Chandra. "It's okay," her sister whispered. "I helped set this up."

"You what?!" she yelped.

Jeremy and Chandra both quickly shushed her.

Jaycee covered her mouth with both hands and stared from one to the other.

"Stay here," Jeremy quietly commanded.

Jaycee's brow creased as she watched him leave. "Chandra?" she whispered.

"Yes?"

"I say we follow him and see what's going on."

Chandra pressed her lips together and looked in the direction where Jeremy had disappeared for a long moment. "Let's go, then," she finally replied.

When the girls caught up to Jeremy, he glanced over at them and sighed deeply, not seeming the least bit surprised they hadn't listened to his directive to stay put. Jaycee frowned as she watched him peer down the dark street and was about to ask him again what he was looking for when a figure appeared out of the shadows.

Beside her, Chandra gasped, then moaned in distress as she stepped forward. "I was right, then, wasn't I?" she whispered.

Lunging forward, Jeremy grabbed her by the arm and drew her back to his side. "Not yet," he hissed, sharply shaking his head. "We still don't have enough evidence."

Chandra reached up and wiped her eyes as Jaycee looked from her sister to Jeremy in confusion. "Who is it?" she whispered.

Even by the dim light, she could see Jeremy's expression was imploring as he once again raised a single finger to his lips. Reaching over, he squeezed her hand before motioning for them to follow him even deeper into the shadows of the trees. Intrigued, she followed, careful to tread lightly. Chandra sniffled and stumbled once, but after a warning look from Jeremy, sighed heavily and steadied her steps.

Jaycee frowned and squinted, trying to get a better look at the person they were following. He was short and moved quickly, despite being dressed in heavy winter clothing. The only color she could see came from the occasional flash of his bright white running shoes. His hair color and facial features were all obscured by a dark-colored baseball cap.

Jaycee crept closer to Jeremy, who, without breaking his gaze on the man they were stalking, tugged her down to crouch beside him. Cloaked by the darkness, she watched as he reached into his jacket pocket and slid out his cell phone. Holding it in one palm, he swiped open the camera, and the phone quietly hummed as it clicked into video mode. Jaycee winced at the sound and held her breath. Her shoulders dropped in relief when she saw the man they were following hadn't noticed.

Jeremy filmed the man as he strode over to the pretty, white picket fence that divided the properties of two residences. After a quick scan of the two houses, the arsonist withdrew a small plastic bottle from his pocket and, unscrewing the lid, poured some of the liquid from it onto the fence slats. He then turned and crept up one of the home's front steps and onto its wide lemonade porch, continually spilling fluid behind him as he shuffled along. Jaycee held her breath as the sharp odor of gasoline wafted toward her. Wrinkling her nose, she watched him stop on the porch and toss the bottle into the front hedge before retreating down the stairs.

Jeremy rose slightly beside Jaycee as the stranger tugged a pack of cigarettes and his phone out of his pocket.

Chandra gasped and reached up to cover her mouth as the man lit a cigarette and took a long drag. He then took a few steps away from the house and stopped to smoke for another minute before flipping his smoldering cigarette behind him and turning to jog away. As it hit the home's staircase, there was a loud whoosh, and a sudden rush of wind as the surrounding air turned orange.

Jeremy grabbed Jaycee's arm and hauled her upright. "Get back," he yelled.

"No, Jeremy! Wait!"

"Call 911! It shouldn't catch, it's been too wet, but still stay away," he shouted, ignoring her and tossing Chandra his cell phone before he turned and headed off after the arsonist.

"Go after him and help, Jaycee! I'll call the police and get everyone out of the house!" Chandra yelled.

Jaycee shook her head, her eyes streaming from the stench of gasoline. Moaning softly, she used her fists to knuckle them clear. "Jeremy?" she called out, struggling to catch her breath as she oriented herself. Gulping hard, she stumbled off in the direction she had watched Jeremy disappear and gasped in surprise when, after only a brief run, she spotted two people struggling in the street. She reached them just in time to see the arsonist was attempting to escape Jeremy's grasp by throwing several unsteady blows at his head, which Jeremy easily warded off with one arm. He was much taller than the other man and quickly got him under control by wrapping both arms around the arsonist's shoulders and twisting sideways to bring him down to the pavement with a solid thump.

Leaning over, he forced him onto his back and pinned the man's arms over his head, leaving the arsonist thrashing his legs.

The two men were exchanging loud words when Jaycee ran forward and grabbed the man's feet to ensure he couldn't kick his way free. "Stop it," she cried. "Just stop it! Dammit, we've got you! And you're not going anywhere. You. Will. Never. Start. Another. Fire. Again," she yelled.

Jeremy turned and shot her a grateful but somewhat amused look before returning his attention to keeping the man under control.

Placing all her weight on the arsonist's legs to immobilize them, Jaycee gritted her teeth and focused on keeping him still. Finally, after a few more minutes of struggling, he seemed to recognize that he couldn't break free and went limp.

"Are you okay?" Jeremy called over his shoulder to her.

She nodded. "I'm fine," she assured him. The adrenaline that had energized her for the last few minutes was now dissipating, and she relaxed slightly.

"Are *you* okay?" she asked Jeremy.

"Finger hurts a bit," he replied, with a smile in his tone as he teased her. As he shifted some of his weight to one side, Jaycee craned her neck to get a better look at the man they were holding. His baseball cap had been knocked off in the struggle, causing a cascade of thick, dark hair to tumble out. Her eyes widened when she realized the arsonist wasn't a man—it was a young teen, a boy who had protected and disguised himself in large, oversized men's clothing.

Jaycee's mouth then gaped open, and in her surprise, she almost let go of his feet when she realized this teen wasn't a stranger at all.

Chapter Thirty

As Jaycee and Jeremy disappeared to chase down the arsonist, Chandra ran through the smoke until she reached a place where she could draw an easy breath. Shoving the phone Jeremy had thrown at her into her coat pocket, she carefully zipped it shut. Pulling out her own cell phone, she called the 911 operator.

"Where am I?" she asked, repeating the dispatcher's urgent question aloud. Spinning in a circle, she searched for something to help orient her to an exact location. The racing of her heart slowed slightly when she realized that the fire seemed to have blown itself out as quickly as it had started, and she could now see through the lingering smoke into the distance.

Jeremy was right. The fire didn't catch.

Gasping out an enormous sigh of relief, she located the street signs at the corner of the block and relayed this information to the operator.

Once she was assured that help was on the way, Chandra turned and ran up the front stairs of the house she had watched being licked by flames only minutes earlier. The wooden stairs she pounded up were scorched and discolored, but no flames were evident.

"Hello? Can anyone hear me?" she called out as she crossed the wide wooden porch. She used both fists to pound on the front door. "Can anyone hear me? Fire! Fire! Hello?" she yelled.

After a minute, she was overcome with a coughing fit and stepped back to catch her breath. Glancing behind her, she saw that only a light gray haze now remained as evidence of any fire. She considered her options for a few seconds, then returned to banging on the door. Although the family inside probably wasn't in any immediate danger, they would still want to know what was happening. She sighed in relief as she heard sirens in the distance.

Reaching over, she found the doorbell button and pressed it repeatedly. Finally, a light switched on in the house, and the door cracked open. An elderly man peered out at Chandra, adjusting a hearing aid and glaring at her as she sputtered out what had happened. Reaching over, he snapped on a light switch and the front yard was immediately lit up by carriage lamps.

The man's lips pressed into a thin line as he clutched his bathrobe closed and stepped out onto the porch. "What are you saying?" he demanded. His eyes widened as he took in the haze of smoke still lingering in the air and a curse left his lips when he saw the blackened steps and scorched front lawn.

"The police and fire department are on their way," Chandra struggled out before doubling over in another fit of coughing.

"Are you okay?" the man asked, leaning over her, his expression now one of concern.

Chandra nodded before turning away and running back down the front steps, where she saw a police car was now blocking the end of the driveway. "They went this way," Chandra called out to the policewoman, who was climbing out of the driver's seat. She gestured down the street and set off in the direction she had seen her sister and the arsonist disappear.

A moment later, she found Jaycee and Jeremy in the middle of the road and her heart fell when she saw they had the arsonist. A moan escaped her lips as she hurried to Jaycee's side. She pushed her sister's arm out of the way and fell to her knees.

Looking through her tears at the boy she had once thought was her forever person, Chandra fought back the urge to strike him. As he turned his face away and closed his eyes, she leaned forward and sobbed. "Dean, it was you! How could you? I knew it. I just knew it. What is wrong with you? What the hell were you thinking?"

Later, Jaycee hugged Chandra as they huddled together on the edge of a wet concrete curb. The girl was shaking and Jaycee tried to transfer as much warmth as she could to her sister as she whispered comforting words into her ear.

She gave a small, relieved smile as she saw Betty coming toward them. "Girls!" the older woman cried, holding out her arms as she closed the distance, her step hitching when she saw Chandra was crying. "What's happened?" Betty asked, reaching out to pull the teen to her for a long hug before wiping away some of her tears. "Are you hurt?"

Chandra shook her head and took a long, steadying breath. "I don't think so. I mean, I'm not hurt, but I'm also not okay, either. I just feel so bad, and I'm so sorry about everything."

"What are you talking about? What do you have to be sorry about?"

Chandra gulped back a sob. "I didn't tell you or Jaycee, but I've suspected for a while that Dean was setting fires. I didn't think I should say anything because I didn't have proof, but maybe if I had told you or Jaycee about him, none of this would have happened!"

Betty shook her head and rubbed a comforting hand across the teen's trembling back. "It's okay, darling. I'm sure you did what you thought was right, and honestly, you didn't cause any of this mess. If it's true that Dean is the arsonist, then this is all on him, not you."

Chandra sniffled and stared at the older woman. "It *is* true. Jaycee and I saw him. We saw him start a fire tonight, and it was awful. I used to think it was so pretty, but it's not. It's terrifying, and it could have hurt so many people. He was lighting fires at people's homes while they were asleep inside!"

Betty looked over at Jaycee, who nodded in confirmation.

Jaycee bit back a yawn as she got to her feet. "Betty's right, though, Chandra. This is on Dean, not you. And you *did* tell the police, didn't you? You told Jeremy what you suspected, and he was leading the investigation. There was no way the police weren't going to keep a close eye on Dean after you told them your suspicions. You have nothing to feel bad about."

After hugging Betty for a few minutes longer, Chandra stepped back and looked over at the police officer who was still speaking with the homeowners Chandra had helped. She was silent as she contemplated how much worse things could have been had she not told Jeremy what she feared.

"It's going to be okay," Betty said. "Dean will get help. Everything will be just fine, you'll see."

"I hope so."

"We'll make it so," Jaycee said in a firm tone, and Chandra watched silently as her sister walked over to the police car where Dean was sitting alone in the back seat.

"Can I talk to him?" Jaycee asked the officer standing next to the police car.

The man called her request over to his superior, and after receiving permission, he opened the rear car door. Sliding in next to Dean, Jaycee took his curled fist between her hands and lightly ran a fingertip across the bruises forming on his knuckles. Looking over at him, she studied the cut on his cheek and winced. Dean didn't pull his hand away nor look over at her.

She sighed. The psychologist who had come to the house before the police cleared Chandra had explained to her that fire-setting was a behavior, arson was a crime, and pyromania was a psychiatric diagnosis. People diagnosed with pyromania didn't need just jail time—they needed medical help and psychological support as well. Jaycee put her arm around the boy's shoulders and smiled at him with compassion as Dean collapsed against her.

"I never wanted to hurt anyone," he whispered tearfully. Using the sleeve of his jacket, he wiped his running nose and eyes. "Everything was so good and I just didn't want things to change. I love Chandra so much, I couldn't just let her leave. But, you have to know, I wasn't trying to hurt you."

Jaycee didn't reply, but she stroked the teen's hair away from his brow while she considered his words.

"I tried to stop lighting the fires. I really did. And I did for a bit. But then I'd just get so mad that I had to light another one. It's like an explosion inside me," he said and dissolved into noisy sobs that left him heaving in pain against her.

Jaycee leaned over and hugged him, trying not to dwell on the destruction and the heartbreak he had caused, but instead focusing on the fact that he was a scared and hurt teenager. "It'll be okay," she reassured him. "I'll help you. We'll figure it out and make sure nothing like this ever happens again."

Dean sniffled, and as Jaycee leaned her head against the back of the seat, she held his hand and waited to see what the police would do next.

A short time later, alerted by the authorities, Dean's mother arrived. She thanked Jaycee for comforting her son, and silent tears ran down her cheeks as she listened in disbelief to what he was accused of. Jaycee placed a sympathetic hand on her shoulder for a long moment before leaving the family and going back to where she'd left her sister.

"Jaycee! What's going on? Are you okay?" a wide-eyed Lisa asked, leaving Chandra and Betty to hurry toward her. "Is it true? Did you catch the arsonist? What's going on?"

Jaycee rubbed a weary hand across her eyes. "Everything's okay. Or at least it is now. Jeremy wasn't at the celebration tonight because he was in the back alley watching for Dean."

Lisa shook her head in disbelief. "So it's true, then? Dean's been setting the fires?"

Jaycee nodded. "Yeah, but even though both Jeremy and Chandra suspected it was him, they couldn't do much without proof. That's why Chandra broke up with him. She was trying to make him angry enough that he would start lighting fires again and Jeremy could catch him."

"Wow. So Dean was at the bakery tonight?"

"Yes, in the back alleyway. But when he saw Chandra was in the kitchen with me, he didn't want to light a fire where she was, so instead, he came over here to make mischief."

"That's terrible." Lisa frowned. "But, wait, why would Dean want to set fire to the bakery in the first place? Surely he didn't want to hurt us?"

Jaycee shrugged. "I don't think so, not really. But he's also a kid, and he didn't like the fact that I was trying to convince Chandra to go off to college and leave Larkin Bay. Before I came back home, Chandra was planning on staying in town with him after graduation. Somehow, in Dean's troubled mind, he decided that me moving back here and building the bakery had ruined all his plans for the two of them."

"You're kidding me?" Lisa's eyes were wide.

"Nope."

"That's crazy, though."

Jaycee shrugged. "You're not wrong. But that's what he just told me and I think now he might finally be seeing it too."

"Huh."

The two women stood in silence for a long moment as they contemplated everything that had happened.

Lisa finally shrugged. "Well. I think I should take Chandra home. She's exhausted. I'll stop by the bakery on the way and tell Kenny what's happened. I'll also put a sign up saying we're closed for the day."

"Good idea. Probably, the news will have traveled fast, though. No one will be surprised we're not open."

Lisa nodded in agreement.

Jaycee gave her sister, Betty, and Lisa a long hug and, rubbing her eyes, yawned widely as she watched them drive away. A moment later, she headed back to where multiple police cars were parked and found Jeremy perched on the edge of the passenger seat of a police cruiser, holding an ice pack up against his swollen left eye.

She stopped in front of him.

He looked up at her and grimaced. "Hi," he said.

"Hello again," Jaycee answered, giving him a small smile in reply.

A paramedic nodded at her before leaning over Jeremy, quickly checking his pulse, and flicking a penlight into his eyes. "I think you're going to survive," he said. "But heck, I didn't know such a scrawny kid could pack such a powerful punch!" He chuckled and put his equipment away. "I don't think you need to go to the hospital, but the places where he hit you might be bruised and sore for a bit, so you might want to take some acetaminophen before going to bed."

The EMS worker gave Jaycee an appraising look. "You should probably sit down too," he told her. "I hear you've had a long night. And don't either of you leave. The police chief told me he wants to talk to both of you. He should be around in a minute."

Jaycee nodded and sat down on the curb. Jeremy left his seat and groaned as he lowered himself to sit beside her. She slid closer to him, finding comfort in his warmth while being careful not to jar the arm that still held the ice pack against his eye.

"So," she said after a few minutes of silence, "now do you want to tell me exactly what you've been doing?"

"Well," a deep voice interrupted from behind them, "it appears your boyfriend here has been a busy guy."

"What?" Jaycee looked up in confusion at the uniformed police officer.

"It seems that Jeremy took it into his head to catch the Larkin Bay arsonist all on his own. And it looks like he succeeded."

Now it was Jeremy's turn to look up questioningly.

"Yep, Dean has confessed to everything, and he's been a busy boy. He's admitted to lighting most of the fires we've been investigating around the area. And now that we have him in custody, we can make sure he gets all the help he needs so that he can't do any more harm to the town or himself."

Jaycee sighed. "It's all so sad," she said. "I still can't believe any of this is true."

Jeremy shook his head in agreement before reaching over and taking her hand in his.

Leaning forward, she gently kissed him on the cheek, then turned to the police officer with a smile. "I hear you have questions for both of us? Let me know when you're ready. I'll stay here as long as you want." And as she made the promise, she sighed happily and snuggled closer to Jeremy's side, realizing that beside him was exactly where she wanted to be.

Epilogue

Eighteen months later, Jaycee held Jeremy's hand tightly in hers as music and laughter swelled around them at Larkin Bay's Fall Fair. "Let me see the ring!" came the happy request from the many friends they met while wandering through the crowded fairgrounds. And every time she was asked, Jaycee was thrilled to show off the gorgeous piece of jewelry that Jeremy had given her the week before.

"It has a baguette-shaped diamond," Amanda quickly pointed out to everyone. "How perfect is that in an engagement ring for a baker?" Her repeated question caused Jeremy to roll his eyes and Jaycee to blush every time.

After shaking Jeremy's hand, many friends also congratulated him on his promotion to sergeant in the newly expanded Larkin Bay Police Department.

The couple smiled and thanked everyone for their well wishes, but as they admired the fall displays, Jaycee also repeatedly turned to check on her bakery's fair booth. Under Lisa's watchful eye, it seemed to be doing a brisk business selling pumpkin and apple pies as well as small stuffed meat hand pastries that could easily be eaten while strolling through the fair.

"Everything looks great," Jeremy assured her, chuckling and shaking his head as he saw where her attention was continually wandering. "But you've got the rest of the day off, and you're supposed to be forgetting about work and enjoying our time together," he reprimanded her gently.

"Does she listen to you?" asked Amanda from his far side. "Because she doesn't listen to me at all whenever I try to tell her to relax and forget about the bakery for a few hours. I know I encouraged her to go into business for herself, but I'm starting to think I created a monster." Her tone was teasing and Jaycee grinned before sticking her tongue out at her friend.

"It's all good," she assured them. "I was just checking out the booth as we went by. Honestly, I wasn't going to go over, but you can't blame a gal for being curious about how her business is doing, can you?"

Jeremy reached over to pull her close and smiled over her head at Danny, who was pushing little Ava in her stroller.

The good-natured bantering among the friends continued as they made their way through the rest of the fair, interrupted only a short time later when Jaycee's phone pinged. She glanced at it, and a smile lit up her face. "I just got a text from Chandra. It's her college homecoming weekend, and it sounds like she's having a great time with all her friends." Her brow puckered as she added, "I can't believe how much I miss her, though."

"Ah, but that's wonderful!" Amanda said, leaning over and admiring the picture Chandra had sent. "She looks really happy, and homecoming weekend was always a lot of fun."

"It was fun. She also told me when she called yesterday that Rachel, Willa, and Lyndsey are all going down to visit her next weekend too."

"They'll have a blast. And I can't wait to see what they put up on TikTok when they're together. Those girls are so cute, and their social media stuff is hilarious."

"Yup. They definitely have a knack for it."

Jaycee felt her smile tremble as she contemplated how far away her little sister was. Looking over, Jeremy took her hand in his. His eyes were soft, and his tone was gentle as he spoke. "I'm sure she's having a great time. But I'm sure she misses you too," he said. "You should take some photos and send them to her. I bet she'd love to see fair pictures."

Amanda nodded and immediately lined up the small group so they could nab an unsuspecting passerby and talk them into taking a group photo. When they had finished making a few goofy poses, Jaycee quickly sent the pictures and a brief text off to Chandra.

She had just finished pressing the send button when Jeremy's phone rang.

He shook his head as he looked down at it. "It's our favorite author," he said, chuckling and accepting the call. "Hey, Amber. What's going on?" he asked. After listening intently to his sister for a moment, he rolled his eyes and looked over at Jaycee. "Amber wants to know if one of the volunteers from the bakery would mind bringing a bunch of the meat pies over to the bookstore? They are swamped there, and she says she can't leave as she has a book signing, but she's half-dead of starvation."

"I'm on it," answered Jaycee and quickly sent a text over to Lisa to have the food delivered. "We can't let the writers of Larkin Bay go hungry."

"Jaycee's taking care of it," Jeremy said to Amber. "Make sure you tip whoever delivers it well," he added.

After saying goodbye to his sister and disconnecting the call, he looked over at his friends. "Why don't we go downtown and check out the fair festivities at the stores there too?"

They all quickly agreed, and after a short walk, they arrived on Larkin Bay's Main Street. The downtown stores were all decorated with colorful fall banners, scarecrows, hay bales, and many pumpkins to celebrate the autumnal season.

Over the last year and a half, the local businesses and many community volunteers, with the help of a substantial federal grant, had worked together to restore the heritage buildings and revitalize the area into a more modern and even prettier downtown center than it had been before the fires. Today, with the lake glittering in the fall sunshine and the maple trees' colorful fall leaves glowing, the whole town shone.

Amanda and Jaycee happily helped little Ava play all the games the shop owners had set up outside their stores. The friends also did some shopping at the many sidewalk sales and soon their steps were dragging slightly and an exhausted Ava was sound asleep in her stroller.

After a quick stop at the bakery to pick up a few peanut butter cookies for Jeremy and other treats, they walked to Jaycee's house. The women claimed the seats on the front porch swing while the men sat on the steps, where Danny could easily keep an eye on Ava.

"Have you heard anything else about Dean?" Danny asked Jeremy. "I heard he was in touch with the school?"

Jaycee nodded. "Denise told me he emailed her to ask how he could bring up his high school grades so he can apply to a trade school next year. It sounds like things are going in the right direction for him."

"I'm just so glad you helped Dean find the services he needed," Amanda said to Jeremy.

"What I still don't understand," said Danny, "was why he was targeting the downtown in the first place. It doesn't make any sense that he was destroying his hometown. From what I heard, he had lots of friends here."

"It's all part of his sickness," said Jeremy. "He couldn't help himself."

"I've talked to his mom a few times, and I know Chandra still keeps in touch with Dean once in a while. He's got a long road ahead of him still, but at least so far he's not lighting any more fires," Jaycee said somberly.

Amanda slapped a hand against her leg. "Enough with reliving the past," she announced. "Let's talk about something happy."

"Did Jeremy tell you about Bo?" Jaycee asked her.

"No. Has he finished his training yet? Did he pass?"

Jeremy nodded. "He did. Now he's starting his training to be a diabetic warning dog. He's learning how to detect when someone's blood sugars are dangerously high or low so he can get them help."

"That's wonderful."

"It is. I miss him, but it's great to know he'll be helping someone. I even heard his new home might be with a child here in Larkin Bay, so we could be seeing him around town again soon."

Amanda clapped her hands. "That's even better. He's such a great dog."

"He is."

Jeremy looked over at Jaycee. "Are you okay?" he asked. "You're rubbing the scar on your cheek."

"I am," Jaycee replied. "Honestly, I'm still worrying about the fair sales and wondering how Lisa and all her high school volunteers are doing. I feel guilty sitting here enjoying myself when everyone else is working so hard."

"You've spent the last two weeks working night and day getting everything ready for the fair. You have nothing to feel guilty about," scolded Amanda.

"Well, I can't help it. Maybe I should just go over there and see if they need anything."

Amanda smiled. "I'm sure everything is going great. And I know that for a fact, because if there were any problems, Lisa or Betty would have been on the phone with you already."

"True." Jaycee grinned at her friend, appreciating her never-ending support and optimism. "Things have gone well at the bakery since we opened, haven't they?" she mused. "I've been very lucky."

Danny snorted. "Luck has nothing to do with running a successful business," he stated. "You're successful because you work hard and don't give up when things get tough."

Jeremy smiled at Jaycee. "How about we go for a walk?" he suggested. "I think we should leave these two to rest along with Ava while I take you back to the fair. If it'll make you feel better, I'll even let you look at the bakery booth from a distance so you can see for yourself that everything is just fine."

Amanda held a hand up in protest, but Jaycee immediately got to her feet. "This man truly knows the way to my heart," she announced, waving goodbye to her friends as she and Jeremy left for the fairgrounds.

"Everything does look great," Jaycee admitted a short time later as they stopped to look at the bakery stand she had decorated with scarecrows and pumpkins the night before.

The crowd in front of the booth wasn't as large as it had been earlier, but there were still people lined up, waiting to buy some of the bakery's festive fall treats. Jaycee could also see by the empty spaces in the small display coolers that the number of pies and pastries available had decreased considerably too.

"Everything looks fantastic," Jeremy agreed, tugging on her hand. "Now, come over to the grandstand with me. They've got live music over there. We can check out the band, and you can try to relax and enjoy your day off. Maybe we can even dance."

"Dance?" Jaycee's eyes sparkled. "I love dancing! But do you know why Mew isn't a good dancer?"

"Because he has two left feet?" Jeremy asked with a grin. "Or paws?"

"Exactly!" Jaycee replied with a giggle.

After waving to Lisa and all her helpers, they headed off to the grandstand, where Jaycee was delighted to hear the band was playing pop music. There was even a Barry Manilow impersonator making the most of his talent to entertain everyone on a makeshift dance floor.

"Look at him!" Jaycee gasped, then smiled in delight as he began to sing one of her favorite songs. "He's really great! Did you know he was performing now?"

"I did," Jeremy replied, placing one hand on the small of her back. He then held her other hand high in the air, where her engagement ring's diamond twinkled in the fall sunshine, as he led her in an old-fashioned waltz around the other couples on the dance floor.

Jaycee laughed and sang along with the performer, her face illuminated with pleasure. Barry Manilow's songs might be old, and the words were sometimes corny, but they also rang true. Reaching up, she brushed Jeremy's lips against her own and smiled as she held on tightly and danced joyfully with the man she loved.

Acknowledgements

This book has taken me a very long time to write. I love to read, but I never fully appreciated how hard it was to write a book until I tried. To all the authors I've read, I'm in awe of how you make writing a novel and publishing it look so easy. Because it's not. And honestly, I really want to know how the heck you make it look that way.

I also want to thank the many, many people who read this book, edited it and made suggestions for improving it. Jenna Fifield, Mira Park, Dawn Murphy Ryan, and Leah Mol are the four who immediately come to mind. To you and the rest of those who helped, I thank you from the bottom of my heart.

Also, thank you, Jenna, for my amazing book covers and website illustrations. I love them and you.

Thank you to Angela James and the entire Book Boss group. When I didn't know what to do with this manuscript, you guided me. I appreciate all of you.

Thank you, Becca, for all your behind-the-book support and social media coaching. I love you.

To my Mac girls — Sandra, Michele, Mira, and Cindy — one day I'll write another book that includes more of our shenanigans and stories. But just in case it never sees the light of day, thank you for sharing your support, laughter, and friendship while I worked on this one.

To my trio — Jenna, Rob, and Becca — thank you for your years of patience while Mom sat staring at a laptop screen writing this series. And thank you for being the perfect people you are. I love you with all my heart.

And finally, thank you, Dave. I told you when we were kids that I wanted to write a book one day. Look at this! I did it! Thank you for your encouragement and patience while I stumbled my way through my writing and publishing journey. I love you and appreciate your support more than words can say.

About the Author

Leanne writes heartwarming, small-town romance books featuring strong and endearing women who often stumble but always reach their happily ever afters.

When Leanne isn't writing, she spends her free time overseeing her small flower farm, baking cookies (that don't contain raisins) and texting her three adult children.

Leanne also often retreats to her forested home in northern Ontario. She thinks it's the best place in the world to couch-coach the Toronto Blue Jays, spy on hummingbirds and read in the company of her needy dog, indifferent cat and loving husband.

You can reach Leanne at her website
www.LeanneStanfield.com
She'd love to hear from you.

Also by Leanne Stanfield

Return to Larkin Bay!

Kara's Garden Center is now available for pre-order. Releasing June 21, 2024